HEROES OF THE TRANSITION

Volume One

Details of the First Eight Attempts to
Assassinate Luna, Little Dragon

Fred Holmes

Order this book online at www.trafford.com
or email orders@trafford.com

Most Trafford titles are also available at major online book retailers.

Printed in the United States of America.

ISBN: 978-1-4669-0302-9 (sc)
ISBN: 978-1-4669-0301-2 (e)

Trafford rev. 11/03/2011

North America & International
toll-free: 1 888 232 4444 (USA & Canada)
phone: 250 383 6864 • fax: 812 355 4082

Credo for a New World

In the beginning was the Big Bang, which hath
made hydrogen and helium.
Then, in the super nova agony of dying stars,
heavier elements were created.
Unto us a sun was born.
And on Earth, crust forming, plate tectonics, volcanoes,
bacteria, algae, and the green fuse that drives the flower,
as arthropods and Permian lungfish crawled from the sea.
Behold the amphibians, reptiles, dinosaurs and mammals.
Behold the hominids.
I believe in the scientific method, atomism, the United Nations,
and radical action to save our world from warming.

CHAPTER 1
Luna's Conception, Birth, and Early Childhood

In this scenario, China's bourgeois authoritarian 'Communists' fell in 2001. In the following elections a pro-United Nations social democratic party—the Middle Way—won a majority, while the Chinese branch of the New Harmony Party, talking softly and carefully lest xenophobia be aroused, took 19% of the vote and sent 63 members to the People's Congress.

With the advent of democracy, planning for a Han-Spar station to orbit in L-5—a gravitational mid-point between Earth and moon—began in 2006. In April of 2010 contracted NASA shuttles from Cape Kennedy and enhanced Long March rockets from a launch site near Xichuan, Sichuan province, were used to get the prefabricated parts into orbit. It took **Turquoise Ramsey** and six other astronauts ten days to assemble the *Dragon Nest* in its most rudimentary form.

Approaching it in space, with Earth over your shoulder like a blue and white tennis ball, the first thing you would see is the parasol of mirrors, 150 metres long, that heats the turbine generator. Then there are long panels of photovoltaic cells, and utility pods where electricity is stored in nickel-hydrogen batteries, heat in reservoirs of molten salt. The main control room abuts the crew's quarters.

Astronaut Ramsey, daughter of two of the founders of New Harmony, works closely with **Cheng Chou**, 42, a handsome man from a village near Xi'an whom she has known since 2004, when he was a lieutenant-colonel in charge of a UN air unit on the Kosovian-Serbia border. (That was the year his parents, both doctors, were killed in a bus-truck accident.) She and Chou enjoy talking politics and playing chess in their spare time. He has recently given her a book of his poetry for her upcoming 39th birthday, and they have begun kissing and touching in private.

Because of Turquoise's political connections, the rest of the crew has pretended not to notice as their romance deepened, the trysts becoming more frequent. Even Anna Weinstein, the mission physician, kept quiet.

"Meet me in the cargo bay at 1400," Turquoise had said to Chou that morning. (The station used GMT.)

“Turn off the cameras. Lock the hatches,” she reminds him, as she puts on Connie Francis’ version of “Heartbeat” on a small MP, before shucking off her coveralls and underwear, as her long mahogany hair floats freely. “I want a baby before it’s too late,” she tells Chou again, as he clasps her buoyant body to his own. Without gravity, her breasts ride high on her chest, sleek as seals.

*

The news that Turquoise was pregnant raced through the leadership of Han-Spar, the New Harmony planning group, and the capitalist philanthropists allied with them—Bill Gates, Warren Buffett, Ted Turner, the currency wizard George Soros, and many others. New Harmony’s General Council sent a message to the *Dragon Nest.*

“Joy to the world,” was all it said.

The maximum safe radiation for a pregnancy was judged to be 5 rem, whereas an astronaut could get 30 rem in that time with standard shielding. Worse still, solar flares could fling iron nuclei at half the speed of light, killing the human cells through which they passed. Turquoise was relieved of most of her duties in the moon exploration program and ordered to stay in heavily shielded areas.

Han-Spar managers rushed to get pseudo-gravity for her and the foetus. First they sent up a relatively small cyclotron, which was all that was available. Work on the big rotational drum was intensified, and it was installed six weeks later. The heavily shielded drum, 50 metres in diameter and 30 metres long, rotated once a minute and gave rotational gravity on its inner wall. The managers also ordered tests with pregnant cats, hamsters, chimpanzees and rhesus monkeys.

Her work was limited, but Turquoise still did an hour a day on a treadmill. Her daily medical check-up took at least an hour; two while a persistent dehydration problem was dealt with. In her free time she played Scrabble, chess, or bridge with off-duty crew members, or just chatted while they sampled the fruit and nuts sent to the expectant mother on monthly shuttles. Turquoise talked on the coded videophone to close friends on earth and to her mother and father at New Harmony’s first base, northwest of Toronto. She also read numerous books on screen and got caught up on back issues of the *New York Review of Books.*

Public interest was focused on the Green Daughters of the Red Dawn, an all-women American-based eco-terrorist group, and on the new Japanese-American moon base and the promise of cheap fusion fuel in helium 3, found in great abundance on the lunar surface. There was much debate about whether the riches of the moon belonged to the UN or to the mining and energy companies that were planning to extract it.

In Turquoise's sixth month the news leaked beyond Han-Spar and New Harmony. DRAGON ASTRONAUT PREGGERS and MOON CHILD DUE IN THREE MONTHS, the tabloids shouted. ZERO GRAVITY DEPRAVITY—SPACE BABY SIRED BY ALIEN, one claimed. Medical 'experts' interviewed on TV gave contradictory opinions. In Las Vegas the odds of live birth were 2:1 against, and that the child would live one year, 4:1 against.

Most Canadians were familiar with the old pictures of Turquoise that then appeared on TV and Internet. One when she was 20, in grimy overalls, holding a wrench beside her Spitfire at an air show near Hamilton, Ontario, while her turquoise-colored parachute was being folded. Another showed her in flying gear, with co-pilot Molly Moosomin, beside the restored CF-105 Arrow (found in twenty large crates behind a false wall in an old Avro plant in Malton, bought by Han-Spar and demolished in 1998) which they piloted in the CNE air show in August of 2001. There were pictures of Turquoise in the early nineties with the Canadian armed forces, flying F-18's around the base at Cold Lake, Alberta. More recent videos showed her rescuing a powersat and then a comsat for Spar-Nippon, and working in the *International Space Station*.

*

During labor Turquoise screamed in pain muted only by tetrahydrocannabinol and Chou holding her hand. She was in her room in the drum, surrounded by three doctors and their equipment. "Oh, my goddess!" she moaned, clutching a small tin ankh encased in clear plastic in her fingers. "Isis and Hathor, please help me, I beg." In pain, Turquoise—an atheist—temporarily lapsed into the paganism the New Harmony planning group used to undermine Christianity. Then she was quiet and the child's wails filled the room.

"Let the new era begin," declared Anna Weinstein, when she set the washed infant in her mother's arms. Thus **Luna Amaranth Cheng-Ramsey** was born in the *Dragon Nest* on March 11th, 2011, with an inertial mass of 3.3 kg. There were respiratory difficulties, and feeding problems related to the fact that gasses are not easily burped out in low gravity. Naturally the baby protested against the tube which had to be inserted into her stomach every four or five hours.

A week after her birth Luna came to Earth in a shuttle renamed *Stork 1*, which was fitted with a big titanium crashball filled with foam pellets, in a fireproof husk, to surround the mother-child module during landing. The baby wore a supportive ribbed space suit and helmet, and there was a tank of salty water into which she could be put to lessen the power of gravity upon landing. (The crashball, helmet and suit, donated by Han-Spar, are the most visited exhibit at the Smithsonian International Air and Space Museum in Washington.)

The landing at Lop Nur Space Center went smoothly. Once inside the Han-Spar cosmodrome the module was lifted by crane into the new annex of the clinic, where Little Dragon and her parents were guarded around the clock by a Han-Spar security team assisted on the periphery of the base by air force and armored units sent by the People's Congress.

*

Shui Zhe was Han Chinese, born and raised in the Xinjiang Uygur Autonomous Region's capital of Urumqi, where her parents and relatives (factory workers) were killed in 2009 by a mob of Uygurs. She felt guilty for not being there to defend her people or share their fate, having left several years earlier to work on a farm south of the city.

During the summer of 2010, when she was 31, she worked as a cook for wardens in the Lop Nur Wild Camel National Nature Reserve. Tall and strong, big-nosed and plain, with calloused hands and sun-roughened face, she kept to herself and didn't flirt with the men. On a day off she went hiking in the sandy desert, and was raped and beaten by four Uygurs. They were illegal gold miners who drunkenly bragged about setting explosives at waterholes to kill wild horses and asses for meat.

The few local police didn't try hard and never caught the offenders. In the eighth month of her pregnancy, when she could no longer work, she was given some food and money and fired. After living in a shack in a Lop Nur village for several weeks, she heard that a baby from space had arrived at the Han-Spar cosmodrome. Without knowing why, she began hitch-hiking—in trucks and on a motorcycle, walking the last four kilometres in a cold and windy dust storm. Although they had pity on her condition and her thin padded coat, the PLA soldiers outside B87 were suspicious that this unregistered laborer might be a Muslim terrorist from the East Turkestan Independence Movement, and were going to send her by military ATV to the town of Argan, some 220 kilometres to the west. But a female Han-Spar guard and a senior B87 security officer overruled them, and drove Zhe in a cart to the base infirmary.

A boy was stillborn a week later. The only good news was that Zhe had not contracted any diseases from the rapists. Then Turquoise heard of her case and went with Chou to the infirmary.

"We want to help you bury your child when you are able, and make a marker," offered Chou, who spoke the same Hunanese dialect as Shui Zhe. "There is a small graveyard in the base."

"I need your help with my baby," said Turquoise, as Chou translated. "Sometimes I'm too tired from space-lag to feed her properly, especially at night." This was only partly true; there was also a sympathy factor and some political calculation. (Turquoise wanted the child to be as Chinese as possible.) "Han-Spar will pay you, and you can live in the spare room in our apartment."

"I am not worthy of such an honor," replied Zhe. "But I will try."

The arrangement worked out well. As time went by, no one else knew what joy Zhe took in nursing the baby while Turquoise slept, or giving the bottle supplements the doctors prescribed, and changing the infant's diapers and bathing her. No one knew Zhe's dread of the day when an amah would no longer be needed for this special child whose crib of rare hardwoods was carved with ornate Imperial dragons (with sapphire eyes), her cartouche (its hieroglyphics inlaid with gold), and Egyptian deities with turquoise and ceramic details.

*

Within weeks a trickle of cards and gifts became a flood.

"Please save the forests and don't send paper," Turquoise urged on UNTV and on Luna's UNICEF (Children's Fund) websites. "We appreciate the thought, but rather than sending a gift to Luna please instead donate to UNICEF or a local children's charity in her name. This is the best way to celebrate her birth."

Despite this plea, which was carried by media globally, by the end of the year 30 million cards and letters were received in nearly all languages. About 300,000 gifts were sent to the baby from every part of the globe. More than 660 million messages were received on Luna's UNICEF websites and e-mail addresses, overwhelming some of them at times.

On Easter Sunday in St. Peter's basilica Pope Benedict XVI asked the blessing of the Christian god on the baby. "But I fear that secularists around her mother will use this child for political purposes," he accurately predicted. "The lack of a formal marriage is itself a political statement," he noted peevishly.

First Attempts

On April 28th 2011 a bag filled with packages addressed to Luna at Lop Nur blew up in a mail sorting station in Milan, killing three workers. After that every piece of mail to her was screened. Delivery services insisted on identifying all senders to Luna. In the next month three more bombs were found, two quite powerful, in New Delhi, Karachi, and Tel-Aviv. They were removed and destroyed without injury. About four hundred hate-filled letters and five hundred malevolent e-mail messages were investigated by the FBI, Interpol, and UN, Han-Spar, and New Harmony intelligence services. The ideologically motivated were put in one group, the products of mental illness in another. Most hate letters were anonymous and untraceable, but all were searched for DNA and kept in filing cabinets by Han-Spar security agents for possible future investigation.

The serious threats to Luna were identified in Han-Spar security reports.

A shadowy conservative Catholic sect with twenty or thirty people, the 'Sword of God,' originating in Poland, was probably behind the Milan bomb, but they could not be located. The bomb defused in New Delhi was traced to a gang of thugs who worked for Hindu extremists, but there was not enough evidence for charges to be laid. X-ray pictures taken of the bomb discovered in Karachi connected it to a Taliban cell hiding somewhere near the border with Afghanistan, but no arrests were made. However in the case of the Tel Aviv bomb, a young orthodox Jew from a family of 'settlers' on occupied territory, a student at a *Hesder Yeshivot* in the West Bank, was arrested, convicted, and sentenced to ten years in jail. He had been studying the Torah while serving in the Israeli army, and was known to admire the extremist who shot and killed Israeli Prime Minister Yitzhak Rabin in 1995 for signing the Oslo Peace Accords.

Many of the threatening letters came from some of the ten million America First Republicans in the United States. America First was funded and led by reactionary imperialist capitalists who saw that a strong UN world government would severely limit their power and wealth. But it included the Christian right-wing, National Rifle Association members, former Tea Party enthusiasts, and other 'red state' elements.

*

The expensive gifts were given to UNICEF and the UN refugee relief fund for auction. A hundred handmade dolls and toys were accepted and placed around Luna's room—an artful mobile of tin animals sent from a Sudanese (Darfur) refugee camp in Chad hung above her crib. A small blanket knitted by a Palestinian woman in the occupied West Bank was used, and a Thank You message sent. Much of the handmade clothing was accepted, if it came from the maker. The rest of the gifts went to poor Chinese children.

In December (2011) Luna was chosen *Time* magazine's Person of the Year.

Pictures taken three months later at her first (western) birthday party and shown on UNTV and UNICEF websites revealed a brown-haired, almond-eyed toddler. That triggered more messages and gifts, but not the avalanche of 2011. There was some hate mail, but no bombs were sent.

A month later she toured Beijing in a UN convoy and was seen, albeit through bullet-proof plastic, by millions of people. "A thousand years of life for Little Dragon," people shouted. Some children carried Baby Luna dolls, which were just becoming available.

*

The dolls soon became wildly popular: 290 million were sold in a two year period. Highly robotic for her time, Baby Luna came with her moon landing module, crashball, computerette, star maps, space suit, dragon robe and other clothes. She could sing "Imagine," the UN anthem sung to the "Finlandia Hymn," and 26 other progressive songs in 40 languages. She could count to a thousand, do basic mathematics, teach alphabets and phonetics, and talk about recycling, reforestation, global warming, overpopulation, atheism, and the importance of the UN for world peace. "I won't eat shark fin," said the dolls for sale in China and Japan. And she could walk on flat metal surfaces with her alternately magnetized space boots, part of her appeal to little boys. A marketer's dream, she was not easily counterfeited, and advertising was free on Luna's websites.

Made in UN factories in China, India, Indonesia, Mexico and Canada, using Fair Trade standards, Baby Luna was a propaganda tool without equal but also a money spinner. (Han-Spar gave $690 million US in profit to UNICEF in January of 2014.)

*

After being presented in parades in Xi'an, Shanghai, Beijing, and Tokyo, in June (2012) Luna was taken to Canada and kept in seclusion for more than a year at New Harmony B1 near Owen Sound, Ontario.

B1 was called Home Base because it was the first of the New Harmony group's secure (or safe) areas. Most of the 900 acres were purchased when the organization started in 1974. (One of Jamie Ramsey's friends had turned C$220,000 into $28 million by pyramiding first copper and then sugar contracts as commodities ran up sharply. The one hundred and fifty acres donated by Ramsey was the remnant of his great-great-great grandfather's (John Taylor) agricultural commune, started in 1847.)

At one side of the property the Big Head creek meandered its way to Georgian Bay. There were extensive woodlands and wetlands, water purification lagoons, bays of anaerobic digesters, pastures and fields. On a flat part near the eastern border were hangars and a landing strip for small planes and helicopters.

The eleven storey tower rested on the thick steel-reinforced ceramic-covered cement ribs and walls of the large egg-shaped fallout shelter below ground level.

Past the lanes of cottages and barns were a dozen geodesic Fuller-ball buildings of various sizes, near the solar collectors and wind mills. For security the base was surrounded by a tall outer chain-link fence, a perimeter road, and another similar inner fence. Guards at the front gate and in the security room in the tower watched for intruders on bays of screens.

In 2013 there were 260 adults and 160 under-sixteens living on the base; almost fifty of the minors were adopted refugee orphans from around the world.

*

Shui Zhe came to B1 too, at the child's tearful insistence. As Luna was weaned Zhe started to lift weights and learned to shoot pistols at the indoor range. She convinced Han-Spar security executives in Beijing to hire her as a nanny/bodyguard for the child, as a way of maintaining some Chinese influence, and New Harmony leaders unanimously approved.

Luna's second (western) birthday party was a quiet affair in her parents' apartment in the tower, just as the party nine months before to celebrate her Chinese birthday had been—only a few children and their parents over in the morning to play for an hour and eat a little cake. And just a few small gifts, as Turquoise insisted. (Her message on this subject ran permanently on Luna's websites, and relatively few presents from the public were received. {White powder in a box briefly suspected of being anthrax was flour.} But Luna's websites and e-mail answering centers were very busy with birthday messages.)

Luna's grandparents gave her a kitten and a litter box. Her parents, Dr Seuss books. After lunch Zhe helped her put on the red snowsuit over her jeans and sweater, and pulled her on a toboggan past the cottages and utility buildings to the forest. (Being so precious, she had to wear a light sports helmet over her cap.) Anubis Fourth, her mother's German shepherd, wearing his silver and turquoise collar, came too. They went into the sugar maple area, where twenty people were gathered, and tasted some syrup from the big cast iron pot over the fire. Then they left the forest and found a gentle slope clear of trees where they slid slowly down a dozen times, the child always pleading "Again, again," at the bottom, and then Zhe made a snowperson. On the way back they went into a barn and watched cows being milked by machine. "Moo to you too," Luna repeated, smiling.

Later Luna helped her grandfather fill the bird feeder in the backyard of his friend, David Eaton-Gage, a PromTek director. For nap-time she lay on a couch, her head on a pillow, her body covered with a Navaho blanket, watching birds through the big back window of the cottage—blue jays, mourning doves, sparrows, junkos, and a flashing male cardinal.

"Red bird," she said, pointing, her last act before snoozing.

When she awoke an hour later the old men were still playing chess and drinking tea at an antique pine table. What she had come to know as Beatles music—"Here Comes the Sun" in this case—was playing softly on a record player, while a faint smell of marijuana smoke from her grandfather's jacket came to her nose. Luna examined album covers as they finished their game. Then David's wife Janet made her a cup of hot chocolate, and showed her pictures of their adopted daughter Oolayou, who lived up north.

In the following months as the weather improved Luna was taken to outdoor playgrounds in the base. She walked or was pushed in her stroller around the sidewalks. She learned a new word every day, in Hunanese, Mandarin, English, and French. When it got warm in May Chou took her into the woods to see the early flowers and greening trees. She wanted to pick trilliums. "It is better to leave them, or the bulb will die," Chou said gently. Luna respected that; she thought of dead trees and animals she had seen and desisted.

In June Zhe and Turquoise began taking her for picnics near the creek, usually beside the pond near the foundations of the old sawmill where the big weeping willows grew. The women took her paddling in an old green canoe through the yellow water lilies in the shallow end, as Anubis watched from shore. Dragonflies droned by, and flycatchers engaged in noisy defense of their territory. One afternoon a Great Blue Heron flew over. "Big fast blue bird," Luna said, her face 'looking up, holding wonder like a cup.'

Of course Luna was never spanked, and never heard a harsh word. When she disobeyed, reason and child psychology were used.

Young group children were limited to one and a half hours of television a day, censored for gratuitous violence, sexism and racism. Of course there was no religious inculcation in the kindergarten or the other schools.

*

In September Luna was taken to Chicago by Turquoise and Zhe for an Oprah Winfrey special show promoting UNICEF, flown in a small Han-Spar (biofuel) Bombardier jet fitted with a crashball for the child. For this show she wore a light blue cotton dress sent the previous Winter Solstice by a Lacondan Maya woman living in the New Harmony base near Oaxaca, embroidered with stylized birds and animals, with matching slippers. Without prompting Luna got onto Oprah's lap and stayed there for ten minutes.

"I saw you on TV," Luna told the retired talk show maven. "I know you are good and safe. Mommy said."

"Thank you. You are safe here, honey lamb," Winfrey said, enfolding the child gently in her arms, as tears came as she thought of Beloved, and of her own child which might have lived. Luna calmly used a ruffled sleeve of her dress to dry Winfrey's cheeks.

"Where's your daddy?" Winfrey asked, pulling herself together.

"Work in sky," said Luna, pointing up. Cheng Chou was in the *Dragon Nest*, preparing for a moon landing. The studio wall screen showed pictures of him in the station, and at the site on the moon chosen for Apollo City at work on the linear accelerator, a long elevated track to be used for launching vehicles or ore buckets into space.

"Welcome to Chicago, Little Dragon," said Winfrey.

"Chicago, Chicago, that toddlin' town. Chicago, Chicago, a cow burned it down," Luna sang, smiling ingenuously. The audience clapped with glee.

"I don't know where she picked that up," Turquoise said, surprised at the precocity.

"Do you know any other songs, honey child?" asked Winfrey

"Fly me to the moon and let me play among the stars, Let me see what spring is like on Juniper and Mars," Luna sang sweetly. The audience cheered and clapped.

"That we sing in the shower," said Turquoise.

Luna radiated such unaffected cuteness that she stole the show from the UNICEF representatives and Winfrey's other guests.

"Why do you like your Raggedy Ann better than Baby Luna?" Winfrey asked, noticing that she was holding a Raggedy Ann doll.

"Not be careful with Ann," Luna said.

"She's just recently become aware that Baby Luna is modeled after her," said Turquoise to Oprah and the audience. "In the last few months. I feel guilty for exposing her to this shock. She brought her Baby Luna but insisted upon leaving her on the plane. In the crashball."

Turquoise let her walk around the stage and even into the carefully vetted audience to shake hands. Luna was not timid and liked the attention. Back on stage she rubbed the white vicuna-hair dress of Inez Clara Coya, a native leader from Peru who claimed lineal descent from emperor Tupac Amaru. Coya was a New Harmony ally, a director of Spar-Runa, which was bringing electricity to rural areas. Coya was congratulating Jane Fonda.

"I see that he [Ted Turner, a former husband of Fonda's] is changing the name of his baseball team from the Braves to the Dragons, and is discouraging the tomahawk chop and stereotype drum beating and singing," Coya said with a Spanish accent. "I know you've been after him about that." Luna distracted Coya by climbing onto her lap to examine her jewelry. "Mommy stone," Luna said, seeing the polished turquoise in her necklace. Luna went next to Toni

Morrison, the writer, and then to Melinda Gates, Michelle Obama and her daughters, and Sally Ride.

"Hello, Space Girl," said Ride, who with her family was a frequent visitor at New Harmony bases in Canada. "Hello Sally," said Luna, to the first female American astronaut.

Turquoise pitched Han-Spar and Spar-Nippon shares for a minute. Then former UN Secretary-General Ban Ki-Moon spoke briefly. After that there was video of UNICEF projects, including the rehabilitation of former child soldiers in northern Uganda. The show was rebroadcast on UNTV and was downloadable from Luna's websites, and bits of it were carried by world media, altogether reaching over two billion people.

Winfrey invited her guests to supper at her townhouse near the studio. Luna went upstairs with Zhe for a short nap in the guest room before dinner, but couldn't sleep. Coming down the stairs she overheard her mother speaking. "Oprah, you may borrow Luna as much as you want for campaigning, if you run," Turquoise told Winfrey. "And of course New Harmony advisors," she added. "You will have the muscle Barack lacked, . . ."

A furrow crossed Luna's brow, a momentary hurt at not being consulted, soon replaced with a feeling of importance. Only Zhe saw the frown.

On the way to the airport ten cars of *paparazzi* swarmed around the Han-Spar armored sedan. The two motorcycle policemen were unable to control them. Turquoise asked the driver to signal well in advance and pull into an upcoming gas station and restaurant. They stopped under a light pole in an empty part of the parking lot.

"No flashes, okay? Be orderly and you may all have pictures," Turquoise shouted at the photographers. When several stands of lights had been set up, she carried Luna out of the car, putting on her dark glasses. Reporters asked Turquoise questions, as she leaned against the car. She let Luna get down to walk among them, followed by Zhe. Luna was curious about the Paper Ratsies, as she called them.

"A pollster claims Luna is known to ten times more people than was Shirley Temple in her prime," said a photographer to Turquoise. "What do you think of that?"

"I think I must not be a stage mother, and instead see that she has as normal a childhood as possible," said Turquoise.

"Good luck with that," another said facetiously.

"I'm not going to tell her to sparkle whenever she meets the public," Turquoise continued. "Anyway it's almost like comparing apples and oranges, the way the world has changed into a global village."

"Who was Shirley Temper?" Luna asked, provoking a laugh from the photographers. She had gotten a policeman to lift her up and was sitting in front of him on his parked Harley-Davidson. Taking off her sun glasses, she handed them to Zhe. The *paparazzi* knew it was front page material, so cameras clicked and hummed.

After fifteen minutes Turquoise said: "You've met the child. Now we must go." Luna waved goodbye as she got into the car. "Out of regard for her safety, please don't follow us," Turquoise added, and they didn't.

*

Luna was too young for the Winter Ride to Wounded Knee, in December, but Turquoise went with many of her native friends.

For three weeks in May (2014) Turquoise and Luna visited dozens of veterans' hospitals and military bases in the United States, accompanied by former Governor-General Michaelle Jean and her daughter, on behalf of the Canadian armed forces. This was an important part of the master plan. With security provided by the Marine Corps and the RCMP (Royal Canadian Mounted Police), several of whom wore ceremonial red serge tunics and riding breaches, Luna's safety was not a worry.

Luna's next major outing was to Egypt in July to the small New Harmony base on the outskirts of Alexandria for ten days. UNESCO (United Nations Educational, Scientific, and Cultural Organization) officials had invited her to cut the ribbon at the opening of a new wing of the restored library, a disc-shaped building on the seashore that represented the rising sun.

"Now we are faced with the possibility of suicide bombings," Zhe told Turquoise, when informed of the trip. "They need only get close to kill or wound Luna. How are we going to guard her against poor deluded fools loaded with explosives, certain they will fly to Allah's bosom for her murder?"

"When she's out of the base, the Egyptian army will keep people at least 20 metres away, unchecked vehicles at least 60 metres away. They'll have dozens of bomb-sniffing dogs," Turquoise replied. "And the new portable sniffing machines. All known members of the Sword of God are going to be arrested and held for the duration of our visit, under EU anti-terrorist laws."

Security was massive and complex. Han-Spar and New Harmony intelligence services co-ordinated with Egyptian armored and helicopter units, as Luna rode in a parade through huge crowds from the airport to the gates of the base. The base itself—five villas on the same street surrounded by a tall brick wall topped with barbed wire—was surrounded with soldiers. There was no fall-out shelter, but the bunker under the largest villa was well provisioned.

When Turquoise took her to Abydos, the one-time center of Aten monotheism, IdentoCams were used extensively. Hundreds of Egyptian police and soldiers assisted the ten-person Han-Spar team directed by Shui Zhe, as Luna waved from a blast-resistant bubble atop an armored personnel carrier. On the second day crews from UNTV, Egyptian, and international networks filmed Luna and Turquoise as they were taken sailing in a reproduction of a 5,000-year-old royal boat. While the sun set behind the restored Sphinx, Luna said the short evening prayer that her mother had taught her.

"Great Aten dies, so we pray that the boats of night and the scarab roller will bring the God of Everything reborn in the east again tomorrow," she said. She and her mother were wearing royal clothing, some eye make-up, and ankhs on necklaces lent by the Cairo museum.

Reporters asked Turquoise if she really believed in Atenism. "We want to weaken organized religion by showing its roots in paganism. For instance we want to expose Christ as just another sun god, his birthday set appropriately at Winter Solstice by the Roman emperor Constantine," she said. "If I believed any religion, it would be Atenism. But we dismiss most religion as group egotism, akin to tribal identity."

A few days later Luna visited the museum. On behalf of the government and people of Egypt, the director gave her a fifteen-cm-high gold and silver copy of a limestone statuette of Bastet in the form of a cat, its eyes formed by rubies. Luna's cartouche, which described her as 'Beloved of Hathor and sky-friend of Horus and Isis' appeared on both sides of the base. Pictures of Luna's delighted grin as she examined the present made the evening news around the world. (Turquoise didn't have the heart to make her refuse it.) The following day Luna (the golden cat in a pocket of her overalls) visited the garbage dump at Mokattam, six km south of Cairo, where a community of 30,000 lived in shanties of crumbling brick and corrugated steel built on a century of refuse thrown into ancient quarries. The men collected the city's garbage in donkey carts, to be picked over by the women for recoverable material. There were flies, rats, and unpleasant smells. Turquoise and Luna were shown the methane recovery system, the schools, and the medical clinics funded by the Canadian embassy. They were introduced to Dr. Adel Abdel-Malek, the first resident physician of the first clinic.

A little later Luna met a dirty and poorly dressed girl of five, small for her age, who was carrying a scrawny kitten. On an impulse Luna initiated a trade of the statuette for the kitten. Aghast Egyptian officials would have stopped the exchange, which was being filmed by UNTV and several other stations, but Turquoise warned them off.

"Please do nothing," she pleaded. "I will square it with the museum if they make a fuss. For us this is good publicity. I never wanted to accept such an expensive gift."

Next day Turquoise explained to Luna that the kitten, a female, would have to be left at the Alexandrian base because it might have diseases. "We'll have a vet look at her, but tests and papers could take months," Turquoise told her daughter, putting her on the verge of tears. "Perhaps she can be sent to Home Base later on," said Turquoise, who knew that the Executive Council would never permit such an extravagance. It could be used to make New Harmony look hypocritical, warning about global warming while flying a cat around unnecessarily. "You can ask somebody in this base to look after her for you until then."

"I'm so proud of you," continued Turquoise, kissing and hugging Luna. "You have changed the lives of that poor girl and her family and given New Harmony and UNICEF tons of good publicity."

Second Attempt

Several days before leaving Egypt Turquoise attended a conference on the status of women. When the topic came up, Turquoise called for an end to female 'circumcision'—the removal of the clitoris and labia without anesthetic, which was still happening to thirty per cent of young girls in rural areas. "Barbarous!" she thundered. "Just like foot-binding was in China. It is all wrong, . . . the *burqa*, even the veil, stoning for infidelity, belief in the devil, the amputation of the right hands of thieves, . . . all cruel and wrong. Shame on the leaders at al-Azhar University [a Sunni Muslim theological center in Cairo] who have supported these practices. Shame on the Muslim fundamentalists who consider them part of *sharia* law."

For the rest of her life Turquoise occasionally wondered if this outburst precipitated the assassination attempt at the airport three days later. Members of the extremist *Gama'a Islamiya* sect cut down a fence and one of them drove a stolen army truck packed with explosives toward the part of the terminal where Luna was attending a final ceremony. Two German shepherds smelled the explosives and ran after the truck, barking. Police and soldiers fired on the cab of the vehicle, finally stopping it near a parking garage. The subsequent explosion killed ten people, including the four soldiers and two terrorists, and the dogs following the truck. Twenty soldiers and thirty-two civilians were injured. Hearing the blast, Egyptian security officials hurried Turquoise and Luna into the personnel carrier that took them to their Han-Spar biofuel corporate jet. "What was the noise?" Luna asked as she got into the crashball for take-off. "A truck hit a wall," said Turquoise. "When you are older you will understand there are some really bad people," she added vaguely, unable to think of a better evasion.

"Don't blame yourself," said Zhe to Turquoise, seeing her look of guilt. "We have to fight for women's rights, no matter what cost."

Then back to the safety of Home Base.

In the fall there were more trips to US veterans' hospitals and military bases, this time organized by UNICEF and Admiral Brenda Lau, a UN supporter. The right-wing media was suspicious, but didn't connect the dots.

At the end of December Luna rode with her mother in the last day of the Winter Ride to the hamlet of Wounded Knee Creek, South Dakota. Turquoise explained the tragedy in simple terms to her daughter. "On this day in the time of my grandmother's grandmother, some bad soldiers killed three hundred native people, . . . Lakota Sioux, . . . men, women and children. I will tell you more details next year," she said.

Luna turned four in March of 2015, while visiting the base (B3) in the Selkirk Mountains near Lillooet, British Columbia, with her mother. (Turquoise was there for an Executive Council meeting.) B3 was fenced but had no fallout shelter or other defenses, which worried Shui Zhe. She noted that the clumps of lodge pole pine that dotted the base, survivors of the pine beetle ravage throughout the region, might give cover to intruders.

Power for the 15-bedroom manor house, which was high up in the valley and accessible only by cable car or helicopter, and for the 'village' of houses and workshops below, came from a generator at the base of the dam which made a small lake on Cayoosh Creek. (Fish ladders at the side of the dam enabled salmon to return to the headwaters.) The First Air float plane which brought them from Vancouver bobbed beside a dock and hangar.

B3 had been purchased in 1978, and became home to fifteen new New Harmony directors and their families and thirty Vietnamese refugee orphans from six hundred taken by Canada from the *Hai Hong,* a crowded old freighter which managed to reached Malaysia. Luna met some of the 'boat people'—now middle-aged—at her party in the lounge of the manor house. They were doctors, scientists, teachers, pilots, UN personnel, . . . and their spouses and children. "How lucky I am to meet you," a little Eurasian girl told her.

"Thank you for saying a nice thing," Luna replied.

After the party Luna telephoned her kindergarten friends at B1. Meritaten Tat-wing Sit, a blend of Chinese, Jamaican and Egyptian, and Desiderata Jones, from a Celtic heritage, were grandchildren of original directors. Mitsy Mekeke was an orphan who when found as a baby by an aid worker in an arid ditch in Somalia was trying to suckle the breasts of her mother, dead of malnutrition and thirst. Sanjay was the son of Jay Chatterjee, a childhood friend of Turquoise whose father had been abducted and killed by Idi Amin's soldiers, causing the rest of the family to leave Uganda.

At B3 Luna met Carla Robinson, a Haisla/Haitsuk native raised on a reserve in northern B.C., a frequent visitor with many friends at the base. Carla had been an aboriginal channel and CBC news presenter, known for her mellifluous voice and gentle manner, and was to be the next Governor-General of Canada. "You and Chou and Luna must visit me in Rideau Hall," Robinson said to Turquoise, referring to the official residence in Ottawa.

*

In the second week of June Luna visited a base (B26) in Ireland near the Rock of Cashel, Tipperary. Before dawn on the Summer Solstice, Luna, her entourage, and UNESCO officials were driven in five electric vans to a world heritage site, the 5,000-year-old burial mound near Newgrange, north of Dublin. Turquoise and Luna wore long white linen anti-UV sun dresses with long sleeves, and Guinevere visors. They arrived half an hour before sunrise for a ceremony designed to highlight the pagan roots of religion.

About two thousand people were controlled by ten police and twenty UNESCO staff with megaphones. There were old hippies in their seventies, aging New Agers, Wiccans, Stonehenge enthusiasts, and curious locals. Twelve Neo-Druid priests, their naked bodies stained purple with woad, were dancing around others of their sect dressed in white robes. A group of women in blue fatigues prayed to a goddess who was worshiped before St Patrick introduced a patriarchal Christianity. There were also a few dozen liberal Catholics, holding signs for the UNTV cameras which listed the Church's sins against paganism, its mother.

The cairn is eleven metres high and covers about an acre, contained by a curb of stone blocks three metres high. At an average of ten metres outside the cairn is a circle of thirty-five standing megaliths. Turquoise, Zhe, and Luna, were among the fifty people allowed inside the tumulus. They entered through a narrow doorway and walked single file for about twenty metres through a crude passage between slabs of granite roofed with large flagstones. The central burial chamber is almost six metres high, with a corbelled dome. Four and a half minutes after sunrise (a slight wobble in the Earth's rotation had slowed it since the tomb was made) a thin shaft of light from a slit above the entrance illuminated the tomb chamber for seventeen minutes. It reminded Turquoise of the Temple of the Inscriptions at Palenque, constructed so that on the day of the winter solstice the sun appears to sink into Pacal's tomb. She said so when interviewed by UNTV, and Luna recited the morning prayer to Aten. At an outdoor panel discussion UNESCO academics argued that all religions were equally valid or invalid, and that all children have the right to a scientific education.

Turquoise and Luna walked among the crowds, her bodyguards dressed in sandals and brown hemp robes embroidered with the child's cartouche, until everyone had a chance to see them.

On the way home there was a one-day stop in New York to visit the United Nations headquarters as part of its 70th anniversary celebrations. Luna addressed the General Assembly briefly and was given a long standing ovation. (Reps from Saudi Arabia and North Korea walked out in displeasure.) With tight security she and her mother briefly attended a charity ball and a dancethon for the UNHCR (High Commission on Refugees) before flying home. (As usual, trees were planted on and off New Harmony bases as a sort of *mea culpa* for the GHG's produced by her flights despite using biofuel.)

*

In August there were more appearances at US veterans' hospitals and military bases. On a two week tour Luna touched or shook hands and talked with thousands of severely wounded men and women. "Pretend you aren't shocked, honey, even if you are. That's what I do," said Turquoise. The right-wing media impugned the motives behind these visits, complaining that a UN bias was forming in the Joint Chiefs of Staff as well as the rank and file. The right-wing deplored the influence of Admiral Brenda Lau, the first female captain of an aircraft carrier, the *Abraham Lincoln*.

These tours were hard on Luna psychologically. She was rewarded by General Council "for doing her duty," as minutes of the meeting record, first with a refurbished carousel placed near the playground in B1. Then there was a Connemara pony colt and its mother, at first kept in a stall in the barn but then let out with the other horses to graze the back pasture. There was a little blue leather saddle and bridle, boots to match, and a riding helmet, for when the colt, a filly, was strong enough to carry her. Luna named her Moonflower and visited her several times a day.

That fall Luna started two hours of classroom instruction a day, and had a music tutor for half an hour. Shui Zhe patiently took the child from checkers to the rudiments of chess. Luna liked sports; skipping ropes or kicking soccer balls with her friends, and learning to swim in the shallow end of the pool in the Rec center. On several fine days in September she was taken incognito with her friends to Sauble Beach on Lake Huron, with extra bodyguards. On the last of these she made a sand castle with the other children, insisting that she were queen.

"You are just a lucky child," said Zhe twice, deliberately deflating her in front of her friends as the team of psychologists that advised her parents and teachers suggested.

"But I want to live in a castle," said Luna firmly, willing to throw a tantrum.

"You already do, honey," said Zhe, soothing, defusing. "A modern castle with high fences instead of drawbridges . . . . You can pretend to be Queen of the Castle today as long as all the girls take turns, and Sanjay is King for a bit," Zhe continued. "I'll be the Dirty Rascal," Zhe added, which made the child laugh despite herself.

In December, after the gift-giving and feasting of Winter Solstice celebrations, Luna went on her second Winter Ride, this time for the last two days. Her colt Moonflower was too young, and was left behind. Luna rode with Sally Ride, Oprah Winfrey, Michelle Obama and her daughters Sasha and Malia, Carla Robinson, Zhe, Turquoise, and many others. Luna liked the smell of wood smoke from the campfires and sleeping in a tent. Arriving at Wounded Knee, Turquoise told her more about the blue-jacketed soldiers shooting the fleeing Sioux like buffalo, the crumpled bodies of the defenseless women and children, . . .

“I think you should let it wait until she’s older. Don’t burden her with the sorrows of the world at her age,” Zhe said to Turquoise, who thought for a while and then nodded.

Security was heavy, with Secret Service agents around Winfrey and Han-Spar guards around Luna. A phone call warning of an attack by Red Daughters of the Green Dawn was later discovered to be from a right-wing hoaxer.

CHAPTER 2
On Top of the World

It was Monday, July 25th, 2016, at 81 degrees of latitude N. The sun circled like a condor twenty-four hours a day above Tanquary Fjord and the rest of Quttinirpaaq National Park, on the north edge of Ellesmere Island in Nunavut, Canada.

Since their arrival three weeks before, Oolayou, Milly Moosomin, and three scientists had occupied the upper floor of the three-storey residence building used by the seven (Inuit) park staff. Oolayou awoke at 7 a.m., feeling rested but still suffering period cramps, as Milly left the apartment to feed and exercise the huskies. After going to the toilet and showering, Oolayou regarded herself in the mirror as she toweled. *Tall for an Inuk, slim, with light brown skin and the high cheekbones the southern people like, she knew. "You are smart and the world is your oyster," her mother once said, a year before she died, drunk, in a burning house in Rankin Inlet with Oolayou's father.* At thirty-three she was starting to get a bit of fat on her hips, and her face was fuller. She took off the shower cap and brushed and tied back her hair. She dressed in long underwear, jeans and sweater, all synthetic, and the beaded sealskin moccasins she wore indoors. Breakfast was grapefruit, bannock, and coffee.

Oolayou reached across a side table and lifted the top off a soapstone carving of a turtle. She took out a dried bud of marijuana and broke it into the bowl of a small stone pipe shaped as a snake. Holding the pipe, she remembered the morning last winter in the back room of her house in Iqaluit when she made it with her new lathe router. Then she went onto the balcony to have a smoke.

Below, several staff members were hurrying about on the board sidewalks which connected the dozen buildings of the village. Lichens lent the rocks a green hue. Someone went into the old church by the water, now used as a museum, art gallery, and gift shop. A kayak, two red canoes, and three orange zodiac landing craft had been pulled onto the stony beach. White satellite dishes, silver solar collector arrays, and the flashing blades of wind generators shone to her right.

Anchored in the middle of the fjord amid a dozen small new icebergs was the *Kapitan Lebnikov,* a late Soviet-era diesel-electric icebreaker refitted in 1990 to carry a hundred and twenty tourists. (Oolayou knew the ship well, having worked on it as a waitress for three summers in a row during her college years.) The other side of the fjord, two kilometres away, was composed of glaciated cliffs and valleys. Far beyond that she could see Barbeau Peak, the highest of the Nunavut range, and other *nunatuks* well above the remaining ice cap. To the south-east was the ancient route of the paleo-Inuit—the Musk Ox Highway—from the Barren Grounds to Lake Hazen, an oasis in the polar desert, and on to Greenland.

The air temperature on the balcony was 6.5 degrees Celsius, chilly without a jacket, so after five minutes she went inside and watched news stations on her wrist-top. A prominent right-wing academic was speaking.

". . . and as eco-terrorism mounts, becoming as frequent as religious-national terrorism, authorities must adjust their focus. They must distinguish between small-scale terrorism, done with minimal planning by the mentally ill, and others who plan devastation on a large scale. The authorities must distinguish between attention seeking nihilists, the sort of punks you see carrying around copies of Herman Kahn's *On Thermonuclear War*, from real Blasters with money and organization who might be able to assemble enough nuclear weapons to achieve the sort of human extinction they propose, and the prolonged nuclear winter that would cool the planet. That is what the Green Daughters of the Red Dawn ultimately want, with them surviving in shelters. Such Blasters will try to be *agents provocateurs* and start nuclear wars, perhaps between India and Pakistan or in the Middle East," said the academic, from an institute funded by oil companies and America First.

"Religious and political-religious terrorism is localized, but eco-terrorism is global, and rural and urban. We've seen executives of companies running-coal fired generating plants killed in ten states of the US, three provinces of Canada, and across China and India, and now ordinary workers are being blown up," the academic continued.

"That is frightening," said the interviewer.

"Yes, all those men in that bus in China . . . . The four workers leaving a plant in West Virginia last month. This terrorism must be stamped out. We must silence the apocalyptic rabble-rousing Luddites who excite the losers and mentally ill to commit these crimes. When Romney is re-elected I hope he asks Congress to pass laws making it a crime to create panic about global warming. Interpreting every heat wave, every drought, every hurricane and flood, as more evidence for global warming is the sort of alarmist propaganda that must be stamped out. It is like yelling "Fire!" in a crowded theater. Panic is our worst enemy, and will only create anarchy. Romney is our best hope," said the academic. His face, a mask of blandness, annoyed Oolayou enough to change the station.

Fox News was showing pictures of Turquoise, recently made a lieutenant-colonel in the new UN SpaceForce, and Luna, in a matching small uniform, awarding prizes at a UNHCR Somali refugee charity flower show and sale in the orangery of Casa Loma, a castle in Toronto. "Look at the police security," said the journalist David Frum, a prominent supporter of America First. "This left-wing love-in cost Toronto taxpayers thousands of dollars, but no one complains. The cabal of One-World socialists around her mother has mesmerized much of the Canadian public with this so-called most famous child in history. She's kept cloistered in New Harmony bases, and only brought out to charm the armed services or to campaign with Winfrey and the international socialists, and then whisked back to a New Harmony safe area," Frum sniffed.

"Well, to be fair," said Bill O'Reilly, the host, a jingoist American imperialist, "it is a dangerous world for Luna, because of the crazy radical communists and atheists who are using her as their symbol. These people aren't even liberals, they're internationalist socialists as you say, attacking America worse than a thousand 9-11 attacks."

Disgusted, Oolayou turned it off and started working. For an hour she composed reports in Inuktituk and English for the Nunavut Combined Office of Warming Response, her employer, in Iqaluit. Oolayou was a liaison officer who also advised Nunavut's government on national and international environmental law.

While in the park she had been helping three scientists on the Canadian Continental Polar Ice Shelf Project. One scientist was an ozone expert, formerly at the Environment Canada weather and ozone monitoring station across the island in the hamlet of Eureka. Another, George Bell, 42, a glacier and permafrost expert, also worked for the UN Intergovernmental Panel on Climate Change. The third, Susan May, 53, from the University of Toronto, was an expert on Arctic flowering plants. Some days Oolayou helped Professor May take pictures of changes in flora. On others she assisted Professor Bell by numbering glacial core samples and transporting them by battery-powered ATV to the refrigeration hut.

The phone in her wrist-top beeped: an encrypted call with a five second delay. It was Boris Larinov, First Mate of the *Kapitan Lebnikov*, with whom she'd had a fling twelve years before, during the last weeks of her last summer aboard the ship. She'd met him again by chance Saturday morning as he got out of a zodiac filled with tourists on the beach near the church.

"A glorious morning to you, most glorious lady," Larinov said in Russian, in his extravagant way. The camera in his wrist-top sent a picture of his torso and face to the small screen on her wrist-top. "You have been busy, I quite understand, and unable to come over. But we are sailing tomorrow morning and so tonight you must certainly come to dine with me at the captain's table. I'll send a zodiac for you at seven," he said.

"Okay, but I'm bringing a friend as chaperone," replied Oolayou in Russian, intending to stifle any romantic ideas he might have. She knew Larinov, 47, now had a wife and two children in Murmansk.

"The watch said a plane came in last night. More things for the scientists?" he asked casually.

"I don't know," she said. "I can't see the air strip from here. Anyway, I'll come tonight for supper. Goodbye." His expression, on the little screen of her wrist-top, was too Cheshire cat-like for her comfort, so she threw it up on a wall screen. His brown hair was thinning in front, she saw, but his goatee and mustache were as well trimmed as ever, his white uniform immaculate. *Be careful, she told herself. He could be a spy.*

The phone beeped again. It was her father calling from his cottage at B1. David Eaton-Gage, scion of several old Toronto families, was one of the founders of the New Harmony group. He and his wife Janet, unable to have children of their own, had adopted Oolayou when she was eight, and she grew up at Home Base. (Forest Winds, the Eaton-Gage estate in King City (a rural area north of Toronto) had become a reception area where refugees stayed while New Harmony recruiters selected the brightest children and their families.) Always a good student, Oolayou did well at St. Andrew's College, a private school north of Toronto where her uncle Nicky was headmaster, Glendon College of York University, and Osgoode Hall law school.

"Hello, my daughter," he said, also using encryption. "We haven't talked in a week."

"Hello, my father," she said. "How are you?" On the little screen he looked his seventy years, with gray and white hair, wrinkles, jowls, and loose skin around his throat.

"I'm fine. Just a bit of muscle pain in my lower back," he replied.

"Too much gardening," said Oolayou. "You must take it easy. Also you must delegate more work at PromTek."

"I visited the grave yesterday," her father said. Janet Flavelle had died in February, and been buried in a pre-dug hole in a biodegradable shroud in the small nineteenth century graveyard in the forest at B1. (Cremation was considered to add to global warming, and carnivorous beetles followed by a bone grinder was too avant-garde for Janet.) Oolayou had flown down to deliver the eulogy. "It was very peaceful in the glade, and still some painted trilliums blooming," he added.

"You must send me pictures of it," Oolayou said. A few minutes later her father changed the subject.

"I've been told confidentially by Jamie that you are going to be offered an important UN role in the Transition. I don't know what exactly . . . . I'm so proud of you, my heart soars," her father said.

"But there are dangers," he warned. "You may become a target for America First and other reactionary groups. The reformist coalition supporting the UN world government movement may break into factions. As you know, within New Harmony itself the socialists and liberals are suspicious of each other, the Canadian directors feel threatened by some American directors, the vegetarians and Indian block want more power, and some radical feminists still want Jamie expelled . . . . It is into this minefield that you go."

"I'm overwhelmed. But I'll do my best, and rely on you for advice," Oolayou said. Her mind was racing. "I'll keep in touch. Goodbye, Dad."

Oolayou sat thinking. A few minutes later Milly Moosomin returned to the apartment. Milly was a resident director and veterinarian from the New Harmony base (B98) north of Regina, Saskatchewan, where over the last ten years she had reintroduced a herd of four hundred bison on 2000 hectares of land. She was Metis, married to a Cree, a pilot of small fixed-wing craft for First Air. They had a grown daughter, active in aboriginal politics, but no grandchildren. Colonel Molly Moosomin, a cousin, was the supervisor of flight instruction at the Canadian Forces air base near Cold Lake, Alberta. Milly was at the park to assist the staff with the sled dogs, which the three hundred and fifty tourists who visited the park each summer expected to see.

"First, you are excused from work today and tomorrow. Susan May just told me," Milly said, taking off her buckskin jacket and going out to the balcony to brush dog hair from her plaid shirt and ski pants.

"I'm feeling okay," said Oolayou. "I felt logy but I had a few puffs of weed."

"I told you to take a spoonful of cannabis extract in the brown jar, and not get tar in your lungs," said Milly in a motherly tone. "Queen Victoria's Midol, it's labeled. I use it for menopausal symptoms."

"But that's not it," Milly continued. "We have visitors. Turquoise and Luna and her Chinese bodyguard, with a UN official from the environmental protection division. Oh, and a young fellow, a camera person for UNTV. They flew in from Resolute [Bay] late last night on a Nunavut government plane, a DC-3 with new biofuel engines and balloon tires for emergency landings, with some seats removed and a crashball for Luna bolted in. The pilot and a park guy are taking turns guarding it."

"What? Don't joke with me, Milly. It's not kind," said Oolayou, looking hard at the older woman.

"No joke. Turquoise and the others are on the floor below. Still sleeping, the Han-Spar guard told me," replied Milly. "She is Shui Zhe, . . . do you remember? From the Winter Ride last December? Big. A weight-lifter. Thirties. Short hair, leathery face, big nose, pointed chin."

"Of course I know her. She's been with Luna since Lop Nur," said Oolayou.

"On the last two days of the most recent ride to Wounded Knee she coordinated the IdentoCam screens around Oprah and Luna with the Secret Service. Some people thought her officious," said Milly.

"The truck bomb in Cairo made her paranoid, that's all," said Oolayou.

"Anyway, Zhe said to please come down at ten," continued Milly.

"Will wonders never cease?" said Oolayou. "It's been months since I talked to Turquoise [on the telephone]."

For the next half an hour they sat on a couch sipping coffee. Oolayou selected her favorite recording of "Finlandia" on her wrist-top. It was followed by John Lennon's "Imagine," which had become the unofficial UN anthem. The music calmed her as it always did. Then she and Milly went down to Turquoise's apartment, bringing some food. Shui Zhe unlocked the door, let them in and relocked it. Oolayou exchanged greetings with Zhe. The light was dim but Oolayou could see the holster built into her bullet-proof vest, as Zhe led them into one of the bedrooms. The blind was slightly open, making a shaft of sunlight.

"Oolly, it's you," said Turquoise, rising in a bathrobe from the large futon bed. "I didn't call ahead because of security. Sorry."

"That's okay. I understand," replied Oolayou. They embraced, each kissing the other's left cheek and then rubbing noses. Turquoise had been like an older sister when Oolayou was growing up in Home Base. Then Milly and Turquoise embraced.

"You are looking good for an old lady," Milly joked. They were both 45, but Turquoise was a month older. "Congratulations on your appointment to the SpaceForce," Milly added.

"Well, there is a lot of space and not much force, so far," replied Turquoise.

Oolayou sat in an armchair. Luna lay still, her long eyelashes together. At five years of age she had a pretty oval Eurasian face, with almond-shaped eyes, skin the rich hue of walrus ivory, fine reddish brown hair, and her mother's dimples and pert nose. Milly, sitting on the bed, sang softly: "Soeur Luna, Soeur Luna, dormez-vous? Dormez-vous? Sonnez les matines. Ding, dong, ding." The little pixie smiled as she awoke and pushed back the sheets. "Oolayou and Milly," she said gleefully.

The child got out of bed and climbed onto Oolayou's lap. Her flannel pajamas, made in an executiveless UN factory in Nova Scotia which payed high wages to workers and donated profits to UNICEF, portrayed Canadian secular heroes: Terry Fox, Banting and Best, Norman Bethune, Louise Arbour, Alexander Graham Bell, Julie Payette, and herself and Turquoise, among others. (The factories also made clothes for Baby Luna dolls, which were still selling well.)

Luna kissed Oolayou's cheek and rubbed noses, the child remembering how it snowed as she was held in the saddle in front of Oolayou on a bay mare during her last ride to Wounded Knee Creek, South Dakota, last December. And then on Milly's palomino gelding. At night, far from cities, the stars were bright. From the open flap of the tent Oolayou had pointed out the brightest, some constellations, and distant dancing Northern Lights.

Then the girl hugged Milly, asking about her husband and daughter, before saying: "Excuse me, bathroom." Zhe preceded Luna, turning on the shower for her and checking the water temperature with the inside of her wrist while the girl went to the toilet.

"Is Luna being affected by so much attention?" Milly asked Turquoise.

"Sometimes she is a bit demanding, usually when she's tired. Actually she's become quite patient and cooperative at official functions or campaigning. She accepts that she has duties," said Turquoise. "But recently, after seeing an old movie about Elizabeth I, at times Luna tells men to kneel in front of her and be knighted and kiss the back of her hand. I hope the media doesn't get wind of it."

"People would just think that was cute," said Oolayou.

The women chatted for several minutes before Luna returned, clad in a bath towel. As she helped Luna get dry, Oolayou noticed that one side of the towel showed Oprah Winfrey and Luna as they led a tree-planting brigade on a clear-cut hillside in British Columbia last May. The other showed Luna and Shirley Temple Black with panda cubs at the new Han-Spar/WWF breeding station north of the Toronto Zoo, in April on the latter's 89th birthday.

Oolayou blew-dry Luna's hair. The child dressed herself with long underwear, thermal socks, and overalls, and came to eat with the women in the kitchen. Oolayou ladled out a bowl of warmed up left-over chicken won ton soup for her, and cut pieces of bannock and grapefruit. After the child had eaten, Turquoise helped her put on mukluks and a nylon jacket, and smeared UV-blocking cream and insect repellant on her face, neck and hands.

"I don't want it," Luna said emphatically when Turquoise put a wide-brimmed straw hat with a bee-keeper veil on her head.

"You want to get too much sun and get rough skin like me?" Zhe asked. "Skin cancer at fifty?"

"Well," Turquoise said, "for now we could tie back the veil with a string so you can see better, and Zhe will let it down if mosquitoes or flies attack. They can be so bad they drive the caribou quite mad."

Luna accepted this compromise and went off with Milly and Zhe to visit the kennels.

"Let me tell you what is going on," said Turquoise to Oolayou. "[Former UN Secretary-General] Kofi [Annan] is indeed heading up the new environmental protection division, under the Kyoto protocol. The scientists of the Intergovernmental Panel on Climate Change will advise him about abatement, and about whom to charge criminally under the new legislation. After the United States signs on, of course."

"What if Winfrey doesn't win?" asked Oolayou. "She's ahead in the polls, but November is ages away."

"Perish the thought," said Turquoise. "Anyway, Kofi got permission for this trip from Appiah Nungat [Nunavut's Minister of the Environment]. Kofi's director of Personnel and Budget is going to ask you to be in charge of policing for Canada and Alaska. Congratulations, my dear. What a responsibility!"

"I'm going to need advice and help, okay?" said Oolayou.

"Yes," replied Turquoise. "You can have Beloved Morton [a brilliant chess player, mathematician, and military historian] as your chief intelligence officer. You'll work with Interpol and national police agencies. You'll be given relevant information by all UN and New Harmony intelligence services, including Red Hand."

"Jesus H. Christ!" said Oolayou. "All of a sudden I'm working with the professional assassins of Red Hand. All the Gandhians and other pacifists in New Harmony will despise me for that. It is not what Nelson Mandela would do."

"General Council has approved," said Turquoise. "Anyway, Red Hand will not be used to enforce international environmental criminal laws, unless you ask for their help."

"Milly said there was a UNTV cameraman," said Oolayou.

"This is presumptuous, I know. Sorry," said Turquoise, "but Kofi's advisors wanted publicity for the new police force. The UNTV guy is going to film Luna in a little green helmet and green uniform on a deteriorating glacier. Like last year when she wore the blue helmet and camouflage and sat on a tank to recruit for the UN armed services."

"Wow!" said Oolayou. "Double wow."

"The actual site hasn't been selected. Any ideas?" asked Turquoise.

"Oh, I know where!" said Oolayou. "The Hand of God. On the cliffs on the southern curve of the fjord. Photos from the seventies show how the glacier once looked like a mighty hand and forearm, so people called it the Hand of God. But now the features are eroded and hard to discern. It is partly covered with sand and gravel and cut by streams in summer . . . . Milly can bring a sled and team of dogs."

"Brilliant imagery! I'll tell the cameraman," said Turquoise. "Perhaps you can show us this afternoon. Also Kofi's personnel man wants to talk to you, of course."

Oolayou turned in her chair, looking uncomfortable.

"Are you okay?" Turquoise asked.

"I'm on the rag," replied Oolayou. "Just cramps."

"Come into the bedroom," said Turquoise. "Lie face down on the bed."

Oolayou took off her sweater and pulled up her underwear top so Turquoise could knead her lower back, as she used to do when Oolayou first started menstruating at twelve. "Monday Monday" and other hits of the Momas and Papas played softly in the background. Turquoise rubbed some flower-oil perfume onto Oolayou's skin as they talked.

"What if your father dies?" Oolayou asked, half of her face on a pillow. "He keeps the various factions in line. Without him the leading directors will quarrel."

"His prostate cancer is under control." said Turquoise. "He should live at least ten years. By then the transition to world federalism should be well under way, and also the key moves against global warming."

"Of course I want to avoid extremism," said Oolayou. "I want an approach to enforcement that acknowledges that we are all guilty of causing warming, but some more than others. That there is a big web of guilt and alienated indifference in most industrialized countries."

"Yes, that is the line New Harmony and the UN will follow," replied Turquoise. "It can be expected that increasingly bad natural disasters, earthquakes excepted, will raise panic and lead to mob action and scapegoating. The UN must remain even-handed on a twenty of thirty year plan of emission reduction and population stabilization. The UN must work with offending corporations and governments, not threaten them."

"I'm feeling better," said Oolayou, "I'll go to the loo, and then make some notes."

"The UN guy is probably close by. Shall we go find him?" asked Turquoise twenty minutes later, as Oolayou had finished writing on her wrist-top.

I go to meet my fate, thought Oolayou as they walked down the stairs.

When questioned, a park employee pointed them to the former Catholic church. It was a small maroon wooden building, with solar panels over the original tin covering of the roof and spire. Half the pews were gone, to make room for wood and glass cases displaying stone carvings, from mythological (a cannibal spirit, Fart Man, and the sun god *akycha*) to realistic. Profit went to the hospital in Iqaluit. The sun-bleached skull and jawbone of a bow whale was where the pulpit had been. Old bone-tipped harpoons and several caribou antlers were fixed to the walls, next to aerial photos of local glaciers.

Watched by half a dozen tourists from the *Kapitan Lebnikov*, the UNTV cameraperson and the UN official were playing chess on a card table at the back near the pot-bellied stove, sitting on folding chairs. The board-case of leather and wood, and the white and green stone pieces were a set made by Oolayou. The pawns were seals, rooks were rampant polar bears, with male and female Inuks in parkas for king and queen. There were seahorse knights and fish standing on their tails for bishops.

Turquoise and Oolayou were much better than the players, but they watched politely for fifteen minutes without kibitzing until the game was over. Then a whistle blew and the tourists left. The young park attendant by the cash register announced that he was going for a coffee break, leaving the four alone to talk.

Turquoise introduced Oolayou to Ira Swartz, the cameraperson. His long hair was gathered in the back with an elastic. Born into an orthodox Jewish family in Toronto, Swartz rebelled in his teens and began reading Philosophy. At 28 he was some kind of Marxist, and carried a copy of the *Economic and Philosophical Manuscripts of 1844* in his backback.

Ravindar Naran was in his mid forties; thin, balding, medium height, wearing wire-rimmed glasses. He was dressed in long-legged khaki safari gear, complete with jacket and white pith helmet against the sun.

"Delighted to meet you," he said to Oolayou. "I was born near New Delhi and educated there. I have stayed at B14, your base near Chennai [Madras], and have friends there. But that is another story, for another time . . . . I have come from New York bearing greetings from Undersecretary-General Annan and the United Nations Ecological Criminal Offenses Police. UNECOP. I'm the Director of Personnel and Budget Management."

"I'm overwhelmed, but flattered by your notice of me," said Oolayou, as Ira Swartz went off to get his gear ready.

"I won't beat about the bush," said Naran to Oolayou. "Mr Annan wants you to head enforcement for Canada and Alaska. You'll have fifty inspectors, thirty uniforms, and legal staff of twenty, if things go as planned. Maybe more later. You'll have contact with Interpol and UNINTEL. The accused will come to The Hague, until the International Criminal Court sets up other branches."

"I'll do my best," said Oolayou. "But I feel trepidation . . . . If I begin to feel used as an instrument of terror when reason and persuasion are required, I shall quit," said Oolayou.

"Of course," replied Naran. "It's going to be 99% carrot, 1% stick. We are democratic socialist humanists, after all. There is the example of Gandhi and Mandela, of living simply and using non-violence to bring social change."

"Good," said Oolayou. "Count me in."

"This letter from Mr Annan contains the details. Welcome to the UN and the Transition effort. Sign here. You are a UN eco cop, starting now."

The three talked for half an hour about the main goals of the planned transition to world government: stopping all wars and demilitarizing, except for UN and African Union forces; stabilizing the population at nine billion by 2050 by providing at least ten years of education to all children, especially girls; weakening most organized religions to lessen religious-territorial strife and liberate women. The New Harmony leadership considered these to be necessary steps in stopping deforestation, pollution, and global warming itself.

Then Luna came in with Milly and Zhe, who showed her around the room, naming objects and explaining their use, lifting her up to see into cabinets and cases. Ira Swartz brought in sandwiches from the cafeteria for lunch. Oolayou was eating when her wrist-top beeped. Boris Larinov. She turned away from the others.

"Venerable lady," said Larinov, "I find out second and third hand that you have a wonderful visitor, really out of this world, because you do not tell me." He paused. "But I shall forgive this negligence if you can bring all the visitors and your scientists too, with you this evening. The captain is very desirous of meeting the Little Dragon and her mother."

"It's not my decision to make," said Oolayou. "There is always a worry about security. So I'll ask and get back to you."

Oolayou turned to Turquoise. "The First Mate of the *Lebnikov*. He and the captain want you and Luna, and the rest of us, to dine on board tonight."

"Yes, I want to go," said Luna.

"No," said Zhe. "Security would be a problem. Just to give some tourists a thrill. Han-Spar won't like that!"

"You are not the boss of me," said Luna, glaring at Zhe. Turquoise thought for thirty seconds before speaking.

"Zhe, could you go over to the ship after we get back from the glacier?" Turquoise asked gently. "You'll meet their head of security and go over the passenger list and the crew list for anything fishy.

Insist that everyone who enters the dining room tonight goes through an IdentoCam check. If something looks bad, we'll cancel."

Oolayou wondered if Zhe would threaten to call Han-Spar officials at Lop Nur or Beijing, but she just nodded curtly. Oolayou called Larinov and made the arrangements.

"Okay," said Turquoise. "If we are all set, let's go to the glacier."

"I've got my camera stuff and Luna's uniform in one zodiac," said Swartz, "and there is another for the dogs and sled. A park guy with a rifle is coming in another in case of any problem."

Life jackets were put on and the zodiacs pushed into the water. Luna's silver-colored survival suit glinted in the sun. The zodiac carrying Milly and the dogs had a tarpaulin to protect the rubberized fabric of the craft from canine toenails. The batteries that powered the motors were checked. Going slowly near shore for safety, it took half an hour to reach the valley next to the Hand of God. Then another half an hour, walking over gravel, stones, and mud from melted permafrost, following the slope beside a fast-flowing stream of melt water to the side of the glacier.

They passed several weather vanes on tripods, tall as men, their propellers into the breeze. In addition to wind speed and direction, the devices recorded air and ground temperature.

Pink moss campions, yellow poppies, white bell heather, and purple saxifrage blossomed amid low grasses and lichen. The dogs watched Arctic hares in the distance and murres and terns above. At the top of the glacier Luna got into the sled and six huskies in fan formation pulled at Milly's command. The camera showed the deterioration of the glacier—its surface was mostly gray and brown, and only white where a break had recently occurred or where streams of meltwater cut channels. Old photos and satellite pictures from NASA's Earth Observatory satellite were shown.

"The Hand of God," Turquoise said to the camera, "once looked like a mighty white forearm with giant fingers and upraised thumb stretching down the slope. Now all that is eroded. Lubricated by meltwater, the glacier is slipping ever faster into the sea. Yet there are still sceptics who say that the world's climate has changed drastically many times in the past. For instance not far from here at Stenkel Fjord is a petrified forest of Paleocene-Eocene, fifty-five million tears ago, with trunks up to one metre thick, so it must have been warm then.

Further south on Ellesmere Island scientists recently found a fossil three metres long of *tiktaalik roseae,* a Permian lobe fish making the transition onto land to evolve into the first tetrapod animals. That was 375 million years ago, and the climate was tropical."

"And at one time, 600 million years ago, the earth was completely covered with snow as carbon dioxide decreased," Turquoise continued. "So sceptics say there was a lot of change in temperature, and that is normal. But this is different. Unabated, the greenhouse gases will render our planet uninhabitable, creating Venus-like conditions that are irreversible. That is the threat. It is up to each of us, particularly in developed countries, to prevent this terrible outcome."

Professor Bell spoke about the great amounts of natural gas burned to heat the large amounts of water necessary, the vast holes, smoke plumes, and glistening slicks on immense tailing ponds around the tar sands operations in northern Alberta. He warned about the methane released as permafrost melted. He pointed to recent developments such as polar bears mating with grizzlies, caribou herds diminishing, and robins appearing.

Luna had the last word. "Together we can save the world. Vote for politicians who help the United Nations," she said, sitting in the sled.

After they returned to the village, Luna and Turquoise had a nap. Oolayou wrote in her diary. At 5.20 Zhe was picked up by a black zodiac from the *Kapitan Lebnikov.*

Zhe called Turquoise at 6.30. "There are eight suspicious passengers and two crew members with criminal records," Zhe said. "For some reason there are three former Blacktide contract workers on board. You know that Blacktide is owned by Joel Atkins, a wealthy America First supporter who made big money providing mercenaries in Iraq after 2004. Of course he hates the UN for limiting American 'freedom.' There are also two thuggish-looking characters with connections to Russian oil and shipping interests who want the Arctic Ocean ice-free year round. Several passengers have mental health problems, including one woman who has not been taking her medication. I think we should cancel."

"No," said Turquoise. "We have an obligation to share Luna with the public. Tell the ship's head of security to make sure the suspicious ones have no weapons. Post several armed guards around the captain's table. That should be enough. See you soon."

Luna wanted her hair gathered up with Chinese combs at the back. She chose to wear formal slippers and a dark blue silk jacket and pants, all embroidered with dragons. Oolayou wore a beaded sealskin skirt and blouse, Milly the same in buckskin. Turquoise put on a black knit dress which seemed formal enough for the occasion, a Sinai turquoise necklace, and beige vicuna-hair shawl. The male scientists and Ira Swartz borrowed jackets and ties from park staff, while Ravi Naran was dressed in Nehru jacket and trousers. Two of the ship's zodiacs picked them up on the beach at 7.30.

Soon the long black hull of the *Kapitan Lebnikov* loomed above. At the bow were several cargo cranes above the hold. The passengers' cabins were amidship in a big white box five storeys high, topped by the officers' cabins and the main bridge, in front of the stack. The helicopter pad and a hanger housing two Russian-built Mil-18's for sightseeing, were at the stern, where Luna and the others came up on the lift. They were met by the captain, Serge Rafalovich, a short man in his sixties with a beard and bulbous nose. Oolayou and Boris Larinov did the introductions. Crew members and passengers cheered as Luna made her way to the auditorium on Deck 7 for pictures. She smiled and waved as passengers snapped her photo. (No flashes allowed.) Held up by Larinov, she examined pictures of the Antarctic, which the ship visited every year.

The dining room was on Deck 4. When everyone was seated the captain stood to introduce Luna and the others.

"In China she is known as Little Dragon. As Moon Child she is worshiped, against her parents' wishes, as a sky goddess in western parts of India. She is UNICEF's best ambassador and Oprah Winfrey's best campaigner in her run for the US presidency. Here is Luna. Also let us welcome her mother, Turquoise Ramsey, who needs no introduction, and the others who honor us with their presence here this evening." When the clapping died down, a dozen people asked to come forward and have Luna print her name on copies of the evening's carte de fare. Then everyone was served fresh broiled char from Lake Hazen in sauce with vegetables from the ship's greenhouse, and the captain said grace. An agnostic, he did not want to offend Turquoise and the other atheists of New Harmony by reference to a god. "As the Innu do, we humbly thank the spirits of these fishes for this sustenance," he said simply.

Luna ate with gusto. "Very nice and delicious, and thank you to everyone who helped with dinner," she said, when the chef came out of the adjacent kitchen to shake her hand. Dessert was Baked Alaska. When she was finished eating, Luna insisted on taking a sunflower stalk out of a big vase on the table, removing the heads.

"What are you doing, little monkey?" asked Turquoise. Without answering, Luna walked over to the captain's chair. "For loyal service I dub thee Captain Serge Braveheart of the North," she said, touching the epaulette on his left shoulder with the tip of the sunflower stalk, and then extending the back of her right hand to be kissed. The captain complied and people clapped.

Third Attempt

Just then a woman ran at Luna. No one had reacted when this woman got off the elevator and entered the dining room, clad in an overcoat, her disheveled henna-red hair covered with a kerchief.

"She is a little Caligula, the devil in the form of a child, the Anti-Christ Stalinist who comes to destroy belief in God," the stout, middle-aged woman screamed in Russian, pulling a carving knife from a pocket of her coat. One of the ship's security guards grabbed at her but missed. Zhe got her pistol out quickly and hit the woman in the abdomen with a single shot, causing her to fall to the floor about five metres from Luna. Zhe took off her protective vest and wrapped Luna in it, handing her to Turquoise, who went to the corner of the room nearest the elevator. Zhe, the other guards, and Oolayou and Milly, all circled Turquoise like musk ox as she descended to the main deck and prepared to disembark. The captain accompanied them, wringing his hands, apologizing profusely, until the visitors were in zodiacs.

The DC-3 was ready to go when they reached shore, and the luggage was soon packed and stowed. "I shall communicate with you soon about finding your headquarters, getting your staff, and meeting your counterparts," Naran said to Oolayou.

"We'll stop in Resolute and report to the RCMP," said Turquoise, embracing Milly and then Oolayou. Zhe said nothing but Oolayou impulsively embraced and kissed her cheeks and rubbed noses. A sob shook Zhe, who hurried into the plane. Luna was already in her crashball, testing the communications system, with the hatch still open, as the DC-3 readied for takeoff.

Boris Larinov came to Oolayou's apartment an hour later. "She was one of the passengers on Shui Zhe's list," Boris said, sitting in the kitchen with Milly and Oolayou. "Olga Petroff, poor wretch. Traveling with her aunt, looking to meet a man on board and always being rejected. She was carried to the infirmary on a stretcher but the doctor was unable to save her life. The bullet must have torn her abdominal aortic artery and hit her spine, so the doctor said. She had a history of depression. Her father raised her very strictly and religiously after her mother died, her aunt said. In Vladivostok. Some crazy letters were found in her cabin, one addressed to [former president] Putin." He paused and drank coffee.

"The cell phone pictures exonerate Zhe completely," Boris continued. "From where she was sitting, she could not have risen and lunged in time to intercept Ms Petroff. The relevant pictures will be sent to the RCMP in Resolute Bay with the witness statements the Captain took, so Zhe will be in the clear."

Oolayou told Boris about her new job.

"Splendid! No one is better qualified," he said.

"But many people will come to hate me," Oolayou said. "I was going to tell the captain that the diesel engines of the *Lebnikov* are a problem and should be replaced. Or better emission control in the stack."

"Those engines are what, forty-five years old?" replied Boris. "I'll notify the company. Perhaps something can be done that is not prohibitively expensive. But you must not be afraid of tough measures. Perhaps all unnecessary use of fossil fuels in travel will first become very expensive and then be curtailed at some point."

They talked for another twenty minutes. Boris could see that the women were tired, so he took his leave. Oolayou walked with him to the water's edge. "Someday we'll meet again, my love, somewhere . . ." he said, pretending to strum a balalaika. "Lara's Theme" had been their song. They kissed goodbye, a friendly, mutually generous kiss that lasted longer than necessary. Back in the apartment, Oolayou couldn't resist stepping out onto the balcony to watch his zodiac become tiny in the distance as it approached the ship. A small shaft of loneliness and self-doubt went through her body, as the sun poured down like cloying honey.

Then she slipped into bed and sleep came quickly, a healing balm.

CHAPTER 3
The Fourth Attempt, from Deep in the Heart of America First

A week later Oolayou returns to Iqualuit. She gives notice and ties up loose ends at work—the prosecution of an iron mine for air pollution, and the owners of a ship for discharging bilge water outside the harbor. To prepare for her new job she telephones other regional heads. Terry Seale, 47, is an Afro-American professor of environmental law at Harvard Law School who grew up in Buffalo, N.Y. and therefore knows a lot about Canada. He is in charge of the continental US. Maria Sanchez, 41, is a Oaxacan criminal lawyer put in charge of Mexico and Central America. Oolayou puts her in touch with several residents of the New Harmony base (B9) near Oaxaca.

In bits of spare time Oolayou reads about the ecological disaster, due to deforestation and rats, that befell the inhabitants of Easter Island. She exchanges e-mails with Boris Larinov every few weeks as he moves about the oceans.

August turns into September. One cold rainy afternoon near the end of the month she takes a hydrogen-powered taxi to the village of Niaqunnut, five km south east of town, to visit the women's shelter and kindergarten that is funded by her carvings. She buys more bone and stone from the old men who collect it for her. Five minutes after returning there is a fully encrypted call from Turquoise.

"I can't speak on the phone, it's too important," she says. "Meet me in Montreal tomorrow, Room 227, the Travelodge on Herron Road near the Trudeau Airport in Dorval. Bring your passport. I'll be registered under the name Mary Craft."

Oolayou doesn't hesitate. She writes down the information, says goodbye to Turquoise, and packs a suitcase. Next afternoon she takes a taxi to the Iqaluit airport, which has many good runways from its DEW-line days and because plane manufactures winter-test their products there. After going through the terminal building, which is painted in a school bus yellow she has never liked, she catches the old Boeing 727 that First Air runs to Montreal every few days. The flight is uneventful and she leaves the airport by taxi at 6.30.

They can't be sure the room isn't bugged, so they go for a walk along the busy, noisy, street. Turquoise is incognito, in sun glasses and kerchief, and talks in a low voice.

"Harry Katz [New Harmony's intelligence chief] has an agent in touch with a high ranking CIA officer. Formerly the head of the Russian, Ukranian, and Georgian section, now Chief of Counterintelligence. He's on the point of defecting, but is afraid. Hugo Mann is his name."

Gusts of wind blow a piece of newspaper past them.

"Mann told our agent that the director of the CIA is plotting to kidnap Luna and bomb B1, using former Blacktide personnel who are working freelance, but making it look like the work of Sunni terrorists," Turquoise continues. "But he doesn't know more details."

"But listen," she says. "Harry Katz secretly pays some of the convenience stores and gas stations owners around Owen Sound for links to their surveillance tapes. Yesterday the Identocam computer noticed a guy who was one of the former Blacktide mercenaries aboard the *Kapitan Lebnikov* in July. Jason Kurtz. He somehow avoided conviction for the manslaughter of several Iraqi civilians. Here are some pictures of him. This one was yesterday, buying gasoline."

"Sometimes a coincidence is just a coincidence," says Oolayou. "I know the CIA leadership is mostly America First and hates the UN, but that is too monstrous. Some planner got carried away in a moment of hatred, . . ."

"Such terrorism, so close to home, would help the Republicans," says Turquoise. "Maybe get a suspension of elections. George W. Bush may have a hand in the plot, still trying to justify his war in Iraq." They were walking back to the Travelodge.

"So where do I come in?" asks Oolayou.

"Well," replies Turquoise, "Mann won't come for money, but he might come for love. Harry Katz had a comely young beauty from Magus Players ready to go to Washington, where the meetings with Mann occur. But she underwent an emergency appendectomy three days ago. Could you play Mata Hari?"

* * *

Under a hidden moon Hugo Mann is fleeing to Canada. It's raining, with distant flashes of lightening, as the rented hydrogen-powered BMW he's driving rolls up the west side of the beltway around Washington, past Baltimore and north on Interstate 83. Hugo has final decided, and he's running north to meet the New Harmony team that will get him across the border. The woman beside him says little, watching to see if they are being followed. By overcast early morning they're in Pennsylvania, following the valley of the Susquehanna River to Harrisburg. Pasture lands appear, disappear, in the misty haze. He remembers three nights ago, when he decided to go, how her smooth body, her gentle hands, her Russian poetry, transformed a tawdry Washington motel room into their summer palace.

He's a short man, balding, bearing the facial acne scars of his youth. If you passed him on the street, you wouldn't give him a second look. Yet today he's someone with a pocketful of CIA secrets.

Just before noon a helicopter appears above them. A half hour later two black Lincolns come close behind. It's raining heavily, on a winding mountainous single lane highway on the eastern border of the Allegheny National Forest. State and local police are refusing to help catch Mann. They see it as a power struggle between left and right, and wish to remain neutral.

The first agency car opens fire with a window-mounted Gatling, aiming at the BMW's tires. The BMW swerves out of control on a hilly turn, careens through a fence, and plows into a large field of pumpkins. Bullets throw up bits of pumpkin, the orange skins spewing innards like pale yellow flesh. Through gusts of rain the pursuers see Mann in a business suit, carrying a briefcase, sprint through a clearing and jump a stone fence. There is a woman with him. They enter a thick forest of hickory, walnut, ash and pine. Lightening cracks and the helicopter returns to base. Agents follow the fugitives on foot but lose them, finding no tracks on the sodden red, brown, and yellow carpet of leaves.

*

It's 8.35a.m., Tuesday, October 18th. George Hawkins, director of the Central Intelligence Agency, strides back and forth in the operations bunker deep below the marble floors of the CIA headquarters building in Langley, Virginia, across the Potomac River from Washington, D. C. Hawkins has an urge to smash something. He scowls at the screens that are his windows on the world. He hasn't been this angry since February 1994, when Aldrich Ames, also the agency's Chief of Counterintelligence, was arrested (by the FBI!) for betraying all major sources in the Soviet Union in the final years of the Cold War and beyond for a paltry total of $2.7 million.

"Find Mann, debrief him, and terminate him with prejudice," Hawkins shouts at an assistant. "He'll probably head for Canada. Use the special squad. Ten helicopters. Retrieve those files! We are warning and recalling all affected agents until we can assess the extent of the damage." The director's drawl has been quickened by many decades in the Washington area. Growing up in oil wealth in Dallas, he joined the CIA in 1968 with and M.A. in Economics from the University of Texas in Austin.

Hawkins strides to and fro, his tall frame in a rumpled grey flannel suit, his face a bitter grimace. *Could it be true, as a memo left in Mann's desk contended, that the CIA was indolent, morally bankrupt, a club of mostly white Anglo-Saxon males, . . . middle and upper-middle class Republican who were tools of the rich right-wing?* Doubt creeps into Hawkins' mind. Then he is angry at himself for doubting the agency and the conservative cause.

"Every top level member of the firm is still solidly America First," he tells Jesse Helms Jr, when the son of the former senator from North Carolina enters the room.

"I don't know how Mann found out about the Luna project," he continued. "Or how he didn't hear that we called it off."

"Mann is a turncoat, plain and simple," says Helms. Helms likes to quote the motto carved on the wall of the lobby far above them, that "Truth shall make you free." It is obvious to Helms that conservative values must be upheld. Allegiance to God and country. Not to international socialism.

"Just a few weeks before the election, and Mitt is trailing Oprah, and now this," Hawkins says to Helms. "If we can't stop Mann, this will finish Mitt. Bush's war in Iraq is a millstone around his neck, and now this. The plan to grab Luna will look bad. All the details of our extraordinary renditions, our support for the Serbian fascists over Kosovo, our arrangements with the Hindu extremists in India, the Corredato mob, the deal with Putin to keep New Harmony out of power in Russia, the weapons sent to Cuban right-wingers and the Brazilian oligarchy, . . . if we don't catch Mann before he breaks and distributes the files, Jesus!"

"You all screwed up big time," drawls Helms. "You all shudda shot Mann months ago when we ah realized he was maybe unreliable. And you ah think it's this Commie Eskimah bitch he's run off with. One of these here eco-freak UN police that's that's gonna shut down the economy. Ya shudda had 'em all in Gitmo by now. Specially that pinko Obama, . . . he's probably calling the shots for Oprah."

Jesse Helms Jr is the founder and leader of the ten million members of America First, many of whom are former supporters of George W. Bush and the Tea Party. Helms is famous or infamous for concluding every speech by saying "The UN must ah be destroyed." He is well into his seventies, frail, with a fondness for wearing red, white, and blue seersucker suits. Despite spending half his life in Washington, he speaks with a distinct Carolinian accent.

"If only the ah Joint Chiefs were with us," sighs Helms. "And the rank and file. We all shudda stopped these Commies from taking Luna to so many military bases. Those little sailor suits and military fatigues . . . . Everyone's li'l dawlin'."

Hawkins too sighs bitterly. "If the Chiefs of Staff were with us, we could institute martial law under the Patriot Act, and suspend the election," he says.

"Bloody traitors!" Hawkins continues. "They want to give our best troops to the UN and get rid of the rest, and stop the use of mercenaries."

"We all allowed our best officers to be ah brainwashed into wanting a UN whar against dictators, when we can't even handle Eyeraq and Afghanistan," groused Helms. "A whar to end all whars and bring democracy everywhere. What a crock of pious glib shit."

"Pinko dupes," hisses Hawkins. "Most of Congress too."

Helms and Hawkins aren't reactionaries in their own minds. They are conservative Republicans who feel sure that a United Nations world government would soon turn corrupt and dictatorial. They refuse to trust these liberal utopians, Frankfort-school Marxists, Trotskyists, socialist feminists, Barack Obama liberals, and their fellow-travelers.

Helms gives Hawkins a cigarette and lights one himself, in front of a No Smoking sign. They sit at the videoconferencing table and drink coffee. Helms takes a flask of bourbon from his jacket pocket and pours some into his coffee. He is pessimistic.

"The conference is starting," says Hawkins to Helms. The Executive Committee of America First is meeting by encrypted teleconferencing. Faces of the various members appear on the big screens at the end of the table as they sign in.

"Hugo Mann, Chief of Counterintelligence, has defected," says Hawkins to the camera. "He's defecated on the American Way and is going over to the frigging pinkos. The son of a bitch copied a whole lot of restricted files. He's made contact with New Harmony and is probably headed for Canada. If we don't catch him, and if his new friends can decrypt the files, they'll have the details of every district officer and ongoing operations."

"The FBI claim they will help," continues Hawkins, "but we all know the director is a closet liberal." (The FBI had been attempting to stay neutral, expelling agents with left or right leanings.)

The Executive Committee members begin giving advice to Hawkins and Helms. From Oklahoma City comes the image of Ted Link, director of the Drug Enforcement Administration. "These leftist idiots will dismantle the DEA [Drug Enforcement Administration] and legalize all drugs. Our kids will be hooked on heroin in kindergarten. You must get the Supreme Court to arrest Winfrey and stop the election." He pauses, thinking. "Let's try again to plant hard drugs in New Harmony bases and Reformed Democrat leaders."

"That dinn't work last time your morons tried it," snapped Bob "Hawkeye" Venzetti, president of the National Rifle Association. "But we gotta do sumpthin'. These bloody Communists will take away our guns and enslave us. Make us all drive small foreign cars and be vegetarians like Hitler. Better we should take over the govamint an' stop 'em."

John Hagee, head of the Coalition for Christ, is with Benny Hinn, another evangelical preacher. "These atheist bastards will tax us out of existence and destroy religion with secular education," says Hagee, "and try to get us on hate mongering charges for claiming that only saved Christians will go to Heaven with Christ, and the rest will die gruesome painful deaths and suffer eternal damnation.

They'll stop Israel from regaining its size under Solomon, a condition of the End Time coming to bring the Rapture. They'll charge us with fraud for faith healing . . . . You've got to use the Supreme Court to stop these Stalinists, and get Congress to hold emergency hearings on Unamerican Activities. We have lots of money if you need it."

Next to speak is William Hubbard, grandson of the science fiction writer who founded Scientology. "The mantle of religion won't save us if these fascists of the Left get into power. We have thirty million dollars set aside if America First needs it."

Jack Meyers is the president of Philip Morris and spokesman for the tobacco industry. "These Commies will try to put us out business, Jesse, even as they legalize the heavy stuff. So be a good ole boy and stop 'em gettin' into power. The industry can make two billion dollars available to you, if you need it. Spare no expense. Smash the New Harmony bases with drone bombs, whatever . . ." Meyers says angrily.

Representing Big Oil and the rightist mining companies is Bud "Chip" Munk, a lobbyist. "Yeah, just tell how we can keep these dangerous dreamers out of power. These sneaky liberal cunts are using the hoax about fossil fuels causing global warming to take over the world. Real energy conservation and switching to alternative energy sources will devalue our resources by many trillions of dollars. If we can't use the police and armies of the Third World to keep unions and environmentalists away from our mines, and prevent strikes, costs will skyrocket."

Jacob Swartz, a Washington lawyer who represents the cosmetics industry, speaks next. "There is a rumor that the beauty industry will die during the so-called Transition. When women are 'really' liberated. We can give you money and attractive young models to use against these fanatics."

Next is Alex Gregory, a lobbyist for drug manufacturers and health care insurers. "These damn socialists want Canadian-style health care, which would drastically cut our drug profits and ruin the HMO business. We have ads set to air next week, the same Soviet Canuckistan themes we used against the Clintons. Also, if you need a couple of billion dollars to bribe their leaders or whatever, you can have it."

Joel Atkins, president of Blacktide, once worked for Halliburton and had often gone hunting with the late former vice-president Dick Cheney. He represents arms industries and companies providing mercenaries. He's in his mid forties, an overweight chain-smoker with a fondness for steaks. "An attack on B1 could have worked," Atkins claims. "But we needed more time to recruit young Muslim hotheads to take the blame, through the 'imam' we set up in Mississauga last month. The plan could still work, if Mann can be silenced."

Ari "Uzi" Kushner, who represents the one of the Israeli lobbies, is last. "Israel will be reduced to the size of a postage stamp," he says, "if these anti-Semitic Arab-lovers sever American support."

Hawkins ends the meeting. "Okay, that's where we are at. We'll meet again this evening for updates. We'll consider ways to defeat this new Red Menace."

* * *

The wrecked BMW comes to rest in a pumpkin field. Bullets puncture the pumpkins, bleeding yellow snow. Oolayou sends an emergency signal to their contact. "Go northwest. Anubis Fourth will find you," they are told. They jump a stone fence and run through sheets of rain. From the suitcase Oolayou takes two anti-infrared umbrellas, hiking boots, compass, waterproof ponchos, and pistols. When they reach the hardwood forest they run for another twenty minutes, amid trees swaying in the swirling air. The storm has grounded the helicopters and temporarily blinded the CIA's satellites. Oolayou and Mann sink panting to the wet mat of leaves, ferns, and humus, not daring to use their position locator or mobile phones. Then they walk northwest until nightfall.

Fitful sleep under an overhanging ledge.

Oolayou wakes in the dark, because an animal is licking her face. As adrenalin subsides, she switches on a light and sees it's a large German shepherd with turquoise stones and engraved silver on its collar. Anubis Fourth. The dog's shoulder harness carries a food/water pack and a deployed infrared umbrella. Hugo holds the dog's tail, stumbling occasionally, sometimes using the flashlight, as Oolayou follows the sound of his footsteps. They walk for hours as the dog retraces its steps, resting briefly at dawn.

The storm continues, downing trees and power lines. Oolayou and Mann scramble through undergrowth for several more hours, following the dog, eventually coming upon Highway 219 and a restaurant parking lot. There Anubis brings them to an armored truck belonging to Snelgrove Security Transfer, a small company secretly owned by a New Harmony subsidiary. As they are dried and given dry clothes, the truck heads north for Canada and Mann's debriefing commences.

The driver is Leona Montoya, 47, head of Red Hand, and there is another Red Hand agent, a cryptologist. The contents of Mann's microchips are e-mailed to the base in Ontario and to UN headquarters in New York, where UN intelligence officers await them.

The truck passes through Buffalo. Oolayou and Mann are dropped off at a marina near the small town of Olcott, on Lake Ontario. They go aboard a large motor launch which carries sonar jamming equipment and a mini-submarine. After dark, near the border, the submarine is lowered over the side. The operator dives and takes them to a boat waiting off St. Catherines. From a nearby marina Leona Montoya and two heavily-armed Red Hand agents take Oolayou and Mann in an armored van along the Queen Elizabeth Way, past Hamilton, and up the Ontario heartland on Highway 6. The storm abates. Mann wishes it were day so that he could see more of the farms they were passing.

Then a delay. Near the town of Mount Forest a motorcycle gang, the London and Windsor chapters of Satan's Choice, is stopping traffic in order to find Mann. But the provincial police have been alerted and are making arrests with the help of Canadian Armed Forces units from Camp Borden. Two cruisers are hit by rocket-propelled grenades provided to the bikers by the CIA the day before, and three officers are killed. Six bikers are shot to death, fifty-five arrested.

The van is given an escort of ten police and army vehicles and takes a detour. By sunrise Mann is twelve kilometres from Owen Sound and can see Georgian Bay as a line of blue above the hills in the distance. A cement tower juts into view around a turn. They have arrived at New Harmony's Home Base. Mann notices the two tall chain-link fences surrounding the base, patrolled by Han-Spar guards and part of an armored unit of the Canadian army.

Inside the gate, the van follows a gravel road another kilometre, past windmills and solar collectors on a hillside and in fields. Geodesic domes look like giant tennis balls.

They pass a landing strip and hangars, tennis courts, and outdoor chess plazas, the pieces made of old wooden telephone polls. "I came here when I was eight," Oolayou tells Mann. "I didn't know how lucky I was, in foster care only a few weeks when fate brought me here."

Only a few people are about. In the atrium of the tower, Mann pauses to scan the stained glass windows honoring secular heroes. Turquoise appears, and wraps her arms around Oolayou and hugs her, and takes them by elevator down eight floors into the 'egg' below the tower to an apartment with a spacious living room. Three walls of the bedroom are covered with oil painted copies of Cro-Magnon cave paintings of horses, oxen, bears, bison, and mammoth.

Having checked that the refrigerator is provisioned, Turquoise takes her leave. Oolayou and Hugo sleep all day and into the evening. After eating, Oolayou tells Mann about a major factional dispute within New Harmony.

"The pacifists, including Gandhians and Theosophists in the Indian bases, feel betrayed by the growth of Red Hand . . . . For good reason Leona is often called the Lioness. Leona was born into a poor family in Mexico City. After her mother died, Leona did her best to protect her little brother from their stepfather, who was often drunk. One night when she was nine the stepfather beat her brother badly with a belt. Later when the man was asleep, Leona hit him an the head with a rolling pin. She and her brother walked to a Catholic orphanage. The man suffered a slight concussion but survived. In the following days the nuns insisted Leona pray for forgiveness, so she left with her brother. They came to an orphanage funded by New Harmony and eventually to Harry Katz's notice."

"You said Katz was a Trot in his youth?" Hugo asks.

"In highschool and as a student at York University in the mid 'sixties. He led the Committee to End the War in Vietnam," replies Oolayou. "Jamie Ramsey met him at an anti-war rally on campus."

"How did Leona Montoya get started?" asks Hugo.

"When she was sixteen, Harry started letting her run small operations, using Maya refugees in our base near Oaxaca whose mothers had been raped and killed by Guatemalan soldiers," says Oolayou. "Some early operations were to avenge street kids murdered by police in cities in Central America and Brazil. Then other cases where the evil ones could not be brought before a court. Now, with General Council approval she has at least two hundred agents world-wide. Thirty are skilled assassins."

"At the CIA we knew something was happening, but we could never catch any of them. We did identified some Green Daughters of the Red Dawn, but they only did ecological stuff," says Hugo. "If I get back into the CIA I'm to communicate with Leona once a week so we don't work at crossed purposes. She gave me her most encrypted numbers."

"One of the founders of the Green Daughters was briefly a member of New Harmony, before she was expelled," says Oolayou. "But that is another story." She pauses for a minute. "There's a gathering up near the top of the tower, in what we call the Aerie Lounge," Oolayou continues. "We can shower. You'll find a razor and everything in the cabinet in the bathroom, and clothes that fit in the cupboard and drawers in the bedroom."

"As long as it's not the Eagle's Nest," Hugo jokes.

They shower together, washing each other's back. He puts on slacks, a plaid shirt and moccasins. She wears the same.

She leads him to the elevators at the center of the egg and they ascend. The Aerie Lounge is a large octagonal room with big windows near the top of the tower, providing a panoramic view of the countryside and the starry sky above. Many of the founders of New Harmony are present, including Herschel "Hairy Harry" Katz, Jamie Ramsey, and David Eaton-Gage, Oolayou's father. The later is sitting next to Noam Chomsky, an historian of US imperialism.

Hugo also meets Mikhail Gorbachev, 85, who is in poor health. He is helped about by his daughter Irina, a WHO epidemiologist, and Garry Kasparov, a former world champion chess player and social democratic Russian politician. Hugo meets Sally Ride and Julie Payette and their families. Dr Larry Brilliant and other Google Global Projects people are there. Robert Kennedy Jr., and Maria Shriver, rise to shake his hand. Then Hugo is introduced to Bill and Melinda Gates and their two children, and to Ted Turner, T. Boone Pickens,

George Soros, and Warren Buffett, the 'Oracle of Omaha.' These progressive capitalists have been meeting secretly at B1.

At one side of the room are Francine Baxter and her husband Kevin, in their late sixties, chatting with Barack and Michelle Obama and their children. "The Baxters are both founding members, both pacifists," Oolayou explains to Hugo in a low voice. "Francine is a former Salvation Army officer who tries to bring liberal religious types into New Harmony if they deconvert. He is a musician and former United Church minister." At the other side of the room, near Stephen Lewis and Louise Arbour, Leona Montoya is talking with a young woman in a silk blouse and *longyi*, a Burmese (Myanmarian) resistance leader whose cell under Leona's direction recently removed Aung San Suu Kyi from many years of house arrest and took her to France to be reunited with her family and members of her party, in advance of the UN liberation of Burma.

Turquoise hugs Oolayou again, then Hugo. Cheng Chou is beside Turquoise, grey hairs at his temple. Luna, dressed in shorts and T-shirt, her hair in a pony tail, is above Mann on a circular staircase. She is sitting next to one of Al Gore's grandchildren, a boy of four. She has taken a cat-tail from a big Chinese vase of flowers, and as Mann approaches she touches his left shoulder with the tip of the cat-tail.

"For very brave service I dub thee Sir Hugo the Fearless," says Luna. She extends the back of her right hand to be kissed, and Mann obliges.

Turquoise admonishes Luna mildly. "You are not a queen," she says. "You are an ordinary child. We want to get rid of kings and queens so everyone can be equal."

Luna sticks out her tongue at her mother for a moment, and Turquoise prepares to say something stern. But instead she breaks into a little smile which ripples around the room.

Some people are watching screens in an alcove, getting the latest news. There have been ten sniper attacks in a week in Ohio on older vehicles and SUV's. The bullets seem to be aimed at the vehicles' engines, not at occupants, but two people have been killed. A local radio station has received a letter claiming the shootings were a training exercise for Green Daughters recruits on bicycles.

George Hawkins and twenty others at the CIA have been arrested by the FBI, while America First backs away from the debacle at full speed, badly damaged, denying any connection to Joel Atkins or Blacktide. But America First is not powerless, as attack adds against Winfrey begin to appear in right-wing media. The worst are 'testimonials' on Fox stations from men who say they had sex with her when she was a promiscuous teenager. But spontaneous polls show Winfrey widening her lead in the popular vote into double digits. Twenty million lower-income Americans, two thirds of them women, have registered to vote for the first time, surpassing the Obama surge of 2008. Hillary Clinton's efforts were bringing results with Chicanos and blue collar whites, while Barack Obama delivered his core—affluent and educated liberals. Obama's hand on the tiller of the new ship of state would reassured moderates frightened by the far-left ideology, it was felt.

Tables of bridge and chess and bridge are started along the north wall. "Could you play bridge for an hour?" Melinda Gates asks Turquoise and Oolayou. Between deals, they talk.

"What happens now, Bill?" asks Turquoise.

"Well," says Gates, "as we expected, many investors and fund managers are panicking and pulling their money out of North American stock and bond markets. When prices are low enough, we'll start buying strategic companies—grain and other food staples, in case America First tries to create shortages next year. Strategic HMO's to guarantee health care during its transformation, to be later nationalized. We already control enough clean energy to keep the lights on. My foundation and other big pools of American money, including property insurance companies, are ready to pounce. Big loads of Chinese and Indian capital are available to us. The UN has some cash too, and can borrow on its shares of PromTek and Han-Spar. Of course, we have to keep the SEC off our backs."

The Gates's bid and make Three No Trump. "European Union countries will be the least affected by the coming economic changes, since they have pretty much demilitarized and are getting off fossil fuels, so we are expecting their political support. We have to get New Harmony elected in Russia in 2018, and sort out the troubles there. Our five small bases in Russia are rather vulnerable, yet are key parts of the Transition." He pauses. "India has never really had nationalism, and can go painlessly into a world government. Pakistan, Indonesia, and Brazil will eventually follow. Africa gets peace through the African Union Armies. Supervised elections in Zimbabwe, Nigeria, Somalia, and elsewhere."

Then the Gates's bid and make Six Hearts. "America will be the toughest," Bill Gates continues.

"Yes, as the fossil fuel guys and the smoke-stack capitalists lose their power, they are not going to go gracefully," says Turquoise.

"The armaments and imprisonment people, and the border guards union, are against us. But partly thanks to Luna, we have the armed forces with us. And most academics. Many communications and other high tech companies," says Melinda Gates.

"It's the intelligence services I worry about," says Oolayou. "Thirty in the US alone. All the agents and managers axed for political cause will be out there, perhaps with rogue leadership, with America First funding, and perhaps joining with religious extremism. Or working with mercenary providers. We'll have to track them all, Hugo says. Also the heavies at the DEA after it's shut down. We can jail them under Patriot Act legislation if they conspire."

The Gates's reached Five Diamond Doubled. On the lie of the cards, it's a difficult but makable contract with a squeeze end-play. But Luna, her mouth smeared purple from grape juice, climbs onto Bill Gates' lap and distracts him with a cattail she's holding. "Don't cut yourself on my sword, Bill. It's very sharp," she says. He goes down two tricks, but doesn't mind.

Soon after a re-routed call for Mann comes on a secure line nearby. When he hangs up he comes to Oolayou. "That was Oprah," he says. "She wants me to be the next director of the CIA, if she wins. I accepted."

"Another piece of the Transition is falling into place," says Melinda Gates. "Now we are going to ride the big snake." Her tone is subdued. Oolayou doesn't know if it is a reference to The Doors "The End" or to the Feathered Serpent of the Maya religion, and doesn't want to appear gauche by asking.

Later, back in the apartment deep underground, Oolayou lights a pipe of marijuana. "I'm spinning like a top with all the things that are happening," she says. "I need to slow down." They smoke and listen to several choral versions of "Finlandia," including ones with Sibelius's theistic words.

Then they go into the bedroom. Naked, she lies on her back on the big bed, the cave paintings making her feel primitive. She helps him with the condom, as she isn't on the pill. He kisses her breasts gently and enters her slowly, reverentially. For fifteen minutes, with a hand on the small of his back, she speeds him up like a vibrator, to a mutually satisfying climax.

Then a bit of guilt. Oolayou almost says something about Boris Larinov, but doesn't. *Really, what is there to tell?* she asks herself.

"I know we can't be together all the time, and I'm not the jealous type," says Mann, as though she had spoken. "I stopped thinking about women sexually ten years ago when my wife died. You have changed that and charged up my batteries tremendously. But in a few days we'll part because you have your work and I have mine. Our duty to the Transition trumps subjective feelings such as love."

They sleep. Next day she shows him around the base, visiting her father in his cottage and walking into the woods to her mother's grave. Two days later Mann starts back to Virginia. He is driven by Leona Montoya in an electric armored sedan to Pearson Airport, in the northwest corner of Toronto. Oolayou comes for the ride.

"Where are you going to live?" she asks as they part.

"I'll fortify my house in Washington," says Mann. "Then in January when I take over the CIA I'll use the little apartment at headquarters that was built after 9-11."

They kiss, a long reassuring hugging kiss, and rub noses for the first time. Mann gives her his most encrypted telephone numbers and a code-pass and key to his house.

"You already have the key to my heart," he said knowing it sounded corny.

CHAPTER 4
Velvet Gloves, Hands of Steel

Many readers will remember when (Tuesday, November 1st 2016) Oprah Winfrey was elected 46th president of the United States. She won 66% of the popular vote, as 72% of eligible voters went to polling booths. Only eight states, all in the south, went to Romney. Enough Democrats, Reformed Democrats, and New Harmony members were elected to give them filibuster-proof majorities in both houses of Congress.

"It is a vote for world federal action on many issues, and an end to American imperialism," said Winfrey, as she thanked workers at her Chicago headquarters. "It is a vote for equality of race and gender." Vice-president elect General Colin Powell was tearfully humble. "I will prove myself worthy of this chance to redeem myself. My life has been a torment of guilt since I assured the UN there were weapons of mass destruction in Iraq. But Oprah believes there can be redemption through good works, and we will support the UN plan for peace throughout the Middle East. Thank you." Republican cynics believed that Powell was chosen to please the Joint Chiefs of Staff. Barack Obama, designated Secretary of State, put a comforting arm around Powell.

Oolayou watched this great event on TV with her father in his cottage. Next day she drove back to Toronto, continuing to search for a southern headquarters. Shui Zhe, unarmed and unvested, accompanied her, as did Oolayou's new chief of intelligence, Beloved Morton.

(Morton, then 31, knew Toronto well. As a child she had lived with an aunt and her four children in a small apartment in the Regent Park housing project on Dundas Street near the Don River, after her mother died of a heroin overdose. (Her father had gone back to Jamaica, denying paternity.) As an overweight, moon-faced girl of seven, with unmanageable wiry black hair, she was teased at school with taunts of 'Ape Girl' and 'Jungle Bunny.' She learned to play chess sitting on a pile of old telephone books watching the elderly Swedish janitor and his Polish friend in the furnace room in the evenings. There was the pleasant smell of Sail tobacco in their pipes, as smoke curled up to the naked lightbulb hanging above the battered card table. When they let her play, she lost the first eight games. Then she drew the next eight, and began winning after that.

"Another Capablanca maybe," the men said in amazement at her quick grasp of tactics and strategy. Six months later they entered her in a tournament in New College, U of T, and watched as she sliced through her age group. She played in several more tournaments and a year later her picture appeared in a national chess magazine. She was contacted by 1-e4, a New Harmony recruiting tentacle, and given a room of her own at the residence of the Toronto Chess Club. She got an allowance, chess books, a new Pentium computer with chess programs, and a tutor—a local International Grandmaster.

At ten she was the third best Under Twelve in Canada. She began attending St Andrew's College on one of the school's twenty chess scholarships, two years behind Oolayou. At twelve she was adopted by a New Harmony couple and came to live at B1when not at school. Harry Katz recruited her after she gave up competitive chess at 25, just after she finished a Ph.D. in Mathematics.)

After several hours of searching the three women were walking down Jarvis Street, below the nightly 'track' of prostitutes to the north.

"It's perfect," said Zhe when she saw the building. "A fortress."

It was a former RCMP regional headquarters, build in 1990.

"That sure is solidly built. Small arms fire would just bounce off," said Beloved. "Our vehicles would be secure in the underground parking," she added.

"It's way more space than we need," said Oolayou. The steel-reinforced concrete structure was fifteen storeys high, with a communications mast on top. "Ravi Naran will never approve."

But when she phoned Naran, he seemed interested. He checked the building on the Internet and got more interested. He flew to Toronto the next day and booked into the same cheap hotel as they.

"The federal government is willing to lease it for twenty years at a reasonable rate, if they can have some space in it," he said. (A New Harmony, Green, New Democrat, and Left-Liberal coalition was in power in Ottawa.) They walked down Jarvis Street, past a park and two large churches.

"I only need three floors," said Oolayou, as they inspected the building with the leasing agent. "One for a jail cell and records and research. One for administrative offices and reception. One for liaison and intelligence officers."

"Okay," said Naran.

"It is a zero-emissions building," said the leasing agent. "We can retro-fit it with solar panels on three sides, and you can have a roof garden. Electrical heating, and we will install a Han-Spar fuel cell co-generating and backup power plant system. Cooling is from the city's pipes in Lake Ontario."

There were eight penthouse apartments. Looking south from one of them they saw St Lawrence Market, a fixture since the early 1800's, and the lower east side. A few sailboats and a ferry braved the choppy water of the lake. The downtown skyscrapers and the CN tower rose on the right. "We'll take it," said Naran.

"You can share the building with UNTV and UN forces recruitment," Naran told Oolayou when the agent was gone. "The International Criminal Court needs a floor. Environment Canada needs three. You'll have access to their scientists any time. PromTek and General BioTek will take two floors and pay for offices of some NGO's with roles in the Transition. Doctors Without Borders, Greenpeace, Amnesty International, World Wildlife Federation, Nature Conservancy, Carnegie election monitors, and the land mine cataloguers and removal trainers. Also a floor for a lounge, exercise room, small cafeteria, and daycare."

"I can't thank you enough," said Oolayou.

In the following weeks Beloved worked with Harry Katz's experts to ensure the building was not bugged and that communications were secure. In the middle of December Oolayou moved into one of the small penthouse apartments, Beloved into another. Oolayou began interviewing secretarial and legal staff who answered her ads. Beloved screened the applicants, identifying a young woman as a CSIS (Canadian Security Intelligence Service) agent. (It is now known that New Harmony had five spies in this civilian spy agency.) A young man who had recently held membership in America First was dropped from consideration as a security guard.

Oolayou chose Polly Weldon, a well-educated, middle-aged single mother active in the Sierra Club to manage the office. Ms.

Weldon, an avid bicyclist, lived in a decrepit mansion in Rosedale with her mother and teenage daughter, and took in borders. Harold Geary, 56, a former PromTek executive recommended by her father became the financial officer. Jenny Wing, 32, a recent graduate with a Ph.D. in Environmental Studies from York University, became chief inspector, and was told to hire twenty more inspectors. Professor George Bell, with whom she had worked in Quttinirpaaq Park in July, was seconded to her from the UN Intergovernmental Panel on Climate Change. Paul Agnew, 64, a former vice president with the Philip Morris tobacco company, became chief constable. Still eager to atone for his sins, Agnew had been a NHP member for twenty years, and done a lot to foster a zero-discharge mentality in European businesses. His major 'weakness' was his sympathy for others who wanted redemption. Agnew insisted on hiring Svend Robinson, a homosexual former NDP MP from British Columbia, even though Robinson had compulsively stolen an expensive ring in 2004. "The right-wing media will make hay of it," said Oolayou, but Agnew insisted. "Robinson wasn't given a criminal record, because he turned himself in soon afterwards, and it was so out of character," said Agnew. He also hired a young woman, Rita Akiwenzie, a Anishnawbe from the Cape Croker reserve near Owen Sound, recently fired from the Windsor police force (drug squad) for smoking marijuana while on vacation. Rita's daughter, Bliss, age five, played with several other children in the daycare center while she was interviewed. By chance Bliss looked a lot like Luna.

The elevators were busy with other organizations moving in when Turquoise and Zhe brought Luna to visit the building one afternoon in the third week of December. Oolayou's office was on the fourteenth floor. "Director for Canada and Alaska, United Nations Ecological Criminal Offenses Police," Turquoise read to Luna, seeing the sign on Oolayou's office door, also in French and Inuktituk. Some rooms were decorated with native art, including her own soapstone carvings of narwhals and nunatuk picas. Then Luna surveyed the city from Oolayou's apartment and had a nap in her bed with Bliss Akiwenzie. Later Beloved Morton joined them for a twenty minute walk to the Riverdale petting farm in Cabbagetown, where the barns were still open despite the cold weather. Luna and Turquoise, their heads covered by beaded anoraks, went unnoticed as they watched and touched the animals. Several people recognized them during supper in a local vegetarian restaurant, but were too sophisticated to do more than glance over occasionally.

*

Oolayou's first move was to lend personnel and some of the unmarked new hydrogen fuel-cell sedans and vans to the Ontario Department of the Environment, which had an office on St Clair Avenue near Yonge Street, to assist with inspection and enforcement of egregious cases. Communications were opened with all other provincial, territorial, and First Nations Departments of the Environment. Only Alberta, home of the tar sands, refused her advances. The provincial Conservatives would do nothing to offend the oil and natural gas industry.

*

Then there was a pause for Winter Solstice holidays. "Come with us on the Winter Ride," said Luna on the telephone. "We're taking Moonflower and her mother in a trailer to the base in Nebraska."

"Sorry, not this year, honey," replied Oolayou. "I've got to go to Washington to see Hugo Mann." She took the train and spent ten days with Mann, at his fortified brick house in the city and in his apartment at CIA headquarters. They copulated frequently and discussed her inevitable battle with the oil industry and its supporters in Alberta. Mann worked on his list of potentially troublesome former CIA and DEA personnel.

When she got back to the UNECOP building in January Oolayou set up her carving equipment in a large storage room in her apartment, and purchased soft stone and bone from an Inuit artists collective on Bathurst Street. She didn't want to come empty-handed when she met the Lords of the Tar Sands. Her gifts would signify that things could be done in a civilized way, without war.

Meanwhile, Luna had been in the column of Amerindian women on the Winter Ride across the prairies to the Pine Ridge reservation at Wounded Knee, using the Cowboy Trail. They started from a New Harmony base near Omaha build around several decommissioned

Minuteman missile silos. The weather was barely above freezing, the snow light. Luna, wearing padded clothing and a helmet, proudly rode Moonflower for several hours each day, until she got tired. Then she rode with Inez Cara Coya, Beloved Morton, Shui Zhe, Milly Moosomin, Melinda Gates, Michelle Obama, Carla Robinson, Sally Ride, Oksana Gorbachev, or Turquoise. When she wanted a nap Luna got into a horse-drawn travois with the baggage or into one of the small electric all-terrain covered vehicles in the rear with the wise old women—Aung San Suu Kyi, Jehan Sadat, Rosalyn Carter, Buffy Sainte Marie, Jane Fonda, Louise Arbour, Bianca Jagger, Rigoberta Menchu, and the others.

Oprah Winfrey joined the pilgrimage for the last forty kilometres, making a short speech over loudspeakers at the end about Big Bear and the failed magic of the Ghost Dancers, and the horror of Dec 29, 1890, when bullets spit from the rifles of the soldiers of the Ninth cavalry and bursting grapeshot from their Hotchkiss revolving cannons hit the women and children in the teepees. The museum showed pictures and other evidence.

The numerous Secret Service agents present, men and women, stood out by their poor riding abilities and new boots. Because Winfrey had announced normalization of relations with Cuba, there was fear of an attack by Cuban exiles from Florida. Israeli irredentists were another threat, inflamed by Winfrey's "Down with the wall!" election slogan and her support of a two-state settlement with extensive 'right of return' for Palestinians and the relocation of 150,000 Israeli settlers from illegally occupied land. Three Mossad agents with sniper rifles arrested by the Secret Service in Bismark, North Dakota, a week before, had been returned to Israel as a precaution and the ride concluded without attempts against Winfrey or Luna.

*

Inauguration week in January set the new political tone. On Sunday the 21st,Winfrey's electric-powered busses took the route of Jefferson's carriage in 1801; from Monticello on a hill outside Charlottesville, Virginia, where she was joined by dozens of descendants of Sally Hemings, Jefferson's mulatto second wife, and by the elderly Essie Mae Washington-Williams, the illegitimate daughter of the late senator Strom Thurmond (who came to office as a segregationist) and a black maid. The city of Washington was decorated in red, white and blue, with many UN symbols present. The weather was mild.

Luna watched on TV in her parents' apartment at B1 as Chou and Turquoise explained things, while Oolayou followed Internet and TV coverage on wall screens in her office in the UNECOP building with Beloved Morton. Hugo Mann, with the cabinet on one of the buses, sent photos and text from his wrist-top. The blind former governor of New York state, David Patterson, was Attorney General. Hillary Clinton, now with enough power to do the job, had the task of completely reforming the healthcare system, eliminating HMO's and private insurance companies. Barack Obama, as Secretary of State, had already been briefed by the UN Secretary-General on many details of the Transition. Domestically, George Soros would lead a team of economists charged with leading the economy through disarmament, the switch from fossil fuels, revised health care, and other shocks. Bill Clinton, Jimmy Carter, and Al Gore were aboard as senior advisors. Admiral Brenda Lau, the choice of the Joint Chiefs of Staff, was Secretary of Defense.

Unlike her predecessors, Winfrey did not visit any places of worship. This was consistent with her campaign. "Religion is a private matter," she told reporters, "and must not be mixed with state functions if we believe in separating church and state."

On Capitol Hill Winfrey first visited the Lincoln Memorial. From a platform in front of the Capitol she greeted hundreds of thousands of people spread around the Reflecting Pool and west along the Mall half way to the Monument. "We are going to improve America and the world," she declared over a system of loudspeakers. "War, preventable disease, famine, ignorance, tyranny, pollution, and global warming, must all be stopped," she said, expanding into a ten minute speech about the coming changes to the UN. As the sun was setting the new president led a walk across Memorial Bridge over the Potomac to ring a replica of the Liberty Bell. The usual fireworks over the river had been cancelled because of its slight contribution to global warming, or at least as a signal that the new administration would curtail custom to control warming. There were a few fist fights when bellicose America Firsters and Neo-Nazis destroyed pro-Winfrey signs or shouted "Nigger." A skinhead was arrested for throwing a beer bottle, while the police ignored people openly smoking marijuana.

After that Winfrey and her retinue went off to attend the first of many balls.

At eleven-thirty on the 22nd of January a Marine band played "Hail to the Chief," as outgoing President Romney, a decent man but a tool of reactionaries, walked out of an archway on the west front of the Capitol. Then the UN anthem was played. At noon six members of the Supreme Court, wearing black robes and black wool skull caps, walked over and shook hands with the new president. Winfrey kissed Clarence Thomas on the cheek, but he was stern and unsmiling, resentful that Fate seemed to be conspiring with the Leftists. For suddenly, with the retirement of Chief Justice John Roberts and Justice Scalia's heart attack, Winfrey's appointments would give a 6-3 majority to liberals.

Winfrey then rode two kilometres along Pennsylvania Avenue, waving to the dense crowds from the back of a personnel carrier powered by lithium-ion batteries.

When Congress reconvened, the Fair Trade Act was passed, eliminating subsidies to large agricultural corporations and setting global standards for labor, taxation, and environmental care. It eliminated tax havens such as Liechtenstein and the Cayman Islands, and opened banks everywhere to UN scrutiny. New leadership at the Environmental Protection Agency diminished the power of industry representatives and lobbyists. The Department of Homeland Security was dismantled. Laws against most illicit drugs were repealed, as Canada had done the year before, and the DEA disestablished. The late Harry Anslinger, head of the Federal Bureau of Narcotics from 1930-62, who made a career out of demonized marijuana with such movies as "Reefer Madness," and who had enjoyed rousting Billie Holiday out of bed at 2 a.m to be imprisoned and strip-searched by male officers, with photographers ready to put his picture in the newspapers, was posthumously deprived of his many Congressional awards. It remained an offence to provide such drugs to children, but adults were expected to decide for themselves what they consumed, just as they did in the Nineteenth Century and before.

Federal gun control laws phased in restrictions over the next five years, prohibiting the export of small arms except to the UN. Winfrey made the issue her own, and there were clever advertising campaigns to counter NRA propaganda.

The notorious prison in the base at Guantanamo Bay was ordered completely shut. "There will be no more mistreatment of detainees," thundered Winfrey. "Remember that in the War of Independence, General Washington insisted that his soldiers treat British prisoners well, even though the British had shot surrendering American prisoners, and starved others to death on navy brigs in Long Island Sound. Washington insisted that America have the morals of the Enlightenment, and so must we. The way to defeat religious terrorism is to remedy the poverty, ignorance, religious egotism, and actual grievances that spawn it.

"As part of our detente with the Muslim world, we are going to prosecute George W. Bush-era criminals."

Other new laws prevented lobbyists and wealthy special interests from funneling money to the lawmakers that regulated them, as public financing of state and federal election campaigns was introduced. Hillary Clinton presented a bill which allowed more generic drugs, limited advertising to the public, and used the buying power of the government to lower drug prices. The bill eliminated HMO's and provided funding for hundreds of new hospitals and clinics. Merged Medicare and Medicaid would cover everyone, shrinking mountains of paperwork.

America belatedly committed to the Kyoto protocol and the same week signed the Stockholm treaty to eliminate nuclear weapons. A week later the US joined the International Criminal Court. Legislation took prayers out of all public schools, and ruled that religion be taught from an anthropological viewpoint. The Pledge of Allegiance was dropped in favor of the UN anthem or "Imagine." For all unemployable, there was a basic living wage. Those left temporarily unemployed by Transition changes were also given the BLW. The defense budget, larger than that of all other countries combined, was cut by 15% a year over eight years. 750 military bases were closed, including most overseas bases not leased to the UN, leaving 250 bases with reduced roles. 165,000 troops and several aircraft carriers were assigned to the UN Military Services Committee. None of them were sent to Iraq, where the UN eventually had 500,000 troops engaged in secularizing and rebuilding the country, trying to repair the damage done by the inept American invasion. In Afghanistan 400,000 UN soldiers tried to keep the peace while supervising rebuilding of infrastructure in the secure zones. Opium production fell as black market prices tumbled, weakening the warlords and the Taliban.

With American and British urging, the permanent members of the UN Security Council agreed to include India-Pakistan, Brazil, Indonesia, and Egypt. The Vatican lost its observer status, and the Constitution of the UN was amended to guarantee every child a liberal education grounded in science.

CHAPTER 5
Early Stages of the Battle of Alberta

Meanwhile, when Alberta's Minister of the Environment again rebuffed her attempts to meet, Oolayou e-mailed the CEO's of the five biggest tar sands companies and asked for an hour of their time. All five agreed, and a date was set for an afternoon in the middle of February in a conference room reserved by Oolayou in the Palliser South office tower on 10th Avenue, south of the Calgary Tower.

To show some muscle, Oolayou and her team made their first arrest just before going out west for the showdown. Beloved Morton and Chief Paul Agnew tracked down two brothers, 45 and 47, who had filled a rented farm near Sarnia with hundreds of thousand of tires. When their shredding business failed in 2015, the brothers resorted to arson. The fire raged for three days, causing billowing clouds of black smoke. The men were traced to a trailer park near Petrolia, Ontario, and arrested with much publicity by UNECOP officers and local police. The mayor of Petrolia insisted on showing Oolayou how the town, the birthplace of the oil industry in North America as the museum and a few wells still pumping a barrel or two a day attested, was developing silicon-collector solar 'farms' technology, and solar cookers for export to Africa and India. "If women, I mean people, can use the sun to cook, they won't have to go searching for wood so much," the mayor said earnestly. "Is there any way Luna might visit us next year when we open the prototype plant to use solar energy to make hydrogen from super-heated water?" he asked. (After a trial in Sarnia on provincial and federal offences seven months later, the brothers appeared in Toronto to face UN government charges.)

Back in her office, Oolayou got official confirmation from the UN and the International Criminal Court that to meet the Kyoto Protocol targets to which Canada agreed in 2002, the country must not undertake further tar sands developments. The Canadian government had accepted the ruling. "Of course this will strengthen the Alberta Independence Party," Beloved said.

"Some Conservatives are for Alberta separation too," added Oolayou.

That same day a pair of non-migrating red-tailed hawks settled into the nesting box in an alcove near the base of the antennae atop their building, above and opposite the garden area and the spruce trees. "Well, that will solve our pigeon problem. Perhaps it's a sign of good luck for us," said the unsuperstitious Beloved, as they watched a relay from a security camera.

But the next news was bad. In northern Alberta terrorists had attacked five oil sands installations with dynamite, killing ten workers and inflicting extensive damage to a Royal Dutch Shell upgrader operation near Peace River that was processing 350,000 barrels of bitumen per day. Because they were heavily guarded the nuclear reactors used to generate electricity for the deep limestone projects were not damaged. Three hours later it was reported that four firemen injured in the conflagration at the coking plant at Exxon's Firebag in situ operation had died in hospital in Fort McMurray. Five women suspects had swallowed cyanide pills when cornered by RCMP at a small airport north of Edmonton. The Green Daughters of the Red Dawn were claiming responsibility.

"This is a major complication," said Beloved. "The fact that one of the founders of the Green Daughters was once in New Harmony will be used against us and damage our cause." (Gundrun Wolfe, once a resident of the NHP base near Redstone, Colorado, was expelled in 1991 for conducting an unauthorized 'action.' She and two friends had kidnaped a vice-president of Dow Chemical and 'educated' him about Dow's dioxin contamination of the Saginaw River by tying his hands and feet and dragging him several kilometres downstream behind a motorboat, before releasing him. Gundrun's friends, Regine Muller and Marlene Kurras, were also daughters of women who had been part of the Baader-Meinhoff group in Germany in the 'seventies. They described themselves as radical eco lesbian vegetarians whose credo was that "Intercourse is rape. Logging and mining are rape." The trio started the Green Daughters of the Red Dawn two years later. An article in the *New York Times* in December had revealed Gundrun's identity, and much of her past.)

"We can go after them for the ecological crime of causing the fires," said Oolayou. "I'll announce our intention to arrest them, to show we don't condone their methods."

"We need to do more," said Beloved. "We must contact Leona Montoya. A threat from Red Hand might get the Green Daughters to stop their campaign in Alberta, and give us a chance to move against the tar sands legally. Shall I call Leona tomorrow?"

"Alright, yes, and keep Hugo Mann in the loop," said Oolayou, after a minute of thought. Then she called her father to say goodbye. "You have the numbers I gave you for PromTek people out west and the address of the office in Calgary, if you have trouble," he reminded her. Luna was in his cottage with her grandfather. "Be careful, `cause I love you," said Luna, who had heard many negative things about the tar sands. Then Jamie Ramsey came on the line, a bit pompous. "Oolayou, as you go forth to battle for the planet's future, I could say that you are the hand of reason in this crisis, if we believed such Hegelian wishful thinking. More likely humans will overrun the globe like bacteria on a petri dish, as Maltheus thought, until mass extinction caused by global warming. But we must think positively, and I know you'll do your best to defend our planet in Alberta."

"Whatever happens, this is just the first round," Oolayou told Ramsey, ignoring such uncharacteristic pessimism from a Transition planner.

A dozen UNECOP vehicles moved out of headquarters on Saturday, February 11th, leaving chief constable Agnew in charge of the building. Several went east, filled with agents to set up offices in Montreal and Halifax. The rest went west. Oolayou was in the lead van, driven by Professor George Bell, who kept a safe speed in the light snow along slippery roads curving between rock walls topped with evergreens, over ravines, or close to lakes and rivers. After ten hours they stopped at a motel in Sault Ste Marie where reservations had been made. On Sunday the Trans-Canada Highway passed above Lake Superior as they listened to the "Wreck of the Edmund Fitzgerald" and other songs by Gordon Lightfoot as Beloved Morton played a teaching game of chess with Bliss Akiwenzie and then went over the lessons she was missing. West of Thunder Bay they stopped for half an hour at Kakabeka Falls, a roaring forty metre drop into the ice palace gorge, in a park unspoiled by development. Going on past Lake of the Woods, approaching the provincial border, the land flattened into treeless prairie.

After spending the night in a motel on the outskirts of Winnipeg, they left two inspectors and a constable behind in the city to set up a Manitoba office. Similarly, when Oolayou's convoy left Regina on Tuesday, after being joined by Milly Moosomin, several agents remained to start a Saskatchewan office.

It turned colder as Oolayou's party reached Calgary in the afternoon, as the terrain first became hilly, and then high plains and snow-capped foothills rose in the west. Three vehicles went on to British Columbia and Alaska. "Except for some grungy old areas, it's not Cowtown anymore, but a modern city of well over a million people" said Milly, who had attended the university for a Bachelor of Science degree and graduated from its veterinary college. "There are other high tech research centers besides PromTek and General BioTech. Some areas are quite cosmopolitan, and many Calgarians are pro-UN," she added, mimicking a tour guide's tone. Building cranes crisscrossed the skyline, especially downtown, where the squat late-Victorian limestone public buildings were dwarfed by canyons of office towers. The crescent-shaped EnCana Bow was the highest. The visitors checked into the Lucky Dragon, a modest but clean hotel in Chinatown, and ate in a Szechuan-style restaurant in the underground concourse filled with Chinese shops.

In the evening Oolayou's contingent met five members of the Pembina Institute of Appropriate Development in their offices on 7th Street W. Started in 1982 after the Lodgepole sour gas well blowout fouled air in central Alberta with hydrogen sulphide for months, the Pembina Institute was helping companies and municipalities (e.g. Calgary Transit) to decrease emission of greenhouse gases, trying to implement the Kyoto Protocol's Clean Development Mechanism. The institute also kept an Oil Sands Watch, in which it suggested ways to reduce GHG emissions from extraction operations.

Institute members were collecting and recording the ads appearing in local newspapers and on TV stations, paid for by tar sands producers and the Alberta Independence Party, linking UNECOP with the Green Daughters of the Red Dawn. Some ads claimed that Oolayou was a Han-Spar agent, aiming to sell more Han-Spar Candu nuclear reactors by shutting down the tar sands. "Let the Eastern bastards freeze in the dark," one concluded.

Pembina members also explained to Oolayou details of the fight in the provincial legislature over the future of the oil sands, and the likelihood of an election on the issue.

Meanwhile, that evening the chief executives of the tar sands companies were preparing, in various ways, for next day's meeting. Hans van der Haas, CEO of Royal Dutch Shell PLC, Adrian Loader, head of Shell Canada, and their V-P in charge of oil sands operations, were flying back to Calgary from Peace River in a company Bombardier Challenger 300 after attending funeral services for their employees. All three were well educated, decent men, with open minds. They had children and grandchildren. "We will invest as much as possible in GHG abatement technology," said van der Haas. Then he seemed to hedge a bit. "We'll hear what the UN police say and remain flexible. I agree with most of the UN's great plan to reform the world, but it may fail, trying to do everything at once. Particularly with all these bold changes in the States, there will be strong reaction," said van der Haas." He was a tall, thin man with a goatee and horn-rimmed glasses, considered wise by his subordinates.

The CEO's of Syncrude, the smaller Suncor, and the director of the Americrude Syndicate, which represented most nine American oil companies, were more partisan. They planned to argue that the United States needed every barrel of tar sands oil, even if it contributed to warming, to lessen its dependence on Middle Eastern supplies.

The CEO and majority shareholder of Northern Hydrocarbon was Frank Connors, 72, called the Wizard of Ooze in the local newspapers. He was 6'3" tall, his 280 pounds including a big belly and jowls. His hair was dyed black every three weeks, as were his prominent eyebrows. He was wearing an expensive cream-colored Italian suit, a thick leather belt with a large gold buckle in the shape of a bucking bronco, and a purple silk shirt. Sitting in front with his chauffeur, he had removed his tie and begun to drink cognac from the well stocked bar, smoking a roll-your-own cigarette made from a tin of tobacco kept in the glove compartment. It was a habit acquired at seventeen years of age as a poor coal miner in the foothills near the British Columbia border, and kept as he rose to be foreman, attended night school, was made a manager, and eventually joined Syncrude. (Which at the time used (surface) coal mining techniques such as huge buckets on drag lines.) Then he had started Northern Hydrocarbon on a shoestring.

Connors had been volcanically angry all week. His company's shares were sinking in value along with all other tar sand producers, while light oil stocks were rising considerably. Investors feared that the UN would succeed in curtailing oil sands production, or at least make it more expensive. Coming home from his office in Calgary, he was still angry.

Its headlights piercing the darkness, Connors' black matte carbon-fibre composite armored Rolls-Royce Conquistador hurtled along the highway thirty kilometres north of the city, propelled well over the speed limit by its V12 490 hp engine on 24inch diameter rims and Yokahama snow tires. The vehicle was driven by Brad Lyons, 31, a former stock car racer, whose brown hair was slicked back into an Elvis Presley duck-tail with sideburns. After a turn onto a side road, the line of evergreens masking a tall spiked fence around Connors' estate came into view. The gatehouse guards waved and raised the barrier.

Lyons lived on the grounds in an apartment above the garage and looked after the three guard dogs and the vehicles, which included two Hummers, three SUV's, three Lamborghinis, two Ferrarris, a Bricklin, a Maxwell, a black 1938 Duesenberg, and five vintage Corvettes. He also ran a goon squad for Connors, and liaised with Bud Munk, the America First oil lobbyist. Lyons was sending twenty burly Northern Hydrocarbon 'workers' to picket outside the meeting next day, and fight with pro-UN forces if possible.

"Tell Mrs Hudson I'll have Mandy tonight, in the classroom," said Connors to Lyons as they parted. Mrs Hudson was his housekeeper, a stout taciturn widow, a former Newfoundlander in her forties. She was as well paid as the others, and sent money to kin in several outport villages. Mandy Elaschuk, 18, was the most submissive of the harem of four women kept in one wing of the ten-bedroom mansion. Sexually abused by her stepfather, she left home at sixteen, working in donut shops. Lyons recruited her six months before on her first day of work as a lap dancer, in Calgary. One of the 'play rooms' in the basement was fitted out like a rural schoolroom of the middle of the last century, containing two dozen student desks with sides of cast iron lattice, ink wells, nib pens, slates, and text books. There were maps from that era beside the blackboards, and a (non-functioning) pot-bellied wood stove at the back. A coronation picture of Queen Elizabeth hung at the front.

It was an attempt to reconstruct the one-room country school where Connors had been punished in Grade Five, bent over the teacher's desk and caned with the pointer from the map case for cheating on a spelling test. All these years later Connors still replays it over and over, but the roles are reversed, as he takes his endless revenge on the woman who hurt him.

Mandy is sitting at her desk in the classroom when he comes in. Connors plays the teacher, inspecting her grooming and her uniform as she stands straight before him, hands by her side, eyes to the floor. She's wearing a tight white blouse, showing a lot of cleavage, over a new robin's egg blue brassiere made specially for her by a small shop in New York that specializes in large cup sizes. A short, pleated, plaid skirt covers her ample hips and thighs, above white knee socks and brown penny loafers. He 'notices' the folded paper protruding from one cup of her bra. "You were going to cheat on the spelling test, weren't you," he said accusingly

"No, sir," she pleads.

"Don't lie to me," he replies. "Bend over my desk."

She complies and he flips up the back of her skirt, revealing a smooth creamy white bottom almost as round as the globe with the British empire in red on other side of desk. He pulls the waist band of her robin's egg blue panties up the small of her back, pushing the fabric into the crevasse and enlarging the orbs.

"I'm going to put a little pink into those cheeks," he says.

It was a typical session. Between sips of an 1886 Armagnac, he spanked Mandy with his hand and with the back of a hairbrush. He took off her panties and spanked her in various positions. Then he removed her clothes and ordered her to lie face down on the cot at the back. He admired her natural Ukranian ash blond hair, her hairless body, her smooth shaved vulva and pretty legs. Her small waist gave her body an hourglass outline. Sitting on the teacher's chair, for twenty minutes he gently massaged her buttocks with expensive oils, moving to the delicate contours of her back, and the backs of her legs. Then Mandy put on a robe and they took the elevator to the master bedroom. He was fairly drunk, fumbling to remove his clothing, but so excited that he got a good erection, and managed to put on a condom. Putting a rubber glove on his right hand, he used one and then two fingers to lubricate her anus with Vaseline, carefully removing the glove inside-out and throwing it in a waste bin. Thus prepared, he slowly inserted his large penis and sodomized her for five minutes before ejaculating. He carefully disposed of the condoms, washed quickly in the bathroom, and sprawled asleep. She returned to her room, thinking of the $4000 (taxes already paid) that was automatically deposited into her account at a bank in Edmonton every two weeks. And the watch and jewelry after Connors had special visitors he wanted to impress.

*

At noon on the day of the meeting the UNECOPs left their van in an outside parking lot near the hotel, and took a bus to the Calgary Tower. The women and child wore mukluks, beaded leggings, and quilled anoraks. Professor Bell wore a hydro coat over his suit. Up in the Tower, Milly Moosomin pointed out the sites she recognized, including the Exhibition Grounds and bits of the frozen Bow River. Beloved experienced some vertigo after glancing straight down through the glass floor to the swirling snow on 9th Avenue and Centre Street far below, but soon recovered by looking to the horizon. They splurged and had lunch in the revolving restaurant.

The meeting was at 2 p.m. Professor Bell led them along the walkway over the rail lines running through the center of the city to the Palliser South building. On the sidewalk opposite the entrance hundreds of protesters were carrying placards, shouting, and throwing rotten fruit across the street. Some were really oil workers, while others were minor criminals Lyons had met while in jail for assault. There were aggrieved shareholders, some quite elderly, and America First agitators bussed up from Montana. “UN Stalinists,” one old man repeated on a megaphone. Others shouted “UNECOP Communists not wanted here.” Conservative, Wildrose Alliance, and Alberta Independence supporters strutted righteously while member of the Alberta Freedom Party spewed their skinhead Neo-Nazi opinions. TV vehicles, ten RCMP and city police cruisers, and local press and *paparazzi,* milled around.

On the pavement in front of the building roughly the same number of pro-UN people had gathered behind a cordon. They finished singing "Imagine" and begin the UN anthem to the tune of the "Finlandia Hymn." Their numbers were swelling by the minute because of a rumor that Luna was with the UNECOPs. "Luna is at her home in Ontario. This is not Luna," said Oolayou, picking up Bliss and pulling back her hood. "She looks a bit like Luna, but this is Bliss Akiwenzie, the daughter of this officer," said Oolayou, presenting Rita to the throng and the TV cameras.

Then they went into the building and up the elevator, escorted by city police. In a women's washroom Rita, Beloved, and Oolayou changed into white blouses, dark green vicuna-hair business suits with knee-length shirts, pantyhose and low-heeled brown leather pumps, all of which had been carried in a suitcase with the gifts. They wore silver dream-catcher earrings but no make-up. Their New Harmony identity bracelets had been left at the hotel.

The small conference room was half-filled with an antique oval bird's-eye maple table with eight cabriole legs. The names of participants were on cards in silver holders in front of walnut and mahogany armchairs with dark red leather seats. A long window had a western view of the foothills. Professor Bell and Beloved Morton sat on Oolayou's left, Rita Akiwenzie on her right. Milly and Bliss sat at the back in an area reserved for aides. Bell introduced everyone, and Oolayou gave her gifts to the executives. A dark green jadeite polar bear stalking a seal on ice went to Hans van der Haas of Royal Dutch Shell, a bluish white soapstone of an Arctic fox with pups to the CEO of Syncrude, sleeping walruses in flecked grey limestone to the head of Suncor, and the nunatuk picas piece from her office to the director of Americrude. To Frank Connors Oolayou gave a basalt Inuk with harpoon in a kayak.

The first four men thanked her graciously, but Connors had been drinking in the Wranglers' Lounge of the Cattlemen's Hotel and was rude. "Why are you giving me this tourist shit?" he snarled, as she set the carving on the table beside him.

Oolayou was shocked by his words, and hesitated for a moment. But then she turned and went back to her chair. She spoke to the four other oil men, not looking at Connors.

"Al Gore's "An Inconvenient Truth" came out more than a decade ago, showing every thinking person that the GHG reductions set by the Kyoto Protocol had to be met. But carbon tax trading and voluntary action by industry has achieved very little. Revisions in 2007 to the Canadian Clean Air Act to require compliance to Kyoto have not been enforced. Other federal legislation in 2007 aimed at cutting overall Canadian emissions to 6% below 1990 levels by 2012 was equally ineffective. Your industry is the worst offender. In 2003 Alberta tar sands emitted 25 megatonnes of GHG's, while last year 126 megatonnes were released." She paused.

"So now come some Draconian measures. The United Nations, which is now the government of the world as the nationalist-imperialist era ends, decrees that no new tar sands operations be started. Existing extraction and upgrading capacity may not be increased. Projects no more than ten per cent started must be halted, and compensation will be paid. You must reduce harmful emissions by ten per cent per year over the next five years, and all operations must cease within twenty years." Oolayou stopped and had a sip of water.

"It's not just oil sands producers," she continued. "The petrochemical industry and power generators will face new rules too. With criminal sanctions. For consumers there will soon be a prohibition on the use of all non-vital small internal combustion fossil fuel engines. Boats, lawn mowers, leaf blowers, . . . Stringent GHG emission standards are coming for all vehicles, everywhere. We will implement the California standard of a tailpipe emissions cut of 25% of 1990 levels by 2020. Short-haul jet flights will be curtailed, and aviation fuel taxed heavily with cap and trade as in Europe, with the money going to develop non-polluting alternate means of travel. Unnecessary vacation and pilgrimage flights will be especially heavily taxed. The Vatican airline will be shut down. Everyone will be affected because this is a total war to reduce GHG emissions. Even if there is wide-spread economic recession as we curtail warming emission, it must be borne."

Then Professor George Bell spoke, relaying more of the position of the Intergovernmental Panel on Climate Change. "There will be no increase in the amount of water your operations are taking from the Athabaska River. You will not get any natural gas from the Mackenzie Valley pipeline, because the National Energy Board has agreed that it should go to convert the coal-fired electricity generating plants in Alberta. There must be complete replanting of the boreal forest in all stripped areas and restoration of watershed streams which have been drained or polluted. All tailing ponds must be cleaned."

"My company has planted five million trees in the last decade," said the CEO of Syncrude, somewhat indignantly. "We've drastically reduced sulphur dioxide emissions. We filled in a pit at Fort McMurray and sowed grasses and a herd of bison lives there now. We've done a fair job of cleaning up, but we will improve. I do not oppose the UN, but only hope that all fossil producers will be treated equally. If there is a provincial election, Syncrude will not finance or otherwise support parties that oppose the UN and Kyoto."

Then the CEO of Suncor spoke. "We too are serious about reducing our environmental footprint, and will do our best to cut emissions going forward. But if we can comply, we shouldn't be penalized more than light oil producers, who will not all be shut down in twenty years. Anyway, isn't it up to the people of Alberta to decide in an election? And what about the fact that the United States needs this secure source of oil, especially as it loses control of the Middle East? The tar sands produce four million barrels of synthetic crude per day, most of it going to the States, and it will not be easily replaced. What of NAFTA [North American Free Trade Agreement], which prohibits such limits as the UN proposes?"

"NAFTA has been superceded by the Fair Trade Acts, which encourage environmental protection," replied George Bell. "The new American administration has a plan to replace this fossil fuel energy with other sources, so don't worry about that."

"You Canadians are very quick to deprive us of this safe source of oil," said the Americrude director, "and very quick to relegate America to small nation status. But US companies have big investments in these tar sands, and we aren't going to just walk away. We will support the provincial Conservatives financially, and we will take this to court, all the way to the Supreme Court of Canada. The constitution of Canada gives control of natural resources to the provinces."

"The Canadian constitution was designed in 1867 and didn't foresee global warming," replied Bell.

Hans van der Haas spoke for Royal Dutch Shell. "I am a Dutchman," he said wryly, "and so I understand what rising sea levels would mean. So Shell will do what the UN wants. Not with rancor either, but in a spirit of duty. For we are all links in the Great Chain of Being, caretakers for future generations. We don't want the curses of future generations over our graves."

Then Frank Connors spoke, loudly, slurring his words occasionally. "I will bet anyone a million dollars there will be widespread anger and rioting when Americans run out of gasoline and there are line-ups at the pumps and the prices skyrockets, and there is rationing and hoarding. Then the oil companies and Republicans will blame the UN, and soon retake political power from Winfrey and her One-World tree-hugging international socialist friends. She'll be impeached by Congress before her term is up. I bet anyone a million dollars." He stopped to take a drink from a flask made of gold, bearing his initials in emeralds and diamonds on one side.

"Can't you see," Connors continued, "that this is just more of the National Energy Program shit the pinko Trudeau put us through in the 'eighties, but much worse? Just eastern bastards stealing from Alberta again, this time threatening us with jail if we don't obey them. Well, I'm here to say I don't give a flying fuck if tar sand oil operations produces three times or ten times the greenhouse gases of light oil production. I think climate change is probably the biggest hoax of all time, but if not, well, apres moi, the heat or the flood, I don't give a shit. Let me tell you why. Who was gutting it out in the mid 'eighties when oil prices were so low, ten dollars a barrel, that we lost money in the tar sands with every barrel we produced? I was with Syncrude then and it almost went bankrupt, and the NEP hurt us even more and Alberta lost hundreds of billions of dollars, stolen by . . . Even the managers had to pitch in. Have you ever been out in 30 below wind for a shift of cleaning calcified soot out of coker ovens with sledge hammers?" (Connors stares at the UNECOPs.) "Fuck you all! I'm not worried about global warming. In fact I hope the ice cap over the Arctic Ocean melts real quick so we can get the oil underneath before the greedy Russians do." Connors stood up.

"That's why we need a deep water port at Bathurst Inlet," he shouted, glaring at Oolayou, as though it were her fault the project was being delayed by environmental reviews. He picked up the basalt carving, throwing it down onto the table with such force that it broke into a dozen pieces. "No fucking UN Stalinist Eskimo cunt, with eco-terrorist friends, is gonna tell me how to run my business and threaten me with jail."

His tirade finished, Connors walked unsteadily out the door. In the silence that followed, Oolayou searched for words.

"The UN does not exist to bring heaven on Earth, but to save us from man-made hell," was all she could think to say, quoting Dag Hammarskjold, as the meeting ended. Milly put the bigger broken pieces of stone into the suitcase.

"If the UN fails, and natural catastrophes cause chaos, Green Fascists will put oil executives into concentration camps," Milly muttered to Oolayou. "They will execute people like Connors."

Slipping by demonstrators, they took two cabs from the line and returned to the Lucky Dragon Hotel. To their dismay they saw that the green UNECOP van had been splattered with red paint, its tires slashed and flattened. Oolayou walked into the parking lot towards the vehicle, but Beloved pulled her back.

"There might be a bomb," Beloved said, as she called city police on her wrist-top.

Several cruisers came within minutes. The police took pictures and cordoned off the area until the bomb unit came and checked, finding nothing.

Oolayou went up to her hotel room and started to cry. It was a premonition of failure, and, she realized, pms. "It was my fault, leaving the van unattended," she repeated to Rita Akiwenzie.

"No. It was my fault," said Beloved, coming in ten minutes later. "I should have seen it coming," she added.

Beloved hugged Oolayou as they sat on the bed. "Anyway, we've arranged for new tires and a paint job," said Beloved. "Milly has a friend whose son-in-law owns an auto body shop and will do the work tonight. So it will be ready in the morning." As she spoke Beloved handed a tissue to Oolayou.

When Hugo Mann telephoned from CIA headquarters a few minutes later, Oolayou had regained her composure. Beloved listened to the call.

"How did it go?" Mann asked.

"One of the tar sands guys, the owner of Northern Hydrocarbon, is going to be a problem," replied Oolayou. "Also I left the van unprotected and red paint was thrown on it and the tires slashed.

My fault. The police are looking at surveillance tapes but the vandals probably wore balaclavas."

"You've got to be careful, my love," said Mann. "Joel Atkins may be in jail but there are Blacktide contractors and mercenaries in the city. Bud Munk is using America First money to fund the Alberta Independence Party, as I mentioned, and they could come at you. Also the Green Daughters have a lot of dynamite left, remember, from the theft at the road construction site in Quebec." He paused to sip from a cup of tea, and continued.

"I have some interesting news," he said, savoring the giving of it. "Agency satellite photos have been showing activity at an abandoned tar sands operation, a ghost town of about thirty wooden buildings from the 'forties, near the Athabaska River north of Fort McMurray. A place called Bitumount, after the bitumen. I had an agent check it out. It is some weird collection of victims, and old hippies from several communes, Theosophists and New Age vegans, former mental patients, Rosicrucians, Jains, Hindus, and some former Catholics, all with an aura of non-violence, . . . They have been coming since last fall with an influx in the last few weeks, making several hundred now. It seems that every morning and evening many pray to ankh symbols and a sun disk of Aten, and a Baby Luna doll set up in one of the old buildings. They believe Luna is a descendent of Aten and Isis, or Osiris, and that she will come to visit them if they pray enough. They believe she is a sky goddess come to "cleanse" Bitumount and then save the world from destruction from GHGs. This rumor, now on the Internet, is luring people from all over the continent."

"No way!" said Oolayou. "How very strange! How are they managing in the cold and dark? Are there children?"

"They have several wind-up radios and some battery operated lights," replied Mann, but mostly they burn wood in stoves the workers made of forty-five gallon gasoline drums welded together, and burn homemade candles for light. Yes, at least a dozen children. They have an ancient school bus and several old cars for transportation."

"This may yield good publicity," said Beloved.

"Or bad," said Rita.

"We mustn't tell Luna," said Oolayou. "It would swell her head. I will send Milly up to check it out and see what they need. I'll call

Turquoise and she'll put a message on Luna's websites, discouraging this nonsense."

"Keep in touch, my sweet," said Mann, as the image of his face faded from the screen of her wrist-top.

*

The drive back to Toronto was uneventful. A few days later at the invitation of Ontario Power Generation (formerly Ontario Hydro) Oolayou attended a ceremony in the town of Nanticoke, on the north shore of Lake Erie, and watched from a distance as the eight giant smokestacks of the coal-fire generating station, the largest single source of air pollution in southern Ontario, were toppled by explosives. Luna, Turquoise and Shui Zhe were visiting Toronto to judge a UNICEF charity flower show in the Horticulture Building of the CNE that evening, and at the last minute decided to come along with Oolayou to Nanticoke. Delighted OPG officials insisted Luna give the signal to set off the charges. As the dust cleared, news came that the Alberta government had fallen and elections been slated for the 22th of June.

Next day Milly reported by e-mail on the people in Bitumount. "Have spoken with the unofficial watchman, Ernie Aitkins, spry in his nineties, who lives by himself in the former manager's house at the north end of town near the Athabaska River, who says the pilgrims, as they call themselves, have no leader. Among the first arrivals was Mary Vincent, in her fifties, who grew up in a succession of foster homes. Had her forearms cut off with a hatchet and left for dead as a teenager. Another woman badly scalded as a child by her mother as punishment. Ivy Redbird, in her mid thirties I would judge, had her tongue cut off by her drunken husband in 2008, for talking to another man without his permission. There are two elderly sisters of Helen Betty Osborne, . . . you know, the Cree girl from a reserve who was living in Le Pas [Manitoba] to go to high school when she was raped and murdered in 1971, and nothing was done to the four white boys responsible until years after, and only then because that book [Lisa Priest's *Conspiracy of Silence*] was written about the case.

Met a young Metis woman, Nitawik, who was raped and beaten. Met five deaf women and a deaf man, in their thirties, from Saskatoon, who use American sign language. Two blind people in their thirties, m & f, with seeing spouses. There are twenty former members of a Green Christian congregation in Winnipeg, and about thirty former out-patients of a psychiatric hospital in Edmonton. Some pantheist Wiccans and several old hippies from communes in the Qu'Appelle valley in Saskatchewan. Many other people I have not met, perhaps a hundred. Maybe some Luddites. The children I saw seemed healthy, but are not being schooled. They are taught to venerate Luna as a goddess, daughter-wife of Aten, and everyone prays at sunrise and sunset to a Baby Luna doll in her Isis robe. "She will come," they chant. The shrine is in a former equipment shed covered with tin sheets still in relatively good shape. They have no electricity nor indoor plumbing, but have fixed up the old latrines, are melting snow for water, and burning wood taken from collapsed buildings.

Taking the old boards may get them in trouble because the area was made an Alberta Historical site in the seventies—the paint on the sign is peeling badly. But the 'caretaker' has not called the authorities about the squatters because he is more desperate than Ben Gunn [marooned on *Treasure Island]* for company, as few people ever visit this inaccessible place.

I trucked in a load on the winter road over the muskeg. Fresh fruits and vegetables, 200 gallons of frozen milk, 200 lbs each of rice, flour, oatmeal, and cornmeal in 10 lb bags, blankets, used clothing and medical supplies. First Air will fly in a small plane on skis to the turf runway south of Bitumount once a week, bringing a nurse and more supplies. Gave $5,000 cash to Nitawik and she is making a list to give the pilot. Told her they should set up a schoolroom somewhere, or child welfare agencies will pounce. I'll send books, education supplies, and a teacher if necessary.

I thought it prudent not to mention any connection to Luna lest it foster rumors and false hopes, but some, I think, have guessed. Several pilgrims saw my New Harmony identity bracelet before I removed it, and may have realized what it was. P.S. Remember that once spring comes, you can only get in by air or the Athabaska River." (End of e-mail)

CHAPTER 6
Interlude

Luna was six years old on March 11th, a Saturday. She had classes in the morning, but in the afternoon there was as a small party for her in her parents' apartment in the tower. Ten friends her own age came over for two hours, bearing homemade gifts. Her parents gave her an expensive child-size wrist-top, justified on grounds of security, and the first phone call was from Oprah Winfrey. In the evening her grandparents brought in a few of their friends. Jack Layton, the Prime Minister heading the left coalition, and his wife Olivia Chow, Minister of Citizenship and Immigration, who was instituting the liberal new immigration policies and taking environmental refugees, had known Ramsey since the 'nineties and were frequent visitors to Home Base when Parliament was not in session. Their gift was a fold-up silk fan with scenes of China, made in a Fair Trade-approved shop. "The last empress had a lot of fans," said Luna, visibly pleased. Layton wanted to suggest that Luna be used in the upcoming Alberta election, but held back. Michaelle Jean, the out-going (in both senses) Governor-General of Canada, who no longer had to keep her sympathy for New Harmony a secret, and her husband and adopted Haitian daughter, were next. Marie-Eden, recently turned twenty, with her hair in an Afro, gave Luna five illustrated Edwardian-era *Girls' Own Stories* and a big book of Krazy Kat comics. Then Leonardo di Caprio, the movie star, entered. He bowed his head and kissed the back of Luna's extended right hand in the way she liked men to do, and gave her an elaborate antique Swiss orrery with a different metal for every heavenly body. "It's possibly a tad over your limit dollar-wise, but so educational I hope you'll accept it," di Caprio told Turquoise. Coincidentally, a few minutes later as the "Titanic" star talked with Luna, a meticulously detailed two metre-long painted wooden model of the *Titanic* in a mahogany and glass case, made by fifteen inmates at Warkworth (Ontario) medium-security prison, was unwrapped. "Dear Luna: We are big fans and put up pictures of you on our walls. Some of us have Little Dragon Girl tattoos," the card said.

For supper there were various Chinese-style dishes. Luna loaded her plate and adroitly used chopsticks to eat, before taking a spoon to a big piece of Baked Alaska. The mood at the party was bittersweet because Chou and Turquoise had just been ordered to Lop Nur for training for a trip to Apollo City in May and June, via the *Dragon Nest*. "We will be part of a Han-Spar team in the excavated area, putting together SpaceForce headquarters, another dormitory and cafeteria, an infirmary, an assay office and an hotel for tourists, to be called the Blue Moon Inn. Then we will use the dozer to cover the segment with three metres of basalt gravel," Turquoise explained. "After that we'll help build radio telescopes on the dark side for the European Space Agency, and use rovers to do some iron ore prospecting for an Indonesian company."

Next day, without prompting Luna used her wrist-top to send e-mails to all people not thanked in person. Through channels, to the prisoners she typed with her right index finger that she especially liked the tiny passengers and crew on the decks, especially the ladies' dresses. Then, her tender age notwithstanding, Luna lectured the inmates about redemption. "Whatever bad you have done, you can do lots of good when you get out, to make up for it. I know because my Mommy read me a story about long ago how a convict who hurt and robbed many people was sent to jail in Australia and he secretly came back to London 25 years later and secretly paid most of them back with money he made farming sheep after he got out of jail," Luna typed. Turquoise helped with spelling, but the words were hers. When they got Luna's message, many of the Warkworth inmates vowed, via e-mail to her, to change.

As usual, Turquoise returned scores of expensive gifts sent from undesirable or questionable sources, or gave them to UNICEF for auction, without Luna's knowledge.

*

Several days after her birthday Luna happened to see a news item on her new wrist-top about the Bitumount squatters. It said that RCMP officers in western Canada were discouraging motorists from picking up hitch-hikers headed to the area. Luna heard the announcer say the pilgrims considered her a goddess. "Is it because of the Luna connection that the provincial government, fearing a backlash, has not evicted the squatters?" he asked in conclusion.

"We must send some help to my people," Luna said to Zhe, who was nearby.

"You are not a goddess, and they are not your people," said Zhe firmly. "Don't let your mother hear you say such things, or she will freak out . . . . But don't worry, Milly has already taken food and blankets and other stuff they need to Bitumount, and arranged for more."

"How long have you all known about this, and not told me?" Luna asked accusingly.

"About a month," replied Zhe. "We thought you would get too big for your britches if you knew."

"Adults!" said Luna, rolling her eyes. "You can't trust them."

CHAPTER 7
Luna Agrees to Campaign in Alberta

A week later New Harmony's General Council decided that Luna be asked to campaign for the Left coalition in Alberta for three weeks in June. The Conservatives had been in power for half a century in the province and sat on war chests brimming with cash. With the outcome being so important, General Council wanted to use every weapon available. Turquoise and Chou had misgivings about Luna's safety, but acquiesced when Han-Spar executives and UN officials supported General Council. Oolayou could not be involved, but Luna's grandparents would travel with her. Shui Zhe would direct the security arrangements.

At bedtime, when Turquoise asked, Luna was still smarting from not being told about Bitumount. The child saw that she had bargaining power.

"Yes, I will go out west and say the tar sands are bad. But I want a TV show of my own, like Emily Yeung." Luna had recently seen re-runs of five minute episodes of a pre-school show made in 2006 featuring Emily Yeung, a pretty and vivacious Eurasian girl living in Toronto, six years old at the time, shown or taught various things by adult guests. Turquoise agreed to twenty episodes of five minutes each to appear on Luna's UNICEF websites and UNTV.

"I'll need some friends to keep me company on the trip," Luna said. "Meritaten. Desiderata. Mitsy. Bliss. Also Sanjay Chatterjee, to have a boy," said Luna.

"That is fine, if their parents agree," replied Turquoise.

"I want to visit a `musement park near Calgary. Bliss heard about it, with Jack Bunny and Jill O'Hare and kid rides," said Luna.

"An amusement park," said Turquoise. "Just tell Zhe, and she will arrange it."

"Also the dinosaur bone museum," added Luna.

"I know the one you mean, in Drumheller," said Turquoise. "I'm sure Zhe can arrange it. Maybe you can do a five minute show with the curator, filmed for UNTV."

"I want to take Moonflower with us, for parades," said Luna.

"Okay," said her mother.

"Most of all, I want to go see my people at Bitumount," Luna said adamantly, stumbling over the name, disregarding Zhe's warning. "You would not let me fly to India to visit the people who pray to me there, `cause it's too far. But we will be close to this place. Please."

"Well, they are not your people," said Turquoise, raising her eyebrows and frowning momentarily. ". . . But yes, okay, you may go for a day after a rally in Fort McMurray. But you must tell these folks that you are an ordinary human child. Not a goddess. You must say that there are no gods or goddesses, that they are just pretend. Human inventions. Promise?"

"Okay, sure," said Luna quickly.

"When we say prayers to Aten, we are trying to imagine what religion was like when it was new, when it was the only explanation for the earth and sky, thousands of years ago. But now we have science. Will you tell them so at Bitumount, or let their cheers go to your head?" Turquoise persisted.

"Okay, Mommy. I'll tell them I'm just a kid. I promise," said Luna.

"Some tutors will come on the trip, so you and the other children won't miss any instruction," said Turquoise. "And I know you'll obey Zhe as if she were me. Milly too, and your grandparents, of course." she added.

"Okay Mommy," said Luna, as they hugged and kissed. "It's a deal."

Then Turquoise read her more of the legends of the Monkey King, stroking her hair until she fell asleep.

CHAPTER 8
Rumors of a War to End All War

Now tyrants around the globe trembled, more so than in the Arab spring of 2011. Some made hasty alliances, frantically bought black market weapons as the arms embargoes came into effect, hired mercenaries at inflated prices, and hurriedly trained recruits. Dictators everywhere knew the UN Military Services Committee was gathering personnel and making audacious plans for a War to End All Wars, to demilitarize the planet except for UN forces.

Military aggressors world wide got nervous when George W Bush, a dozen senior figures in his administrations and four retired generals were arrested in March by teams of officers of the International Criminal Court, Interpol, and FBI, and charged with war crimes stemming from the American invasion of Iraq in 2003. (Henry Kissinger was on the list of American war criminals, for the carpet bombing of Cambodia and Laos, but he died weeks before he was to be arrested.) They were flown to The Hague for trial in a Gulfstream biofuel jet leased from the CIA, an extraordinary rendition cheered around the world. Former prime minister Tony Blair was arrested in England at the same time.

The arrests sparked widespread demonstrations, and rioting in ten southern American cities, the worst being Miami and Dallas. But efficient local police work coupled with FBI arrests of organizers brought the rioting under control within a week. Then a spate of right-wing bombings started. In New York City there were four separate subway bombings, and three trucks filled with explosives went off near the UN building. (Five others failed to detonate.) Trains in the Chicago area were targeted, and six car bombs exploded near offices of UN agencies. Car bombs in market areas of Los Angeles and San Francisco killed hundreds and maimed as many more. Improvised roadside devices and mines on roads outside New Harmony bases killed thirty people, wounding twenty. But unlike religious terrorism, the counter-revolutionaries had no suicide bombers, which limited the damage somewhat. Altogether more than three thousand people were killed, as many as died in the 2001 attack on the World Trade Center towers, although the number of injured was much higher.

This carnage in the spring of 2017 turned the undecided public firmly against America First and the other reactionaries responsible. The FBI and CIA worked together to made arrests in most cases and used the preventive detention of about three thousand right-wing fanatics, (including some former DEA, FBI, and CIA agents, Israeli agents, mercenaries and religious extremists), to disrupt the wave of terror. Ironically, ten right-wing newspaper editors, four Fox News television commentators, and five prominent evangelical preachers were arrested under anti-terrorism provisions they themselves had once welcomed, for urging armed resistance (including Minutemen militias) to Winfrey's pro-UN administration.

CHAPTER 9
Green Daughters in Turmoil

What was going on with the leadership of the Green Daughters of the Red Dawn? Why did Regine Muller suddenly leave Marlene Kurras in charge of operations in Canada and drive to Costa Rica? Why something so risky? Did she love Erica Newby, the younger sister of one of the women who committed suicide at the rural airport north of Edmonton, swallowing cyanide pills provided by Muller as police closed in? Had Newby and Muller shared an apartment in Chicago for several months? Was Newby the woman Muller followed to Costa Rica, driving a rented dark blue BMW Hydrogen 299, and using cleverly forged documents? Was this willowy young beauty, this supple young branch of the Tree of Life, this idealist with an obscure animal rights organization in Chicago, was she disgusted by the manner of her sister's death and angry at Muller? And Muller, plain, buck-toothed, skinny, greying in her mid fifties, always smelling of the cigarettes to which she is addicted, feeling guilty in one part of her mind, not guilty in another, . . . should she be pitied or admired for driving fourteen hours a day, sleeping fitfully in motels, crossing dangerous borders to Costa Rica?

How did the Columbians identify Muller? How did they get her out of the Quetzal Inn, in the old part of San Hose, a town in the Central Highland region close to the white-water kayaking that Erica Newby loved? Were staff threatened or bribed into complicity, as one report suggested? Who administered the needle with the tranquilizer as she lay sleeping? Was it actually a hearse the kidnappers used, putting her in a coffin to fool the Guardia Rural as they traveled down the isthmus to Columbia? The official papers presented at the border, don't they indicate collusion between the kidnappers and the Columbian government? When they switched to the white van that Muller later remembered, and the tranquillizer wore off, did she realize she was in the hands of a right-wing paramilitary group, the United Self-Defense Forces of Columbia (AUC)?

Was AUC doing more kidnaping because their cocaine business had collapsed, or was it a contract job? What was the role of their allies, the murderous Black Eagles?

When Hugo Mann learned of Muller's fate from decoded National Security Agency cell phone intercepts, he notified Leona Montoya and Red Hand sprang into action, using a tramp freighter from Jamaica, a former DEA helicopter with CIA crew, black market cruise missiles, and her best agent.

*

[This is an excerpt from the *Diary of a Red Hand Agent*, which was published anonymously several years ago in the *Heroes of the Transition* series, translated from the Spanish original by the author.]

We are about five kilometres north of the small city of La Mesa, Departmento del Cesar, Columbia. Local Red Hand agents and UN guerrillas have cut power to radar installations from the Atlantic coast to our destination.

It's almost drop time. I take a last drag of hashish and slip into a black bulletproof dragon-armor one-piece of mimetic polycarbon, with infrared goggles built into the helmet. As adrenaline mounts, I check my tools and strap them on. I'm carrying a silenced .22 Beretta, a strangling wire for close-up work, and a flechette gun with toxin darts. If I get noticed I have a double pack of anti-personnel missiles and a small automatic rifle. The pilot gives the warning, "Two minutes to target," she says, taking the four-bladed Super Cobra helicopter up to two thousand metres.

I'm thinking of the people killed by AUC thugs in the last fifteen years, working from this site. Several thousand altogether. Over sixty ethnic Wayuu and Wiwa, and more than a hundred Kankuamos in native communities in the Sierra Nevada de Santa Marta and La Guajira. I think of the union leaders, teachers, environmentalists, New Harmony politicians, UN personnel, and rival cocaine dealers, tortured and killed by these thugs often even when ransoms were paid. (Amnesty International has the documentation.) The AUC leader resides here, with his mistress and about a hundred of his five hundred men, and I'm hoping to meet them soon.

As always I'm thinking of the Guatemalan soldiers who shot my father, and then raped and strangled my mother. When I was seven, hiding under clothes in a closet.

As we hover, the light by the hatch turns green and I drop with outspread arms and legs into the moonlit darkness. I feel invulnerable, an avenging angel of justice.

Drift control is good. I pull the cord at two hundred metres, managing to follow the beacon and land on the roof of the building I want. Soon I'm through an upper window and started down to the cells where the prisoners are kept. Security is poor. I kill four guards with no trouble.

There are twenty-seven prisoners. The youngest is a girl of ten, daughter of a prominent Columbian New Harmony leader, a professor. Ms. Muller has been raped and beaten and needs help to walk. As I lead them to the gate I kill another six guards with my rifle. The local support team has rigged the gates, and blows them off at my signal. We take cover as debris falls. We come under fire but the Cobra sweeps in low and blazes away with gatlings and missiles, and we escape. The prisoners are driven away in four directions, as I set land mines which destroy the first personnel carrier to come through the wall. The second carrier I hit with a double clip of missiles, causing it to crash. Then I set more mines and drive away with Regine Muller in the last car. The Cobra heads back to the old freighter in international waters in the Caribbean from whence it came.

Three cruise missiles launched from the freighter hit the compound two minutes later, pulverizing the buildings and vehicles, creating a red glow I see through the rear window of the car I'm driving. No one survived, I am later informed. Among the dead were the AUC leader and eleven senior federal policemen, the latter there for a weekend of seminars on counter-terrorism techniques. We live in a time rich in irony.

A week later I'm back at the New Harmony base in the Atacama desert on the Peruvian high plains, where Muller is recovering in the infirmary under guard. The phone rings. "Well done, as usual," says the Lioness, and my trip is complete. [End of excerpt.]

*

Oolayou, in her office one morning in the middle of April, answered the shielded and encrypted land line from B1that Leona Montoya preferred.

"We've reached a deal with the Green Daughters. They are going to cease operations in Canada and Alaska for at least five years." For a wild moment Oolayou thought Montoya might be joking, some sort of delayed April Fool prank. Oolayou knew Regine Muller had been rescued and smuggled first to the base on the Peruvian *altiplano* and then aboard a yacht to Mexico and overland to the base near Oaxaca, where Erica Newby (located and invited by Montoya) awaited her. But this was a surprise.

"The deal with Gundrun Wolfe and Marlene Kurras," continued Montoya, "is that we are turning over Muller to a Green Daughters cell in Brownsville, Texas. In return Wolfe and Kurras promise to curtail all activities in Canada, and have disclosed the location of the rest of the stolen dynamite. Hugo Mann agreed, holding his nose, because it would hurt the Left badly to have a wave of eco-terrorism during the election campaign in Alberta. Of course it will look bad that we coddled the Green Daughters, if it leaks out. To make up for it I intend to come down hard on them when I find their headquarters, somewhere in Washington state, and the FBI can grab all of them at once because the cells are not independent."

CHAPTER 10
Goddess or Princess

With her mother and father away, Luna was staying in her grandparents' apartment high in the tower at B1. (Jamie Ramsey and Roxanne McFadden had been part of a twelve-person group marriage involving other founding directors of New Harmony, but in old age were drifting back together.) They were busy making arrangements for the campaign in Alberta. One morning at breakfast Luna had a question.

"Jamie, after I do this gig [at the Hospital for Sick Children in Toronto] on Saturday, may I go to the museum?" she asked. "There are some things from an Egyptian queen. Not Cleopatra." (Luna had many books about Cleopatra, and had watched the movie starring Elizabeth Taylor eight times.)

"The pharaoh Hatshepsut, foremost of the noble ladies," replied Ramsey, who was not as worried as her mother about Luna's queen/goddess phantasies.

"I'm sure we can manage that," said Roxanne. "Although I hate to see the museum building, so mutilated by the aluminum and glass idiocy added ten years ago on the Bloor Street side. Crystal indeed! It looks as if a large jet had smashed into the side of the building. The window cleaning costs are through the roof, I hear."

On Saturday Shui Zhe and Luna and her friend Meritaten, who was part Egyptian, came to Toronto with her grandparents in one of two armored Ford Stardust Cruiser hydrogen fuel-cell sedans purchased for the trip out west. Luna sat in the car-seat/crashball in the back seat with the visor open as the driver, who was also an armed bodyguard, carefully navigated the 400 and 401 highways in light traffic into the city. Despite the extra weight of armor and crashball the 700hp electric motor in the car was capable of 300 kph if necessary.

Shui Zhe and the other bodyguard removed their bullet-proof vests, but carried concealed pistols. As arranged, four uniformed policewomen escorted them past hundreds of spectators outside the hospital, into the telethon center where Luna did an hour and a half on the phones. She answered one hundred and seven calls, getting pledges of $327, 340, a new record for the Sick Kid's celebrity telethon. "Princess Diana in her prime could not have done better," said the hospital CEO, within Luna's hearing. Then she toured several wards, shaking hands with staff and greeting patients. She was wearing a blue turquoise cotton dress embroidered with her cartouche and the main gods and goddesses in many-colored threads, a birthday gift from the family of the Egyptian girl to whom she had given the golden cat. Her moccasins were beaded with ankh symbols, as was the hair band which pushed up her Shirley Temple ringlets.

Leaving the hospital, Luna and her party were driven to the UNECOP building on Jarvis Street and the Ford parked in the underground lot. After lunch with Beloved, Oolayou, and Rita and Bliss Akiwenzie in the cafeteria, they all crammed into two cabs to the Royal Ontario Museum. Escorted by the same four officers, they waited in line to buy tickets and then toured the Egyptian exhibits. As visitors and staff stared at her, Luna stared at a plaster cast of the capstone of an obelisk erected by Hatshepsut, studying the queen's cartouche and getting Oolayou to sketch it on a piece of paper. Then Luna spent half an hour before the plaster casts of two walls of Hatshepsut's funerary temple in Thebes (depicting a trading voyage to Punt), posing a lot of questions.

In the gift shop she asked her grandparents for an expensive half-size reproduction of the gracile Selket, one of four gilded wooden funerary goddesses found in Tutankhamun's tomb.

"How beautiful she is! I really must have one," Luna announced.

"I don't know," said Ramsey. "It's rather expensive. What labor made it?" (The price was $500.) But her grandmother was already reaching into her purse. When Ramsey insisted something be bought for Bliss and Meritaten also, Bliss pointed to a bust of Nefertiti, a ceramic copy of the swan-necked one in Berlin's Altes Museum. A 20cm long resin sarcophagus with three coffins inside, detailed copies of those found in Tutankhamun's burial chamber, was purchased for Meritaten. Then the policewomen cleared a path through the crowd in the atrium and outside the main door as Zhe hailed cabs for the ride back to UNECOP headquarters. The policewomen followed in two cruisers to see there was no trouble with photographers or political enemies.

Upon arrival both of the cab drivers, a well-dressed, turbaned, bearded Sikh and a Hindu with two days of stubble, in a faded Blue Jays T-shirt, old jeans, scuffed running shoes, with an image of Ganesha on his dash-board, asked Luna for her autograph and picture. She obliged, writing her full name and the date on museum brochures, while they snapped her on older model cell phones.

Ramsey took the opportunity to proselytize for secularism. "You know we feel that religion should fade away. That it causes too much trouble," said the New Harmony founder, as he paid the fares and tipped generously. (He had driven a taxi on weekends in Toronto in the early 'seventies while in graduate school at York University.)

"My kids are saying Luna is better than Bollywood movie stars, and I am liking her too," the Hindu man said simply, shrugging.

"She is herself proof of a Divine Being," said the Sikh driver solemnly, as he departed.

After tea and scones in Oolayou's apartment, the Stardust Cruiser was driven back to B1without incident. That evening before bedtime Luna heard a TV announcer say that the Canadian Parliament was "abolishing the Queen." She listened carefully while her grandfather explained why the new government was cutting this connection to England, deleting references to the Queen in laws and taking her picture out of public places, and off the stamps and money.

"Canada is a democracy where everyone is equal, and we do not need royalty. Also we have many cultures now, so it's wrong to put English culture ahead of others," said Ramsey. "But Canada will keep the job of governor-general and the provinces will keep their lieutenant-governors, to open Parliament and give out awards and such."

"But what about poor Queen Elizabeth? It is bad to treat an old widow lady like that. She will be very sad," said Luna.

"I think she sort of understands," replied Ramsey.

"Tomorrow I'm going to write her a letter to cheer her up," declared Luna.

(She did, receiving a kindly personal reply ten days later, just before leaving for Alberta. This document is accessible at *B1archive.com*)

*

Luna was in a cycle of curiosity about human sexuality. She often bathed with both sexes in communal spas in the egg, and had been given lots of information by liberal adults, as you would expect in a planning group that tolerated nude areas in their new base in northern California and on two Indian bases. But inexorably Luna had internalized the genital taboo of the larger society.

Intermittently over the past two years Luna had been initiating doctor games with her friends when they were alone. It was their secret, until Zhe accidentally overheard Mitsy and Meritaten talking. Apparently Sanjay was often the patient, getting his 'willy' checked many times by the girls. Recently the children had started to spy on teenage couples using dim corners of the common sleeping rooms in the egg to copulate. Luna and her friends hid behind stacks of mattresses and watched how 'it' was done.

"What if we get caught?" asked Mitsy. "Could we be punished?"

"Nobody will punish me, or you if I say," Luna boasted.

When Zhe reported what she knew to the three child psychologist who advised Luna's parents, they suggested that no action be taken. Somehow this decision leaked around (B1 could be a fish bowl of gossip, a medieval village) and the teenagers involved stopped covering themselves. So Luna and her friends got a good look.

"That's icky and gross," Luna told Desiderata, as they ran away. "That's what the dogs were doing on the lawn that time in Toronto, and the man put the garden hose on them. I'll never do that!"

"Me neither," agreed Desiderata, rather overcome.

Thus the matter was handled without communication with Turquoise or Chou on the moon. Such messages were supposed to be private, but in practice resembled a rural party line crank-up telephone system, and publicity would have given the savage right-wing media more innocuous facts to distort.

CHAPTER 11
Alberta Bound

The bus, a gift from Bill and Melinda Gates to Luna, was the best available, a modified armored Volvo requiring an assistant who sat beside the *driver* to monitor auxiliary equipment. There was an extra driver and assistant, permitting 24 hours of travel per day if necessary. One of the assistants was also a Volvo bus mechanic, carrying his tools in the two-ton truck that pulled the horse trailer conveying Moonflower and her mother. The behemoth bus was fitted with Ballard hydrogen fuel-cells that ran electric engines powering three rear axles, each with six cellular puncture-proof tires on blast-resistant rims. The front axle, likewise carrying three wheels on each side, had a specially designed steering mechanism.

The light blue vehicle had silver solar panels top and sides, but looked streamlined, even with the upper deck at the back and impact-absorbent snout in front. *Luna Express,* read the display panel above the front window. Decals with her picture and the words "Time to get off fossil fuels," were stuck on the door. The bus could be sealed against gases, smoke, or submersion in liquids, and provide its own atmosphere. Large side windows of anti-UV tinted armored glass were as projectile-resistant as the body. There were infrared and radar systems to counter poor visibility, and jammers meant to prevent the detonation of radio-controlled roadside devices and mines. There were gas masks, helmets and blast blankets for the other kids, and a crashball for Luna next to the twenty-five sleeping berths at the back. The uppermost had skylight domes.

There was even a one-minute shower next to the toilets.

*

This little convoy, which included the two Ford Stardust Cruisers, left B1on a warm sunny morning, the last day of May, skirting around Georgian Bay for several hours to reach the Trans-Canada highway. Then they followed the route recently taken by Oolayou, even staying in the same motels at night. Ira Swartz, the UNTV photographer who'd been on the trip to Quttinirpaaq National Park last summer, made a five minute video of Luna visiting Kakabeka Falls. He still had long hair, and had not gotten his glasses fixed. (A piece of a paperclip was still replacing a missing pin.) Swartz was reading Marcuse's *One-Dimensional Man* in his spare time, when he was not chatting with the tutors or playing chess with the mechanic. Swartz also attended to Anubis Fourth and took him for walks at rest stops, usually when the horses were being exercised.

In the mid-afternoon of the third day, five heavily-armed RCMP officers in two cruisers, directed by an Inspector who had assigned herself to the job instead of a lower ranking officer, were waiting at the Alberta border to provide an escort. They had a helicopter and pilot working with them. Inspector Maxine "Timbits" Tibbetts informed Shui Zhe and the prime minister's three permanent RCMP bodyguards from Ottawa that a man had just been arrested in Grande Prairie, a town in the northwest of the province, after an overt threat against Luna was made in a telephone call to the *Calgary Herald.* Fourteen loaded rifles and ammunition had been seized from his house.

"We don't know how serious he was, . . . probably only a big-mouth. He's mighty angry the Catholics are losing their separate schools, and some other things. At his court appearance tomorrow we'll request that he's held in custody for a month for mental health evaluation. We'll keep you informed," said the Inspector. Her greying hair was wrapped into a bun at the back of her head.

The convoy passed wheat fields and gas wells and then came into Medicine Hat, a prosperous town of 70,000 people and many trees in a river valley with cliffs and coulees made by glacial runoff 10,000 years ago. There was a huge Catholic church reflecting the sun from its shiny roof, and a giant teepee on a metal frame in a park. The town was big enough to have a Wal-mart and a Costco.

Their first stop was at the leper treatment center in Crescent Heights, where the Canadian government paid for treatment of foreigners in the early stages of the disease. Luna gave Baby Luna and Schoolgirl Luna dolls to the younger children. Then there was a rally at the junior college campus. Term was over so its students had departed; only several staff and a few hundred high school students who were playing hooky were on hand. Only one local TV station had a camera set up.

"Where is everybody?" asked Luna.

She asked the same thing at a sparsely attended rally at the Exhibition and Stampede Grounds. Milly Moosomin arrived with David Suzuki (a life-long environmentalist), three Pembina Institute members from Calgary, and four other buses with party leaders, assistants, local supporters, and there were hundreds of people waving Liberal, New Democratic, Green, and New Harmony Party signs in the bleachers. Prime Minister Layton and Olivia Chow gave short speeches. (Town police were keeping a dozen Alberta Independence Party hooligans at a distance.) But half the seats at the picnic lunch in the park next to the grandstand were empty.

However the Stampede Queen, a lanky Metis brunette of nineteen in sequined blouse and jeans, welcomed Luna warmly with a hug. They rode at a trot around the track together, her palomino gelding beside Moonflower. The mayor, a fat little man in a white linen suit and a Stetson, gave Luna a hundred bulbs of new varieties of tulips, gladioli, and irises, and a big basket of such flowers. "From my greenhouses," he said. Then he presented Luna with a cowgirl hat, which fit perfectly. She wanted to wear it while riding, but Zhe ran up and insisted she wear her helmet.

The mayor explained the poor turnout. "You can't really blame them. You folks are about as popular here as skunks at a tea party. The towns around here sit on a huge deposit of natural gas, which we sell to keep our taxes laughably low, and produce cheap electricity to attract industry. For a long time now . . . . Rudyard Kipling was here in 1907 and called Medicine Hat the trapdoor to Hell because of all the wells. But the municipality is making $200 million a year from the gas fields. Gas paid for the new hockey arena. The arts center esplanade cost fifty million bucks, including the new museum. Life is better here than in Calgary or Toronto, because of the gas. We've got so much gas we don't bother to turn off the street lamps downtown at night."

"It is brave of you to greet us, then," said Jamie Ramsey.

"I'm not running for re-election," the mayor laughed, presenting his shy grandchildren to Luna and Prime Minister Layton and Olivia Chow. "Besides, I'm as worried as the next person about global warming. I'm leading a push to use the cold water aquifer under the town to cool homes in summer."

So the campaigners left Medicine Hat in a somber mood. The sole positive was that only one leftist candidate, a Liberal, was running in the riding, by (province-wide) agreement of the leftist party leaders, whereas the Conservatives would be splitting the right-wing vote with successionist and extremist parties. Thirty-five per cent of the ballots might be enough to win.

*

It was midnight. Stops at six mall towns during the day had exhausted her, sending Roxanne to bed at 8 p.m. when the bus parked in a motel lot about thirty kilometres southeast of Lethbridge, on Shui Zhe's orders, for a threat assessment. Most of the police escort and some passengers were sleeping in the motel.

In an upper rear berth, Roxanne was dreaming. It was a memory-dream, where she's in the half-finished students' residence of Founder's College, York University, in the fall of 1965. After seeing Jamie at the wine and cheese mixer, hearing his iconoclastic talk, . . . laughing at his jokes about the Pope after her Catholic upbringing, getting close and tilting her cleavage in her low-cut sweater towards his eyes, her mini-skirt wrapping her waist, her hair thick, long, and lustrous. Saying 'Yes, I want you' with her eyes. Then taking a bottle of Mateus rose' off to her room in the women's residence. Door locked. Candle lit. Wine poured into paper cups. Lights out. Kissing him for the first time, a bit drunk. Not having to worry, after the doctor on Keele Street gave her a prescription for the pills because she had turned eighteen. Her large shapely breasts are a gift to his hands and mouth. She hopes he won't notice that she is the more experienced. "We don't need a safe," she says, reclining on her bed, to this brash callow student leader who is willing to confront the authoritarian master of the college. He is so eager to remake the world nearer to their hearts' desire.

Something awoke Roxanne, jarring her back to her aged body, wrinkled thighs and withered dugs. It wasn't Jamie, who lay beside her, a paunchy old man with jowls, fighting prostate cancer, bald on top, hair in his ears, mouth splayed open in sleep.

It was Luna, who had been in bed below with the other children. She was soft and warm in her vicuna-hair pajamas, crawling into the berth from the ladder. "E.T. phone home," said the child, grinning at her joke on herself, in the dim light. She had been wakened and told by Zhe that the solar flare which had prevented communication was waning and that a call from the moon was being routed from NASA-Houston to the bus.

Luna pushed a button and their part of the observation dome cleared, revealing the starry night sky. The moon was in its first quarter, above a distant grain elevator and ghostly wheatfields, and a railroad track stretching westward to the mountains.

"Let's go out the escape hatch and sit on the top of the bus. We could see more," suggested Luna.

"That might be dangerous," said Roxanne, not mentioning the possible threat. So Luna contented herself with training her bird-watching binoculars on the Sea of Tranquillity, searching in vain for any sign of Apollo City. Then she talked to her parents on her wrist-top and saw them on its screen, with two minute delays, as Roxanne brushed her hair, occasionally bending her head and kissing the back of the child's neck as her hair was drawn away by the brush. Luna woke her grandfather by tickling his feet, and he was grumpy until he saw who it was. Ramsey talked briefly to Turquoise and Chou, who were in a rec room in Apollo City. There was still some static and break-up caused by the flare, when the call ended.

"Jamie, come with me to visit Moonflower and exercise her," said Luna a few minutes later.

"Uh, honey, that might be dangerous, so you must stay in the bus until we get the All Clear," replied Ramsey. "Ira has led her around, and her mother."

"Jamie, why do they want to kill me?" asked Luna.

"Only a few bad people do," said Ramsey. "Because you are helping the United Nations to save the world, and they hate you for that. They know how much it would slow down the Transition if you were gone. Oh, and fossil fuel producers and investors will lose trillions of dollars, so for them it's about money," replied Ramsey, as she slipped her hand into his.

"Do you want to go home?" Ramsey asked.

"No," she said, and soon fell asleep between her grandparents.

*

The original alert came from Hugo Mann to Zhe at 7.30 p.m. Mann forwarded a cell phone intercept from Fargo, North Dakota, made the night before. A drunken women was talking to her sister on the other side of town. The relevant bit was: "Rambo's gotta job in Lessbrook . . . someplace north. He's mighty pissed off wit' the Commies for puttin' Bush an' other patriots in jail." The voice was badly slurred.

"Rambo" was John Norval, 43, who had been making $160,000 a year working for Blacktide in Iraq, protecting US State Department officials. The drunken woman was his girlfriend, a 25-year-old unemployed hairdresser. Norval was wanted on war crimes charges in the deaths of dozens of Iraqi civilians over a ten year period, but had narrowly eluded arrest three months before. He was a NRA member, a sniping specialist when he was in the US army.

In the last hour Maxine Tibbetts has learned that Norval has a deer hunting friend in the Lethbridge area, an Alberta Freedom Party member and gun enthusiast. Al Browning, 42, was not home when his house was surrounded and entered by an RCMP tactical squad. Three rifles were missing from a gun case.

Fifth Attempt

Dawn. The assassins are in the old industrial part of town, on the sixth floor of an abandoned flour mill. Erected in 1933 and long slated for demolition, the building was still standing because of a complicated dispute over ownership and taxes. They are less than a kilometre from the Nikka Yuko Japanese Garden in Henderson Park, as the crow (or bullet) flies.

Stiff from the warped boards beneath his sleeping bag, Norval stands and looks through a half broken pane of glass as he dresses.

The sky is clear. Hardly any wind, because Lethbridge is sheltered below the prairies in a gorge of the Oldman River. The wind meter set up on the roof last night is indicating a slight easterly breeze. "Today is the day" he says to Browning. Norval is wearing jeans, a Yankees T-shirt, and cowboy boots. His brush-cut needs a trim and he has not shaved for three days. His wrist-top shows their pictures, less unkempt, on the local TV news. It is Sunday, June 4th.

They take turns going down the hall to use the old pail in what was once the manager's office, using paper towels for toilet paper, and washing with bottled water and soap. After eating sandwiches and drinking milk from the portable cooler, and each smoking a Marlboro, they carefully descend the staircase next to the silos. The stairs are rotten in places and littered with broken bottles, animal dung, wheat grains black with mold, old newspapers, rusty pieces of machinery, and skeletons of rats and raccoons.

On the ground they walk through dewy weeds, a tangle of burdock, dandelion, thistle, blue lupines, chicory and Queen Anne's lace, leading to an evergreen thicket where the car is hidden. They take more ammunition, two handguns, and another rifle from the vehicle and re-cover it with branches. Back upstairs, Norval readies his weapon. It is a L115A1Longshot with a 3x12x50 scope and a computer-assisted aiming system, automatically firing clips of fifteen 8.59 mm bullets—heavier than most to lessen wind drift—from a 1300mm barrel, accurate within six inches at 1100 metres. It has a front tripod, stock clamps, and recoil shock-absorbers. Norval sets it up on a battered, water-stained, heavy wooden desk near a window with a view of the Nikka Yuko Garden in the distance.

*

Three armored Humvees filled with an RCMP tac squad arrived from Regina in the morning. Each Humvee was fitted with a Ferret, a device consisting of directional microphones, lenses and computer, which determined the place of origin of sniper shots. Two observation drones from the Canadian forces base at Cold Lake had been flown to the Lethbridge airport overnight. A bullet-proof plexiglass cone on wheels in which Luna could walk in public was unpacked from the truck. An offer by Rita Akiwenzie in Toronto to substitute Bliss for Luna was rejected by Zhe as unthinkable.

With all this protection, and no definite evidence that Norval and Browning were close, Zhe decided at 10 a.m to enter Lethbridge. The convoy rolled past the Canadian Tire store, and from Whoop Up Drive they could see the railroad bridge across the Oldman River, coulee, and coal seams exposed in the river valley. "The longest and highest bridge of its kind in the world, the locals claim, and well over a hundred years old and still in use," said Milly Moosomin. On a hill on Mayor Magrath Drive Luna noticed an old water tower that had been turned into a restaurant. Its eight round steel legs, once covered with advertising billboards, now held arrays of solar panels. A windmill was mounted above the tank, which had windows to give diners a panoramic view of the town.

"Can we go there?" she asked. "To see all around."

"As it happens, we are going there for supper this evening," said Zhe. "Just you and the kids and your grandparents. It's a fund-raiser for UNICEF. Three thousand bucks a seat. The politicians are going other places."

First Luna went downtown to a reception at City Hall, and then to a little Chinese monument nearby with Olivia Chow, where she placed flowers. After lunch on the bus she went to the Enmax sportsplex and spent an hour on the curling rink with her friends and local children, learning the game from prairie champions, while three thousand people watched and listened to speeches. The seats were less than half-filled.

Luna's convoy reached the Nikka Yuko garden in Henderson Park at 2.10 p.m. Awaiting her were hundreds of tourists and curious locals, and about five hundred descendants of Japanese-Canadians forced from their homes on the coast of British Columbia during WW2 by the Canadian government and brought by train to work on local farms. Amy Kawamura, 7, great-granddaughter of the Buddhist monk and his wife who conceived the idea of the gardens as a Canadian centennial (1967) project, in a kimono the same cream and russet colors as those the tour guides wore, welcomed Luna and walked with her and the other children into the large *sukiya*-style pavilion made of Taiwanese cypress, abutting the Henderson lakelet. The stadium on the Exhibition Grounds was visible in the distance.

The girl was unable to talk to Luna, who could not hear well inside the conical shield on wheels, until they got inside and the device was removed. After short speeches in the main hall, sixty members of the Buddhist Choir of Southern Alberta sang "Imagine" in Japanese and then English. Next they sang the "Finlandia Hymn," but with the original words by Sibelius. They knew these words were discouraged by Ramsey's Disestablishmentarian Committee because of the appeal to a divinity, but the choir found Lloyd Stone's 1934 international lyrics—adopted by the UN—(itself with the words "Oh, God" twice changed to "to people")—to be rather insipid.

But Luna and her friends, who liked to sing, joined in when the original words by Sibelius began. Ramsey surprised the choir by singing them too, and soon only a few tourists and police officers who did not know these lyrics were silent.

When the music ended, a spokesperson for the choir made an announcement. "I had prepared words which now seem too harsh. Let me say only that we [choir members] are atheists, as all true Buddhists are," the woman said, "but we hope the United Nations leaders will go easy on religious music. After all, a lot of great composers such as Beethoven thought they were talking to a divinity with their music. What we suggest is a contest to get better secular lyrics for the UN anthem. Perhaps Mr. Ramsey could ask the General Assembly for that."

"You overestimate my influence. But such a good idea will probably come to fruition, as this wonderful garden has," Ramsey replied diplomatically.

Luna's patience wore thin as the tour progressed, along gravel paths next to Japanese conifers, imposing rocks, and a falling stream with many pools of fish, to the tea house, the bell tower, a house made of bamboo, various pagodas, and the Zen garden. She was annoyed to have missed the pinks and whites of the cherry and apple blossoms by a month, to be left with hues of green. The hot sun bore down more like an enemy than a friend. When not in the cone she had to wear a helmet and flak suit, and while the suit was (water)cooled, the helmet was hot with the plexiglass visor down. The girls were given little kimonos, which the others put on, but Luna couldn't wear hers because the flak suit would crush it.

"What a botheration," she said to Zhe, who helped push the cone as Luna walked inside it, or flipped down the seat and rode.

*

"If I don't get the little mongrel bitch, then at least I'll nail the Commie prime minister and his Chink wife," said Norval. Still sure of his cause, he was confident they would not be detected. A drone had flown over an hour before and an RCMP officer in a cruiser had checked that the gate was locked. (It was, with a lock they put on after cutting the first.)

With binoculars Browning followed Luna as she came into sight on the path to the Hiroshima/Nagasaki memorial, which was set in a bower of cedars containing a gong two metres in diameter and a log suspended vertically near it. (The log was pulled back every year in a ceremony on August sixth and released to strike the gong.) Luna was out of the cone, wearing her helmet and flak suit.

"Tell me when they start to take her body armor off, to put her in the cone. That's the moment," said Norval to Browning.

A few minutes later the drone returned, this time circling.

"Fuck, they must have a magnetometer indication of the car, or spotted the wind meter. We gotta do this now," said Norval.

"She's taking her jacket off," said Browning, two minutes later.

Norval prepared to shoot. The targeting screen showed her turn to face him, standing beside a large German shepherd. Aiming for Luna's chest, he pressed a button that released the volley—fifteen shots in two seconds.

*

Zhe saw Anubis IV's shoulder erupt. His flesh and blood, and bits of his silver and turquoise collar exploded beside Luna, spattering one side of her body and face with blood and fur. Instinctively Zhe leaned down and pushed the child through the door of the cone. Then a deflected bullet hit Zhe's right biceps and spun her to the ground.

Pandemonium. Another volley, aimed at Prime Minister Layton and his wife, struck a monk and the shield of a female RCMP officer who was covering Olivia Chow with a flak blanket and bear-hugging her to the grass. Zhe crawled to Luna and tried to cover the cone with her jacket. Six other guards musk-oxed around Zhe and the cone. Another fifteen shots smacked into their shields, body armor, and helmets. A slug ricocheting from a ceramic body plate struck the gong. Then a Humvee roared up to block the line of fire, which its Ferret had determined.

From the parking lot, three RCMP snipers had begun returning volleys of shots. The two other Humvees, led by local police with sirens wailing and followed by a local TV crew, were speeding toward the flour mill. The helicopter replaced the drone, hovering above the building.

By now Luna was inside the remaining Humvee with the prime minster and Olivia Chow, who were unhurt. Three of the wounded were being given first-aid. Zhe took off the child's T-shirt, wiping her facc and upper body, looking for injuries and finding only a few small cuts on her chest. Luna was shaking, as Zhe held her closely, covering her again with a flak blanket for the dash into the bus.

*

The police arrived at the old mill in just under three minutes, breaking down the gate and surrounding the building. Browning was killed trying to escape in the car when two .50 caliber machine guns opened fire. Moving around inside the building, Norval shot at the RCMP with a deer rifle, wounding two, until he died suddenly when a bullet passed through his frontal cortex.

*

Zhe washed Luna in a warm shower, helped her into pajamas and into a berth. Milly put iodine from the bus's first aid cupboard on the child's cuts. "From bits of turquoise or shards of bone they are," Milly said to Zhe later. Roxanne took off her outer clothing and slid in beside the girl, holding her closely to her body. Neither spoke for half an hour.

"It was horrible. But you are okay, my precious Sweetie Pie," said Roxanne.

"What happened?" asked Luna in a small quiet voice.

"Somebody, I don't know how many, was shooting at you from far away, and they missed a bit or Anubis moved in front of you, I don't know. Poor Anubis is dead. Now he is with Osiris, his master. But probably he saved your life," replied Roxanne. She thought the ancient Egyptian euphemism would soften the blow.

Zhe stuck her head into the darkened berth. "Two shooters have joined their ancestors. Seven people injured, taken to hospital," she said.

"You should go yourself," said Roxanne, noticing a big bruise on Zhe's upper right arm where her jacket was torn open.

"I'll keep an eye on it," Zhe responded.

"Hot chocolate for a brave soldier," said Jamie Ramsey, passing in a cup. The drink contained a mild sedative. The doctor who had prescribed it looked in for a minute, gently touching her chest with a gloved hand while holding a magnifying glass with a light, searching for embedded fragments. "Nothing. The pieces must have glanced off," he said, withdrawing. Soon Luna was asleep, cradled by her grandmother.

The area around the bus quieted as tourist and visitors left the garden to crime scene investigators. Luna slept for three hours, inevitably waking to images in her mind of the flying blood and fur. Roxanne called the other children in to divert her, and that helped. Just talking to her friends took her mind off the fear she'd felt. Roxanne left them alone for twenty minutes.

"I guess we must cancel the supper at the water tower," said Roxanne to Luna, upon returning to the berth.

"No," said Luna, surprising her grandmother. "It is my duty to UNICEF to go. Tell them I will come. I just want a bowl of pea soup."

"Yes dear," replied Roxanne, marveling at the child's take-charge attitude.

"Anubis Fourth must have a proper funeral. He was my mother's dog, and she is not here, so I must do it. All the kids agreed," added Luna. "Sanjay said the police took Anubis. So you must ask for him, and ask Jamie to put him in a coffin and we will put flowers in. Then we must find a place."

"Yes, yes," said Roxanne. She knew this would be a good way for all the children to deal with the horror at the Hiroshima memorial, although she had no idea where to bury Anubis.

Roxanne spoke to the Inspector Tibbetts, who promised to return the dog's body that evening, after photographs, X-rays and other scans at the Chinook Regional Hospital (for evidence) were completed.

*

The window at Luna's table at the old water tower restaurant gave a view of the mountain peaks into which the sun in a blaze of glory appeared to be sinking, streaking the undersides of clouds with shades of red from pink to vermilion. She was wearing a favorite blue turquoise cotton dress embroidered with her cartouche and many Egyptian gods and goddesses. She has finished her salad, soup, buns, and Shirley Temple cocktail. She has met Gillian Scott, 43, a local high school History teacher and UNICEF co-ordinator for the event, and her husband Ron, director of the Southern Alberta Alternative Energy Partnership, a group of investors in wind and solar power projects. She has met most of the wealthy ranchers, farmers, doctors, and high tech business owners present, whose expensive hybrid, hydrogen, and electric cars sit in the parking lot below. She has met staff and administrators from the university, colleges, and high schools, some who will have to scrimp for a while after this night. An old man from Sun Life Insurance has presumed to pat her head.

Then a woman got up the nerve to come over and address Luna.

"I'm M-Mary, an astronomer at the university. I'm s-so s-sorry about Anubis." She paused to get up the courage to go on. "Would you l-l-like to visit a l-little observatory away from city lights in P-P-Popson Park?" she asked, with a slight stutter so that when she said 'Popson Park' it sounded as though popcorn were popping. She was Mary Mullins, shy, slight, mid forties, whose only family was her aged mother, and whose only friends were the two other astronomers at the University of Lethbridge. She was nervous being in a crowd with famous people. "You could have a l-l-look at the moon, although as you know it's not f-full enough to l-l-light Apollo City. There is a pet graveyard on the hill near the observatory, where I b-b-bury my cats when they die of old age. The children of the other astronomers b-bury their pets there . . ."

"Oh yes," said Luna. "Anubis needs a place. Thank you so much. But I must ask permission from Zhe."

When Luna turned and asked, Zhe took ten minutes to confer with Inspector Tibbetts, who was wearing her red serge dress uniform for the occasion, and the local police escort.

"Yes, it can be done, my brave Little Dragon," said Zhe upon returning. She was pleased the child would have a way of coping with the violence of the afternoon.

"Zhe, please send notes to the people who were hurt," said Luna. "Say I will visit them in hospital tomorrow before we leave."

She asked that food be sent down to the police guard and members of her retinue in the bus below. Only when assured that this was being done would she eat her Baked Alaska.

*

After twenty minutes the bus stopped in the parking lot at Popson Park, a large (133 hectare) grassy flood plain with clumps of cottonwood, bordered by the Oldman River at its far edge. The distant fires of a camping area flickered on the flats. A range of coulees, dark in the moonlight, formed another side of the park. The drones above were almost silent ghostly galleons.

Moonflower and her mother were walked for exercise on a riding trail on the flats nearby by Roxanne and Jamie Ramsey, who went slowly with guides with flashlights because the moonlight was not strong. Luna, a shawl over her dress, went into the observatory with her friends. Three more members of the Lethbridge Astronomy Society had arrived to assist Mary Mullins.

They had the telescope ready. Luna viewed the dark Sea of Tranquillity in great detail but could not see any sign of Apollo City, not even the linear accelerator. Then she and the other children went out on the terrace with Zhe and sat in lawn chairs. Luna sipped a cup of orange pekoe tea with milk while she spoke with her parents on her wrist-top.

"Anubis was killed. Men shot at us and he died to save me," Luna told her parents. "I am going to bury him now in a big park," she said. They were in dressing gowns, in their small bedroom underground. She could see emergency space suits hanging in a corner.

"My precious darling," said Turquoise, worried. "What have I let you in for?"

"Do you want to go home?" asked Chou.

"No, Daddy," said Luna solemnly. "This is my job."

"You just say the word and you are out of there," said Chou. "Ask Zhe to send us a detailed report of what happened."

Luna talked to her mother for a few minutes. "Goodbye, dearest heart," said Turquoise at the end, careful not to show the alarm she felt.

Inspector Tibbetts arrived in a Humvee with Anubis's body. Two policemen dug a grave in the pet cemetery about a hundred yards away on a hillside Four officers carried the thick biodegradable cardboard box. It was open, the damage to the dog's body covered by a UN flag. "We borrowed one from the main library," said Maxine Tibbetts. Flowers of all sorts had been placed around Anubis. Representatives of the florists and pet veterinarians of the town carried an ankh symbol on a stand, two metres high, artfully woven from hundreds of flowers. Ira Swartz filmed the event for UNTV News and Luna's websites.

The coffin lid was attached, and the box lowered into the grave. The children threw down more flowers. Coyotes howled in the distance as "Last Post" was played on a hand-held storage device amplified by loudspeaker. The police officers stood at attention and saluted the grave while the bugle notes spread across the valley. Luna sat on Moonflower and saluted. Then the grave was filled in, and more flowers piled on. The big floral ankh and wreaths were set beside it.

"I and the other astronomers in our group will put up a p-p-plaque so p-people will know about Anubis Fourth, that he was an important dog who will not be forgotten," promised Mary Mullins. Luna stood on a chair to kiss her cheek and hug her.

The road out of the park was lined on one side with hundreds of cars and pickup trucks. People, including many children, had gotten out of their vehicles to wave at the bus, so Luna cleared a window and waved back. There were dozens of German shepherds on leashes. "Please slow down a bit," Luna yelled to the driver, who immediately decreased speed. Many in the crowd had found or made ankh symbols which they illuminated with flashlights. Some had reproduced her cartouche from her website on Bristol boards. "Luna, Luna, Luna," they shouted, a chant which intoxicated the child.

Spontaneous polls taken for the New Harmony Party after the evening news indicated that Luna's 'likeable' rating had gone up five points across Alberta, more in the cities than in rural areas. The figure was almost triple with dog lovers. There did not seem to be a backlash against her handlers for exposing Little Dragon to danger. Her rise was pulling undecided voters to the parties of the Left.

*

Luna's convoy spent the night at two adjacent motels on the Crowsnest Highway, just out of town. The police officers guarding her got a good rest after a hard twenty-four hours. Luna slept with Zhe in a berth in the bus, in the parking lot of the Gold Rush motel. When the child tossed fitfully and cried out Zhe opened her pajama tops and cradled Luna's head on her ample pale smooth breasts, bringing back a rush of memories of China, as they both sank to deep sleep.

At 9 a.m. Milly Moosomin woke Luna with a kiss on her forehead. "I'm taking the horses to stables in Regina on the Exhibition Grounds. I'll see you in a few days," said Milly. At 10 a.m. the bus was driven to the Chinook Regional Hospital. Wearing a WWF T-shirt with the words 'Save the saiga' on the front over a picture of this endangered Mongolian antelope, jeans, boots and cowgirl hat, Luna accompanied Prime Minister Layton and Olivia Chow into the hospital. The head nurse guided them from one victim to another. Four uniformed RCMP officers with sidearms assisted Zhe and Inspector Tibbetts with security inside the building.

The monk who had a bullet pass through his right lung faced a long recovery, but was in good spirits. Two tourists had leg wounds that would keep them in the hospital for months. The Pembina Institute member, a man of forty, had broken bones in his right foot caused by the tire of the Humvee that almost ran him down in the confusion. The young RCMP officer whose left wrist was shattered had undergone amputation. He was awake, making jokes. "Good thing it was my left hand, because I'm right-handed," he said. He was Metis, his short raven hair neatly combed. He introduced his parents. "My name's Eli Ermineskin. I'm glad you are safe," he said to Luna, who sat on the bed to kiss his cheek and hug him for a minute.

"Thank you for getting hurt to save me," said Luna. "If you ever have no money or no job, you may help Zhe look after me."

Another officer had been hit in the jaw, another in the ankle. They expected to be released in several weeks. The female monk had pelvic bruises and lacerations, and the political aide to the prime minister suffered a broken wrist in a fall down the stone stairs leading to the Hiroshima shrine.

As Luna's retinue was leaving the hospital, going through a corridor adjacent to the Emergency department to avoid *paparazzi* at the front, she walked past a door which by chance was half open. Luna glimpsed a man lying still in bed. His face was badly bruised, his head bandaged. There were tubes up his nose and attached to his wrist. Zhe pulled her away from the sight, but a dozen steps later Luna stopped.

"I know that man," she pronounced.

"Don't be silly, honey," said Zhe, trying to move Luna along with her hand. "What are the odds of you knowing someone like that out here in Alberta? It's probably just a bum who got beaten up in a drunken fight."

Luna broke free and ran into the room. She looked at the man for ten seconds.

Then she started crying softly.

"Boris," she said, taking one of his hands in hers. The man was unconscious.

"Don't be crazy," said Zhe, a little irritated. The rest of the entourage waited in the corridor.

"Boris, Boris, don't you know me? On the ship [*Kapitan Lebnikov*] up north?" cried Luna.

"First Mate Boris Larinov?" asked Zhe. "How could that be?"

"He hasn't been identified," said the town's chief of police as he entered the room with Inspector Tibbetts "He was found unconscious in a truck stop parking lot a couple of miles north of town three days ago, labels cut out of clothes, no identification. Hands and feet bound with electrical cord. Many burns from cigarettes on his body, . . . thighs, wrists, and scrotum. White van seen leaving the area. We were waiting until facial swelling goes down to send out his picture."

Zhe carried Luna, protesting, to the bus.

"If it will make you feel better, I'll go back in and Identocam the man, and you can stop your silliness," said Zhe. Taking an Identocam which contained pictures of Boris Larinov from last July in Tanquary Fjord at Quttinirpaaq Park, Zhe walked back into the hospital. She returned to the bus twenty minutes later, a perplexed look on her face.

"Well, I'll be damned," said Zhe. "It *is* Boris Larinov. A nurse shaved off his goatee to get at the cuts on his chin. So beaten up and barely alive," she said sadly. "What on Earth is he doing here? The police are going to guard him round the clock until we find out. A fractured skull and so many burns, from cigarettes. Poor Boris." She paused. "Poor Luna for having to see such things. Can you forgive me for doubting you, my darling?" asked Zhe.

"Yes," replied Luna, in a mood to be conciliatory after her vindication.

"I'm going to call Oolayou right now," said Luna. "I know she likes Boris too. I'm going to stay with him until Oolayou comes."

"Oolayou will be busy. Probably she won't have time to come out here," ventured Zhe.

*

"Boris called me a week ago. He was going to Churchill, Manitoba, to buy a house," Oolayou told Zhe, after speaking with Luna. "The *Lebnikov* is dry-docked in Murmansk where the diesel engines are being replaced with hydrogen fuel-cell technology. Boris had been getting anonymous threats and said he wanted a safe place for his family if things got too dangerous in Russia. He has been working for a information service set up for Garry Kasparov and the social democrats. Maybe that got him in trouble with Putin's gang."

Oolayou put Chief Agnew in charge and flew from Pearson International in Toronto on the first available flight to Calgary. From Calgary she called Hugo Mann on a secure line at the PromTek downtown complex, where she spent the night. Harry Katz and Beloved Morton were also in the loop, as were Interpol and Han-Spar intelligence. The consensus was that Larinov's presence in such condition could indicate that an another plot to kill Luna was afoot.

CHAPTER 12
Sixth Attempt: From Russia Without Love

Larinov was given a twenty-four hour police guard. The decision was made to announce the death of an unidentified man in (the back pages of) local newspapers, in case the assailants were still in the area. Oolayou called Larinov's wife in Murmansk, telling her that her husband was in a coma and asking her to be quiet and wait, not mentioning that she knew Boris from her time working on the *Kapitan Lebnikov*. Oolayou next informed the management of the Far Eastern Shipping Company, Boris's employer, and asked them to keep silent until more was known. Inspector Tibbetts, on intuition, asked the commander of the Canadian forces base at Cold Lake if an attack helicopter could be made available. The thirty-four dime-sized cigarette burns on Boris's body indicated great viciousness to her.

Oolayou remained in Calgary because Larinov was being flown to the city by air ambulance for an operation on his fractured skull by a neurosurgeon and her team using a robot at Foothills Medical Centre. Making sure no reporters noticed, Oolayou saw Boris briefly before he was wheeled into surgery next day at 11 a.m. Four hours later the neurosurgeon came into the waiting room. "He has a better than even chance. We'll know more in a few days," she said, touching Oolayou's cheek in sympathy with the back of an index finger.

The day before, after watching the medevac helicopter bearing Boris leave the roof of the hospital for Calgary, Luna's cavalcade had departed to keep its schedule. It went northwest from Lethbridge, stopping at three small towns—Coaldale, Fort Macleod, and High River, entering Calgary from the south via Highway 2 at dusk. Luna was not allowed to come to the Foothills Medical Centre next morning lest attention be drawn to Boris. So after the operation Oolayou took a taxi to the bus, which was parked in the Exhibition Grounds near the stables, surrounded by police vehicles.

"We can only wait and hope Boris gets better," Oolayou told Luna.

"Is it wrong to pray for Boris?" Luna asked Oolayou, when no one else was close enough to hear.

"I don't see how it could hurt. You could ask Osiris to please not take Boris, to send him back from the Underworld," said Oolayou. "It can be our secret."

"Great Osiris, First God besides Aten your brother to be Reborn, please send back Boris if he comes your way because his family needs him, and Oolayou and me love him. You already have Anubis Fourth," said Luna, with her eyes closed. Her long lashes glistened.

"Oolayou and I," Oolayou corrected, wiping tears from her eyes with a handkerchief. Then Oolayou was driven back to the PromTek tower.

This building, which she had avoided during her previous visit to Regina so that the company not take right-wing flak, looked like dozens of other downtown skyscrapers, albeit more green. The upper floors contained three floors of apartments and amenities. Senior executives, many of whom were friends of her father, welcomed her and made her comfortable in a small suite. Every day Oolayou visited Boris morning and evening, as he remained unconscious.

The day after the operation, once Moonflower and her mother were exercised, Luna wanted to do nothing except just wait in the bus for news of Boris. The children's Math and Science tutor took the opportunity to spent an hour with them. Then their History tutor explained the broad outlines of western Canadian history to them for half an hour. But all children are easily bored, even dutiful ones such as Luna and her friends, and Zhe's late-morning suggestion of a trip to Calaway Amusement Park a few kilometres west of the city on the Trans-Canada Highway was irresistible.

"You can't do anything here, Sweetie. Boris would want you to enjoy yourself," said Zhe to Luna.

So the bus and its support vehicles, joined by a four-bladed AH1HueyCobra attack helicopter armed with two M320 chain guns, laser-designated Hellfire anti-tank missiles, and CRV7 rockets, set out to the amusement park.

Luna and the other children had never been to Canada's Wonderland or Disneyland or other large places because New Harmony Party leaders disapproved of them, and therefore this small park seemed wonderful to them. (Only adults with children were allowed anywhere near, so security inside the park was light. The reasoning was that people with little ones would not be assassins.)

The delighted manager and the mascots, Jack Bunny and Jill O'Hare, escorted the youngsters and dignitaries around as pictures were taken for future use by the park. First stop was the measuring wall, to determine the children's heights. (Rides were graded by height.) All were within a few centimetres of 117 cm. and so not tall enough to qualify for some of the advanced rides, such as the sudden dropper and the saucer twirler. But there were electric bumper cars and boats, a junior roller coaster, and a little Ferris wheel. There was a water squirt gun area, bubble makers, and water slides, with change rooms where the children put on swimming trunks and covered themselves with UV blocking lotion.(New Harmony girls did not wear swim suit tops until they developed breasts, and not always then.) The merry-go-round was not much better than hers at home, but Luna was pleased with the painted wooden wild animals—bison, antelope, deer, moose, and others—available to be ridden. She liked the miniature western town, the tofu hot dog and mango milkshake, and was fascinated with an ornate antique steam calliope decorated with mermaid figures which played "The Daring Young Man on the Flying Trapeze," "My Darling Clementine," "The Whiffenpoof Song," and other old tunes. Her grandparents and the Music tutor taught the children the words to the songs as they listened and tried to sing along.

After three hours they prepared to leave the park.

"Should we go west for a couple of hours and see Lake Louise? They say it's very pretty. You could attend a fund-raising dinner at the hotel if you felt like it," Zhe asked Luna as they got into the bus. "Or we can cancel. The PM and Olivia can go on in the cars." Feeling a little guilty for enjoying herself while Boris lay at Death's door, Luna agreed. "I can do it, if you like," she said.

She and the other children slept most of the way, cheek to jowl like a pile of meerkats in a double berth. They slept through the town of Banff and awoke to the sight of Lake Louise ahead. Angled sunshafts danced off its pellucid turquoise blue and emerald green water, in a dish below several mountain peaks and the (receding) glacier in a valley which supplied it. The HueyCobra helicopter landed on the lawn behind the parking lot, its noise bringing many of the staff of the Fairmont Chateau Lake Louise, an imposing beige-colored three-winged structure, out to the wide stairs to greet the bus. Tourists, political supporters, and reporters took pictures of Luna, Prime Minister Layton, and Olivia Chow as they entered the hotel. The little girls wore moccasins beaded with ankh symbols and embroidered loose-fitting traditional Guayami cotton gowns in different shades of blue, with ruffled sleeves and velvet vests, a birthday gift to Luna from a UN factory in a village in western Panama. Seated in the dining area of the Mount Temple Ballroom with four hundred people, Luna said grace when asked by the MC.

"Let us be thankful for this bountiful food because many people in the world go hungry. Let us hurry up the Transition so soon all people will have enough to eat, and peace also," she said. It was a mixture of two graces spoken by the new model of the Schoolgirl Luna doll. As usual, people who had not seen it marveled at Luna's confidence and poise before a large audience, and her skill with microphones. "She knows we have come to adore her, and it makes her fearless," a reporter later wrote in the *Banff Crag and Canyon* newspaper.

The meal was chicken cooked two days in a sauce of chocolate and hot peppers, wild rice, vegetables from local greenhouses, and Baked Alaska. After dinner Luna gave a short speech, thanking people for coming, and introducing the prime minister. After his brief message, the children led off the dancing with a rousing Bunny Hop—Luna headed a long snake of dancers, each with their hands on the hips ahead of them, hopping and shaking their legs with glee despite their adult Canadian reserve, and it seemed to some participants that the snake grew an electron spine of pure joy from its pretty pixie head, which flowed for several minutes before dissolving into a sunset of self-conscious smiles. Then there was The Twist, and some rock and roll, before slow dancing. The children were proficient at them all, as Sanjay demonstrated with the girls in turn. Before leaving, at her insistence Luna and the prime minister went into the kitchen to thank the chef and workers and shake hands. The affair raised a million dollars for the Left coalition.

The bus got back to Calgary at midnight. Boris was still unconscious, but his vital signs were stronger. Next day the children went as scheduled to the Royal Tyrrell Museum of Palaeontology near Drumheller in Midland Provincial Park, a two-hour drive to the northeast. Approaching the Badlands, the flat fields of the prairie changed to eroded coulees, canyons, gullies, and hoodoos (toadstool-shaped pillars of harder rock), with colorful bands of red clay, white sand, and coal in the exposed strata.

The museum's director, a chubby thirtyish man with blue Lennon glasses and a pink carnation in his lapel, gave the tour. "The exhibits are in chronological order," he said. In the first gallery there were models of the cooling crust, the forming oceans. The next gallery contained cyanobacterial stromatolites made 3.5 billion years ago, found in western Australia. In the third Luna marveled at the diverse weird Cambrian fauna fossilized in the Burgess Shale, once on the bed of the inland sea but now high in the Rockies in British Columbia. As Ira Swartz filmed for UNTV, her Math and Science tutor pointed out the priapulid worm, *Ottoia*, amid the trilobites and *Hallucigenia*. "Our ancestor," she said. (The tutor was Michelle Poulin, 29, who grew up in the New Harmony base (B2) near Nominingue, Quebec.) Next was a diorama of a Devonian reef 375 million years ago where life-sized models of fearsome fishes marauded through the shallow tropical sea covering Alberta. The Cretaceous Garden recreated as much as possible the vegetation of that era, including the advent of flowering plants and their insects. The adjacent exhibit showed a group of *Albertosaurus*, the *T.Rex* of the neighborhood, lurking in a dry riverbed. (Many *Albertosaurus* skeletons had been found in a rich theropod bonebed nearby.) Then the visitors went slowly through the Age of Mammals and the Ice Age.

"There has been a lot of time, . . . such big numbers, so many years," Luna told Zhe as they got on the bus.

"Yes, we are just a moment in the immense space/time," said Zhe, "but that only makes our days more precious."

The children slept on the ride back to Calgary, to be rested for the Glenbow Museum next morning and rallies at the Saddledome afternoon and evening.

"Boris is moving a little, with better EEG's," said Oolayou, calling on an encrypted line, as Zhe sipped cocoa before sleeping.

*

The Glenbow, a worthy museum in many ways, was a disappointment to Luna because it had so few Egyptian relics. But as she left the building a man was stopped for pushing past the barrier and trying to approach her. Since he was an old fellow who looked harmless, he and his package were searched and brought to Zhe and Luna. "He claims he is a retired jeweler, living in an apartment about a kilometre away," said Inspector Tibbetts. "He says he has a present for Luna. It's been opened and scanned. Jewelry. He came here by taxi."

The man spoke. "My name is Saul Morgenstern."

"Thank you, but Luna can't accept expensive gifts. Not while some children have nothing," said Zhe. Luna saw that the man looked tired.

"Come into the bus and rest, and have a cup of tea. It's safer there," said Luna, taking his free hand. Zhe wanted to object but Luna gave her no opportunity. Luna instructed the other children to make tea and bring a tray from the galley, while she listened to Mr Morgenstern and the bus returned to the Exhibition Grounds. It was a sad story of persecution and escape from Germany by his uncle and father in 1935 with a small part of the family fortune. "My wife is dead and I don't have long to live," he said. "Cancer. I have no children or close relatives. Most of my friends are dead." He drank a cup of tea with milk and honey, regaining color to his face.

He took his present out of a plastic bag. Wrapped in a towel was a scarab-shaped polished black teak case with gold, ceramic, and turquoise inlays. He set it beside Luna. "It won't hurt to look," he said, smiling for the first time. "Just a few trinkets."

It was a set made in Vienna in 1821 for a rich merchant's wife. The green silk was a little worn but the pieces would have delighted a tsarina. What caught Luna's eye first was an ankh pendant (15 cm in height) set with rubies, emeralds, and a blue diamond (cut in Amsterdam), with ceramic and turquoise insets including tiny hands of Aten and eyes of Horus, on a yellow gold chain with four large pearls in white gold filigree. Mr Morgenstern had engraved Luna's cartouche in a space at the center of the ankh. There were matching gold ankh earrings, an asp bracelet with ruby eyes and fine chain-mail skin of white and yellow gold links, an Isis wing broach of ceramics and iridescent milky opals, and a delicate gold ring with lotus filigree around a sapphire. Two hair clips, one a gold crocodile with diamond eyes and ivory teeth, the other a gold and silver-gold giraffe, and a vulture hair band of gold, rubies and pearls, completed the set. Morgenstern named for her the jewels she did not know.

"It won't hurt to try on the necklace," he said. Meritaten's nimble fingers doubled the chain so that it fit Luna fairly well. Sanjay held a mirror. Luna imagined how it would look with various of her dresses.

"Don't get attached to that," Zhe warned, trying to end Mr Morgenstern's visit. Sensing trouble, she went to discuss the matter with Jamie Ramsey and Roxane. They were no help.

"After what Luna's been through, with Anubis and then Boris, we should probably cut the poor kid some slack. For now anyway. Tell Mr Morgenstern we'll give it back to him or to UNICEF if there is a fuss. Put that in writing and get a copy of his assent. Find out what the stuff is worth, and we can make a better decision," said Roxanne. Ramsey nodded. "Refer the matter to Executive Council, and let them decide," he said. "Perhaps she will tire of it and . . ."

Sensing that her grandparents did not support Zhe, Luna grew bold. "Mr Morgenstern wants to give the jewels, and I want to have them, so what's the problem?" she asked. "The ankh has my name on it . . . If Turquoise says no way Jose, I can give the jewels back later," Luna said, her face set in a determined pleading/demanding way Zhe had come to recognize. Zhe didn't want to hear the stinging "You are not my mother!" from the child, and so relented.

Luna asked the old man to stay for lunch on the bus, and introduced the politicians to him. Against Zhe's advice Luna gave him one of her private telephone numbers, and took his. She kissed Mr Morgenstern on the cheek and raised the back of her right hand to his lips. Then Inspector Tibbetts drove him home in one of the Stardust Cruisers.

Luna insisted on wearing the ankh pendant to the Left coalition rally in the nearby Saddledome in the afternoon. (She let Meritaten wear the Isis broach, Mitsy and Bliss the hair clips.) There were many waving supporters, some with their German shepherds, and thousands of noisy protesters lining the streets. Luna noticed that the building, which could seat 20,000, was full—even the standing areas. There were other celebrities. She knew Steve Maclean, the astronaut, and David Suzuki, the environmentalist, who spoke briefly, but not Sir Paul McCartney, the Dixie Chicks, or Canadian superstar singers Shania Twain and Measha Brueggergosman, who entertained the crowd. "What a brave little angel you are," said Twain, upon meeting Luna and hugging her gently. "Sorry about Anubis," said Brueggergosman, stooping to kiss Luna's proffered cheek. Both stars admired her pendant and her cowgirl outfit.

Arnold Schwarzenegger, once 'Governator' of California, coming from a long private meeting with the prime minister that morning, bowed his head and kissed Luna's hand in the way she liked, as she sat astride Moonflower.

"Arise Sir Arnold, worthy big knight," Luna said, indulging her fantasy after someone informed her that McCartney had been knighted. "They tell me you are quite famous and do good things," she said in her queenly mode of talking.

"I was just another action hero in the movies, and then just another womanizing politician come late to environmentalism," said the former governor modestly. "But your name will be remembered as long as there are humans, as a brave ambassador of the UN."

"Thank you, but we don't say such things because it will spoil her," said Zhe tartly *sotto voce* to him.

Schwarzenegger put his Stetson back on and mounted a big bay stallion. He and Luna trotted around the ring together amid chuck wagons, a stage coach, various buggies, steam tractors, clowns, acrobats, and the U of C marching band. (All come early to Stampede to see Luna and the other celebrities.) Her friends took turns riding Moonflower's mother.

While the children slept for two hours in the late afternoon, Milly took Morgenstern's gift downtown to a large firm of jewelry dealers and appraisers. She met twin brothers in their sixties, both in white cotton suits, specialists in antique jewelry, who examined the pieces carefully with magnifying glasses. Both half bald, with bushy eyebrows and sideburns to their jowls, they smiled like Cheshire cats. Each had a pocket watch on a fob in the side of his vest.

"We could have saved you the trip, and told you on the phone, but we wanted to see it again," one brother said. He wore a blue tie. "Aren't we bad?"

"Yes, yes," said the other, who wore a yellow tie, "Morgenstern showed us this marvel about thirty years ago. Beautiful craftsmanship, flawless stones. He kept the box in his bank safety deposit box all these years, lest his store be robbed for it."

"He wants to give it to Luna Cheng," said Milly.

"He was talking about that very same young lady in a most approving way, when last we met for chess," said the brother in the blue tie. "He said he hoped to meet her before he died."

"Aye, brother," said yellow tie, "so he said. Claimed she is come to save the Earth from destruction."

"I hate to be crass, but Luna's people need to know approximately what the set is worth," said Milly.

"Four and a half or five million Canadian, at least," said the blue tie brother. "Probably double that in a global auction if Luna uses them for a while, because of the association with her," said the other.

"Oof," said Milly. "I'd hoped it was much less. Can you put that in writing? . . . How much is your fee?"

"No charge," they said together. "We are sympathetic to your cause, although we don't broadcast it because many of our customers are in oil and gas," explained blue tie, dropping his voice, as he filled in an appraisal form on an ancient Underwood typewriter.

*

"The jewels are worth four or five million dollars. They must be insured, and kept in the vault when not in use," Milly told Zhe, when she returned to the bus. (There was a small safe near the galley where emergency cash and the prime minister's papers were kept.)

"Trouble and nothing but," said Zhe. "Now we must worry that the jewels don't get lost or stolen. And just wait until the media gets hold of the story. The right wing-media will twist this . . ."

"Ah, but the baubles are beautiful," replied Milly. "For beauty we risk trouble. Also, the appraisers think they will double in value if Luna uses them."

"That scarab case will be a Pandora's box," said Zhe with a sigh.

The evening rally in the Saddledome was another packed house. There were moments of alarm when firecrackers went off in stands, and were mistaken for gunfire. People in the area surged towards the exits, but Inspector Tibbetts' voice came on the PA system, so full of calm authority that the panic subsided. Two fifteen year old boys were escorted out of the building to police headquarters, to be charged with mischief and attempted arson.

Bits of Al Gore's "An Inconvenient Truth" were shown on the replay screen.(It was showing free at several theaters in the city, paid for by the Left coalition.) The speeches seemed longer and Luna and her friends were tired before the rally was over. Surrounded by a phalanx of police officers, the children were carried to the bus as Measha Brueggergosman softly sang Brahm's "Lullaby" to them. Luna wasn't awake to get Oolayou's report about 10 p.m. that the swelling was going down and Boris was moving more, nor see the full moon above the city.

*

On the fourth day after Boris's operation, the children appeared at a UNICEF charity one-day golf match at the Elks' Lodge and Golf Club in the morning. They were instructed for two hours on the little nine hole course for age nine and under, and played the mini course. In the afternoon Luna and her friends took part in a three inning softball (hitting tee)game on the small diamond with local youngsters. Then Luna threw out the first pitch for a charity minor league baseball game. In the evening she and her friends attended a fund-raising dinner in the Calgary tower restaurant, once again visiting the kitchen afterwards to meet and thank the workers. Zhe took her picture with a dozen sous chefs and waitresses. The prime minister and Olivia Chow were politely received, but as usual Luna was the center of attention. It fell to Milly to be Keeper of the Jewels, putting them away in the safe when the girls came back to the bus.

Meanwhile, a little after nine p.m. Oolayou was sitting in a chair beside Boris's bed when his eyes opened. A minute passed before he spoke.

"I must have died, and this is heaven with my beautiful friend Oolayou," said Boris in Russian, ever gallant, in a hoarse whisper because of his swollen lips.

"Boris," said Oolayou. She began to cry with relief, kissing his hand.

"Where am I?" asked Boris.

"In Calgary, Alberta. Foothills Medical Centre. You were found near Lethbridge five days ago. Luna saw you in a hospital ward and recognized you despite . . . You've had a skull fracture repaired. I call Titania [his wife] every day and there are three armed guards sent by the shipping company protecting your family."

She could see that bad memories were rushing back.

"And the date?" asked Boris.

"Saturday, tenth of June," replied Oolayou.

"Could you get the police, my sweet," said Boris, not noticing the RCMP officer in the corner. Oolayou motioned and the officer came close to record Boris's words on her wrist-top, while a nurse waited. He began in Russian, but started over in English.

"Three Russian mafia types kidnaped me in Churchill nine days ago. In a white van, no side or back windows, Manitoba plates, with the letters BL together . . . I can't remember any numbers. Two big guys, one small. I'd know them if I saw them again. They kept me tied up and gagged most of the time. They grilled me about New Harmony leadership, and security arrangements on Luna's campaign. About Garry Kasparov and social democratic parties. I said nothing. They followed Luna's bus to Lethbridge to get a look at its defenses. I tried to escape, hopping, when we were stopped but one of the big guys, Alexi they called him, came after me with a tire iron . . . . Oh, yes, they had welding equipment in the van. They joked about burning me with that . . . . To avoid restaurants they ate bologna sandwiches with catsup, and gave me the scraps. There were two long steel boxes, military looking, which barely fit in the van."

When Inspector Tibbetts and Zhe arrived, a more complete description of the kidnappers and preliminary sketches by Oolayou were ready for distribution. After ten minutes the nurses told everyone to leave for the night. Tubes were removed. Boris was bathed and fed, and sedated. He then slept for ten hours, awaking to find Oolayou and Luna sitting with Inspector Tibbetts. The child wore shorts and a Calgary Stampeders T-shirt. Incongruously (to Boris) she had a jeweled ankh symbol around her neck. A shaft of sunlight which escaped the blind shone on her hair like a halo and made the pendant glow and sparkle.

"How can I ever thank the best little princess of the universe for finding me in my hour of need?" asked Boris.

"It was just luck," said Luna modestly, pleased with herself. She went to Boris and kissed his forehead. He admired the pendant, and heard its story. After he came back from the toilet, held by Oolayou and a nurse lest he fall, Luna spoon fed him porridge as they chatted. When Inspector Tibbetts showed him photos of twenty Russian nationals spotted in Alberta and Manitoba in the last month. Boris recognized the two big men. Alexi 'The Bull' Orloff and Uri 'AK-47' Sokolow, members of a Moscow based gang of ex-cons known to work with a branch of Putin's secret police that assisted Gazprom subsidiaries with foreign matters. Both spoke heavily accented English, and Orloff had relatives in Vancouver. He had traveled to Canada 'on business' once before. An alert went out to all police in the province, along with the updated description of the white trades van. Two RCMP officers began phoning every seller of plate steel within five hundred kilometres.

Boris slept through the afternoon.

*

With hindsight, we know Zhe should have waited. She knew she might be up against an armored truck, probably filled with explosives, and the long boxes could be surface to air missiles. But Beloved Morton and Harry Katz in Toronto, Hugo Mann at CIA headquarters, and senior Han-Spar intelligence officers in Beijing were confident that the police and the Cobra could adequately protect the bus. The brass at Cold Lake said the Cobra had countermeasures against most missiles unless they were released at very short range. Crew were notified to watch for this possibility, co-ordinating with the drones and spotter helicopter.

So, wanting to salvage the schedule, Zhe and Inspector Tibbetts decided the convoy would leave that (Sunday) afternoon at 2 p.m., three hours late, for Red Deer. All approaching medium and large vehicles were to be detoured around the route of Luna's bus. Same way traffic was to be kept at a safe distance by the Humvees, and more bomb sniffing dogs were enlisted to check trucks.

Luna wanted to wait until Boris awoke, to say good bye. She settled for leaving a note for him with Oolayou, who had purchased a wrist-top with video-phone for Boris and included one of Luna's private numbers in the directory. Oolayou remained in Calgary, intending to take Boris to B1 or UNECOP headquarters in Toronto when he could travel.

The trip to Red Deer was peaceful. The area was aspen parkland, and again there was a river running through it, and numerous coulees amid rolling hills. The road into the community college was lined with protestors. Some rotten fruit was thrown at the bus and several arrests were made for throwing empty beer bottles.

The college auditorium seated a thousand people. Hundreds more were standing at the back, with about a thousand supporters outside watching on hastily improvised screens running a UNTV feed of events inside. Two hours late, the Legion pipe band led Luna, the prime minister, Olivia Chow, and other Leftist leaders into the auditorium. RCMP tac squad officer stood in the corners as chamber singers and the Red Deer symphony orchestra joined Measha Brueggergosman and Shania Twain in "Imagine" and then the "Finlandia Hymn" with some groups singing the theistic words, others the mawkish secular version. The politicians kept their speeches short, and the event took less than an hour.

The four former Catholic high schools and seventeen primary schools in the area were to become public under recent federal legislation. So in addition to oil workers and investors, Alberta independence agitators and other right-wing elements, many stakeholders in the former separate school system were there protesting Luna's visit to the town. But except for a few who threw rotten apples and rocks at the bus as it passed, the demonstration was orderly.

After the scheduled rally at the curling rink, a report came in to Inspector Tibbetts. "Two men answering the description bought twenty 12' by 48' pieces of half inch steel plate two days ago from a fabricator south of Edmonton. They made three trips in a white van to carry it away," she told Zhe. "As we thought, probably they want to armor a large vehicle against small arms fire," Zhe replied. "It's a bad dream, so soon after the Nikka Yuko Garden."

"We are trusting the Cobra a lot," said Inspector Tibbetts. Had she emphasized the 'are,' Zhe might have halted for the day. Instead she decided to proceed on schedule to Edmonton, a decision easy to criticize in retrospect.

*

The assassins had been on the premises of the Western Fertilizer and Feed plant, near the small town of Lacombe, twenty kilometres north of Red Deer, since shortly after 8 a.m. when their co-conspirator, Vladimir Gigov, the watchman, came on shift. Late in the afternoon in the repair shop Alexi Orloff, sweating and feeling his 46 years, looked on his work with satisfaction. One of the firm's twenty-ton gravel trucks had been modified with wheel skirts welded to the body to protect the tires, while steel slabs shielded the cab and most of the windscreen. He thought once again of the money, about six million Canadian dollars (which he had chosen over roubles or Euros) he would get for this job. He didn't relish the task, but if people were willing to pay so much . . . Uri Sokolow offered him a cigarette and they smoked.

"I want to put on a pup too," said Orloff to Sokolow, "to add another ten tons."

"But there is no steel left to cover its wheels," replied Sokolow.

"We take a little chance to make a bigger boom," said Orloff.

Gigov and Sokolow knew better than to question further. The larger man, thick-necked and muscular, had a psychotic temper when opposed. The driver, Viktor Vassilovich, a small thin man suffering from AIDS, also said nothing to this change of plans. (His children were to get his share of the money if the plot succeeded. A former truck driver from Moscow, he had been infected by a young female hitchhiker he picked up outside Novgorod in 2009. Recently he had developed leukemia.)

The others planned to escape in Gigov's yellow half-ton truck, lie low for a while, and then return to Russian and great fortune via Alaska.

Now their hour came. At five p.m. Vassilovich drove the truck into place under the elevator marked Ammonium Nitrate. Diesel fuel was sprayed on as the level of little white beads rose, and ignition wires, run off the truck's battery, were inserted. Next the pup was filled. The two missiles and the automatic weapons and grenades in the van were transferred to Gigov's half-ton, and covered with bales of hay.

Then at 6 p.m. the three conspirators drove a kilometre to watch for Luna's bus near an overpass above Highway 2 outside Lacombe, while Vassilovich awaited their call. After two tense hours they saw Luna's convoy in the distance through binoculars. Orloff telephoned Vassilovich. "Get going now," he ordered.

An inquiring drone flew low over the yellow half-ton. When it passed they unpacked and readied the missiles behind bales of hay. The thumping blades of the Cobra grew near. At three hundred metres Orloff and Sokolow fired. One missile went in looping spirals and exploded prematurely. The other sought the Cobra and seemed sure to hit it. But the pilot of the spotter helicopter, flying near the Cobra, in a reflexive act of heroism veered his craft down towards the missile, which turned and met him in a midair fireball. The Cobra, wrathful in its embarrassment, closed on the half-ton as it tried to escape. A hail of bullets from the chain guns and two anti-tank missiles destroyed the small truck and its occupants. Small bits of body parts were later identified by DNA.

However a piece of metal the size of a fist from the explosion of the observer copter had penetrated the Cobra's fuselage and severed electrical systems. Smoke started to pour from the area as short-circuits sparked. The Cobra had to make an emergency landing on the overpass road to extinguish the fire.

So now Luna's bus was vulnerable to the armored truck, which Vassilovich drove out of the company yard and onto the road, wondering why he had heard no more from Orloff. Five minutes later Vassilovich barreled down the access ramp to Highway 2, slamming two police cruisers and a station wagon out of his way at a roadblock. He could see the convoy pulled over about half a kilometre ahead.

He sped up, trying to reach his target. But Zhe and Inspector Tibbetts, warned of the attack, ordered the bus driver to move ahead and attempt to outrun the threat. The Humvees fell to the rear of the bus to protect it, as the truck gained on them. One of the Humvees slowed to confront the truck, but was hit and flung upside down into the ditch. Two police cruisers were sideswiped and sent tumbling into the field. By then the bus was going 160 km an hour down the center line of the northbound double lane. The truck overtook the next Humvee and tried to bump it out of the way, the Humvee's guns proving ineffective against the sheets of steel on the cab.

Then the third Humvee drove onto the shoulder and slipped by on Vassilovich's right, where his vision was obscured by the armor. Once behind the truck, that Humvee directed .50 caliber fire at unprotected tires of the pup. The rubber on one side ripped and shredded, slowing and swinging the truck as the pup fish-tailed. Sparks sprayed out as steel rims scraped the pavement. The truck careened off the shoulder, skidded diagonally through a shallow ditch and plowed a hundred metres into a wheat field, turning over on its side and sliding to a stop in a gully. For thirty seconds nothing happened. A hawk circled in the distance. Gophers popped their heads out of holes in the fields on the other side of the highway.

The bus sped away. There was a flash of light behind and then the force of the blast pushed the *Luna Express* forward and to the left. The driver regained control and continued, slowing to 100 km per hour to check for damage to the vehicle. A crater half the size of a football field had been created, with a mushroom cloud forming above. Soil and rocks rained down. The sound was heard in Edmonton, a hundred and twenty kilometres away. (Fragments of truck parts were later found, but no pieces of Vassilovich or his clothing.)

The bus stopped briefly to pick up an escort of five cruisers and the remaining Humvee, and then continued past the town of Leduc. During this time the children called their parents, and Luna received calls from Oprah Winfrey, Oolayou and Boris, Secretary-General Ban-Ki Moon, the head of UNICEF, and several celebrity friends. Zhe got a call from Cold Lake. It was Colonel Molly Moosomin, Turquoises' former Arrow co-pilot.

"Should we send an F-35 to escort you to Edmonton?" asked Molly.

"No. I think the danger must be over. We'd be criticized for the jet's pollution by right-wing media . . . . Better just stay on standby," replied Zhe.

Forty kilometres from Edmonton the bus was met by two eight-wheeled mobile gun systems (MGS's), each bearing light and heavy machine guns and a 105 mm barrel loaded with armor-piercing shells, come from the armory of the Princess Patricia Light Infantry regiment in the city. The bus slowed to their pace.

CHAPTER 13
Edmonton and Northward

When the convoy entered the suburbs, wailing sirens and flashing red lights cleared the way. As drivers pulled over, occupants of their vehicles got out to wave and cheer as the bus passed. Luna cleared a window and waved back. By then pictures of the truck and explosion had been on TV and Internet news for two hours, setting off a surge of sympathy and anger around the world. Past the ring road into the older part of Edmonton the streets were lined with tens of thousands of people and several hundred German shepherds on leashes. Many people held pictures of ankhs or little dragons, and chanted "Luna, Luna, Luna."

The bus entered the Connaught Armory, which was surrounded by military vehicles. The remainder of the convoy—the cube van, horse trailer, equipment truck, entertainers' bus, and the Stardust Cruisers—arrived an hour later. After a three hour hiatus Luna's Internet sites announced that her bus was undamaged, and all aboard safe, and that everyone's thoughts should be for the dead and injured—even the misguided assassins.

But as the Russian connection became known, a stone-throwing crowd gathered around the Russian Embassy in Ottawa. In Edmonton the Russian Club and St. Vladimir's Russian Orthodox Church required police protection from angry mobs. A performance of "Swan Lake" by the Moscow Ballet company in the Northern Alberta Jubilee Auditorium was stopped after persistent booing and hissing by the audience. Many Canadians had become alarmed by Russian saber-rattling in the Arctic.

Some cabinet members wanted the prime minister to travel apart from Luna, but in a short evening emergency address to the nation he refused. That night Layton and Olivia Chow sent their aides and bodyguards to the moderately priced Campus Tower Hotel for a good rest, and slept on the bus in a berth near Luna and her friends. (Where, if the world must know, they surprised each other after months of indifference by quietly copulating with the eagerness of young lovers before falling asleep in one another's arms.) In the morning the PM toured the armory and the yard outside with

Luna and talked with some of the soldiers, many of whom could hardly restrain their pleasure at meeting the child. Men and women hardened by years of bloody futility in Afghanistan were eager to kneel and pretended to be knighted, to be touched on the shoulder with the Chief Warrant Officer's parade square baton, which Luna had commandeered, and kiss her right hand in the way she liked. Zhe, taking a shower, was displeased when she found out.

By then the children were in the regimental stable, preparing to take Moonflower and her mother for rides in the little paddock behind the armory, supervised by the Chief Warrant Officer. Luna remembered later in her life that he had a ruddy face and mutton-chop sideburns, salt and pepper hair, and smelled pleasantly of horses and bay rum. He held her up gently, making a chair of his arms as she leaned against his chest, to better see the photographs of Princess Patricia of Connaught, a granddaughter of Queen Victoria who for most of her life was Colonel-in Chief of the regiment, on a wall in the room that served as regimental archive and museum. Luna stared at one taken when Patricia was a girl of seven (in 1893) with long ringlets in late Victorian dress, with her family in Buckingham Palace. Then Luna sent Sanjay to the bus to get a picture of herself in UN helmet and uniform for the CWO to put up on the wall after she printed 'Thank you for keeping me safe.' and signed her name, 'Princess Luna Cheng-Ramsey of Dragon Nest near Moon, also China, and Home Base.' (Zhe was displeased when she heard of this, but did nothing except notify the three psychologists at B1 who were advising her parents on how to prevent megalomania in the child.)

In later years at the smell of bay rum on a man Luna sometimes remembered seeing and touching the WW1 water-cooled and belt-fed Spandau machine gun she saw that morning, and how Bliss read the card which said it fired 450 bullets a minute. "If UN forces can win this so-called War To End All War, one day weapons will only be in museums," the sergeant-major told the children, as they glimpsed the horrors of war in a D-Day montage on a long table. "No one hopes for such an outcome more than this old soldier."

Zhe came to bring Luna back to the bus for an interview with a CBC reporter and a cameraperson. Milly Moosomin prepped her on what the PM wanted her to say. First Luna read a statement of solidarity with the Russian people, needing help from the reporter to pronounce the phrase "imperialist ambitions of the oligarchy." Then the child spontaneously hit upon a healing gesture.

"I have only seen "Swan Lake" on DVD," she told the reporter. "I'm going to phone the Moscow ballet company to ask if my friends and I can come to see their show tonight," Luna said. "Maybe Jack and Olivia will come too, and my grandparents, and people will like the dancers again . . . . If I can get permission from Zhe and Milly," she added as an afterthought.

Then Luna read the list of the injured, which included five civilians and ten police officers, with broken bones, cuts, and bruises. She read a statement thanking the pilot of the spotter helicopter, Lieutenant Jim Prentice, 29, for his heroic act. Prentice left a wife, Claire Brinton, a labor lawyer and NDP riding executive, but no children. (The young couple had been putting it off.) "I would like to come to his funeral, if his wife is not mad at me for bringing bad trouble where I go," Luna said sadly.

Then she, Zhe, and Olivia Chow and her husband, with minimal escort, were driven in a Stardust Cruiser to visit the injured in various city hospitals. Luna noticed that flags were flying at half-mast and that Edmonton was a city of many trees—basswood, lodgepole pine, white birch, and stately old elms which had escaped the Dutch elm disease.

*

Meanwhile, Han-Spar spies in Russia had identified another plotter; a private nurse, Svetlana Mayakova, 36, who had cared for Vassilovich in Russia and paid for his prescription drugs. Interpol used the full disclosure required under new international banking laws to trace the ins and outs of her Swiss accounts. There was a convoluted trail leading back to Zandox Petroleum, a Gazprom subsidiary, also involving Potemkin Aircraft Leasing—owned by a branch of Putin's secret police. There was possibly evidence, depending on how a snatch of conversation in Russian intercepted by Canada's Communications Security Establishment (SigInt) from a disposable cell phone a month before was interpreted, that Mayakova was in the Fort McMurray area.

*

In the afternoon Luna attended a big rally in Commonwealth Stadium, located in a north central 'working class' area of the city. Throughout Northwood people came from their post-WW2 bungalows, row houses, and apartments over stores to line her route and cheer and see the mobile gun systems, the armored Humvees, and a Bison personnel carrier protecting the bus. Some of them brought their German Shepherds. Luna cleared windows and waved from one side of the bus, then the other, darting back and forth every thirty seconds until Zhe made her choose one side. Bliss Akiwenzie subbed for Luna when she went to the toilet. They noticed fewer protesters than in Calgary.

The 60,000-seat stadium was overflowing, including many politically-aware natives from reserves in northern Alberta. "O Canada" (references to God removed) was sung, followed by "Imagine" and the "Finlandia Hymn," the deistic version drowning out its official rival. Before the speeches, Luna rode Moonflower around the cinder track next to the wall, escorted by twenty mounted RCMP officers in red jackets. (Polls showed that its role in protecting Luna in Alberta was dramatically improving the tarnished image of the force with Canadians.) The loudspeakers played Ray Smith's 'fifties hit, "Rockin' Little Angel." Then at home plate she met fifteen captains of women's baseball teams from around the world, in town for a tournament on the natural grass of the stadium, came on the field to meet Luna and the prime minister. Luna gave silk scarves with her cartouche embroidered in the corners to the captains of the Canadian and Chinese teams. There were more in the box so on her own she gave scarves to the Korean, Jamaican and Nigerian captains while Zhe's back was turned. Then Zhe stopped her, scolding. "That's not what was planned. If you are going to be a leader, you must learn not to be impulsive." Someone had told Luna that these teams were underdogs, which she associated with Anubis. Consequently the child made a fuss, threatening tears and tantrum, and another box of scarves was quickly brought from the truck so that she could give one to every captain to resounding cheers. She even insisted on standing on a chair to put the scarves around the women's necks, going on tip-toe as Zhe held her to reach the tall Russian and American.

Then there was a ceremony, involving several leaders of the Inuit Tapiriit Kanatami and the mayor of Edmonton, to rename the Eskimos football team. (The team was owned by the community.) Luna turned a wire bin containing a hundred finalists and then reached in and took out one envelope. "Our team's new name is the Edmonton Starfighters," the mayor said, reading the card. "This is long overdue. After all we don't have names like the New York Orthodox Jews, Chicago Chicanos, or the Edmonton Limey's. We still hear about the Fighting Irish—Notre Dame University's team, but that is a self-given nickname. The fact is that Esquimaux or Eskimo were unflattering names given to the Inuit by the French or by southern tribes. But by twenty-first century standards, every group has the right to be called by the name they give themselves. There are other ugly names like 'squaw' which are just as bad as 'nigger,' still being used as names of places. And 'Indian' should refer only to people from India, and not perpetuate the mistake of European explorers."

The starting quarterback of the team was showing Luna and Shania Twain, the latter in sequined blue denim jeans and jacket, how to throw small rubber footballs on tight spirals.

Then Luna read a message from Turquoise. "We can switch from oil without going back to the Dark Ages. Canada must be a leader in other kinds of energy, and there will be lots of jobs for everyone. Where there are sacrifices to be made, the pain will be shared by all Canadians." After that there were speeches by the prime minister and the candidates in local ridings.

Polls of prospective voters showed the Left ahead in the big cities by four points, about even with the Conservatives in small towns in the south, but down ten points in rural areas and the north. Certainly liberal commentators in eastern Canada were hopeful. "Despite a barrage of alarmist propaganda from the oil companies, she is turning the tide in Alberta. And polls are showing record high recognition and approval numbers for the little pixie worldwide," wrote Antonia Zerbisias in the *Toronto Star*. "Canadians are especially satisfied because she personifies Canada's much increased role in world affairs. Lester Pearson would marvel at this girl, the poised pretty little face of a determined group of revolutionaries with a global master plan, led by Canadians. I'm especially impressed by the brilliant use of Atenism, to undermine religion by showing its pagan roots. New Harmony constantly but never with Red Guard crudeness strikes at a major Old Way of Thinking."

The new owners of the *National Post,* which had been losing readers in all big cities by slagging Luna and what she represented, had just fired the editor and five extremely right-wing columnists and replaced them with pro-New Harmony personnel. The new editor was David Olive, a brilliant liberal columnist from the *Toronto Star*. Shock waves were running through the *Post*, a newspaper which had often supported bloody dictators against the democratic Left, for instance at the time screaming that General Pinochet's arrest in Britain was "judicial kidnaping." Thus its founder, Conrad Black, Lord of a subway stop in London, having recently finished his prison sentence for fraud and obstruction of justice, and rejoined his social-climbing wife, saw the last of his influence wane. The *National Post* ended its policy of no pictures of Luna, and apologized for the departed columnist who recently wrote that Luna was "a perfect Stalinist monster in the making." The paper suddenly found good things to say about the Kyoto Protocol and the UN, and began criticizing many elements of the business community for shortsighted cynicism when it came to action on global warming.

These views were not echoed in most Alberta media. The *Edmonton Journal* fulminated mightily in an editorial against " this cabal of One-World Socialist Atheists from Toronto, this pack of Eastern political hoaxers and thieves who shamelessly risk Luna's life to gain sympathy when she is attacked. Shockingly, the RCMP has never properly investigated New Harmony's connection to the Green Daughters terrorists."

*

The bus left the stadium at 3.30, and again for two kilometres the roads were lined which cheering crowds while the repaired HueyCobra and a police helicopter patrolled the air above the convoy. Again Luna waved as much as she could, excited by the rhythmic chanting of her name and the hypnotic bass thumping of helicopter blades. Back at the armory it was quiet and Zhe insisted the children take a nap, lying in a berth with Luna to calm her down, falling asleep herself for an hour and waking with the sleeping girl soft and warm in her arms.

At 6 pm there was a UNICEF charity dinner at the Fairmont Hotel Macdonald, the most expensive in the city. Luna dressed in a green turquoise huipl—an embroidered jacket—over a cream silk blouse with a blue turquoise pleated vicuna skirt and black patent leather shoes. There were only two hundred guests but a million dollars was raised. As usual Luna went into the kitchen afterwards with the PM to thank the workers and sign autographs.

Then her bus rushed to Jubilee Auditorium where the Moscow ballet troupe was ready to start. The house was full. Aside from a few protesters outside arrested for throwing stones at the windows, the show went off without incident. Sanjay was not so impressed, but the girls were rapt. They met the dancers afterwards, each girl wearing a piece of the Egyptian jewelry to show the ballerinas. Mitsy wore the headband, Meritaten and Desiderata each a hair clip, and Bliss the Isis broach. Luna wore the ankh pendant, of course, while Milly wore the earrings and Roxanne the lotus ring. Inspector Maxine Tibbetts, in her red serge dress uniform, ensured that the large police and army presence did not spoil the evening.

On the second day Luna toured the nearby Fort Edmonton historical park in the morning and visited the West Edmonton Mall in the afternoon. At the latter Luna and her friends enjoyed the little kids' section of the Galaxy amusement park, the waterpark and skating rink. But for Jamie Ramsey, the mall, once the largest in the world, was a palace of consumerism against which he grumbled the whole time. "They once had two Hudson's Bay stores in this place," he groused. In the evening there was a UNHCR fund-raising dinner at the Fantasyland Motel in the mall, and Ramsey found the themed rooms off-putting. When Luna and the PM went into the kitchen before leaving, an old Chinese-Canadian dishwasher in a dirty wet apron shut off the steaming Hobart conveyor belt machine for a few minutes and through his nicotine-stained, crooked teeth sang a passable rendition of "Diamonds Are A Girl's Best Friend." This made his assistants and the busboys and waitresses laugh. (Some tabloid newspapers and blogger websites had noticed Luna's jewels and started the debate about whether she should keep them. Right-wing media were accusing New Harmony of hypocrisy.)Eight

Chinese-Canadian college girls working for the summer crowded around to see the pendant and other jewelry. "You must keep them, Little Dragon," said one waitress. Two grinning Philippine-Canadian bus boys tap-danced with Luna while holding long-handled wooden spoons. "You deserve the jewels for being so brave," said a sous chef six years removed from Goa, as pictures were taken.

At dusk the bus was driven to Hawrelak Park, which is in a loop in the North Saskatchewan, to see the River City Shakespeare Festival's production of "A Midsummer Night's Dream." The Heritage Amphitheatre, covered by a big white tent, protected them from light rain. Hot chocolate and blankets warmed the children against the chilly night air while a nearly full moon reflected in the man-made lake.

Next morning the children and some politicians took a green and yellow street car over the three-decked High Level Bridge over the North Saskatchewan and past the provincial Legislature Buildings. For some reason there was a man-made 45-metre waterfall named the Great Divide by the artist who proposed it, spilling from the mid span of the bridge. They watched contestants in the Sour Dough Raft Race paddle hard to avoid its spray. Squinting into the distance, the children tried but could not see the Rockies (220km) to the west. Then they got ready for the funeral.

*

Far from being angry, Claire Brinton welcomed Luna's participation, as did Prentice's mother, Saxon, 60, a scientist with the National Institute of Nanotechnology (on the main campus of the U of A). She was also a provincial director of Greenpeace. Before the ceremony in the armory they were invited into the bus by Zhe to rest for half an hour and meet Luna. The little girls were wearing matching charcoal jackets and dresses. Luna held Brinton's hand and kissed her cheek, using a handkerchief to wipe tears from the woman's eyes. To divert her, Mitsy brought the jewels. Jay Chatterjee comforted Saxon Prentice by holding her hand.

By chance Ms Brinton was a granddaughter of the late Ed Broadbent, an NDP leader from Oshawa, and shared his ideals. So despite her grief, she wanted to seize this opportunity to showcase the cause and honor her husband. The prime minister delivered a stirring eulogy, hailing Jim Prentice as "a hero of the transition to global government," stressing Prentice's interest in poetry as well as his commitment to social democracy. Luna read a message of thanks and condolence from her mother on the moon. Then Claire Brinton read her husband's unpublished "Credo for a New World."

> In the beginning was the Big Bang, which hath made hydrogen and helium.
> Then in the super nova agony of dying stars, heavier elements were created.
> Unto us a sun was born.
> And on Earth, crust forming, plate tectonics, volcanoes, bacteria, algae, and the green fuse that drives the flower, as arthropods and Permian lungfish crawled from the sea.
> Behold the amphibians, reptiles, dinosaurs, mammals.
> Behold the hominids.
> I believe in the scientific method, atomism, the United Nations, and radical action to save our world from warming.

The regimental band and members of the symphony orchestra played Purcell's slow march for the funeral of Queen Mary, Glass's "Funeral Music for Akhnaten," and other marches, as TV cameras relayed the ceremony to three satellite halls open to the public, one in Calgary, and to the world. The streets were lined with silent crowds as the cortege, including Luna's bus and its escort, moved slowly through the streets to Mount Pleasant Cemetery. On a hilltop overlooking the south-side and downtown, its headstones and monuments dated from the early nineteen hundreds. There were blue skies and scudding clouds above lawns as green as new billiard tables, pocketed with trees and banks of flowers—particularly lilies and geraniums in dozens of bright colors. Banks of early blooming roses in a full pallet of alluring colors rioted beside the broad gravel path upon which Claire Brinton and her mother-in-law led the procession of politicians, aides, Canadian forces personnel, police, RCMP, media and some of the left-wing public. Prentice's great-uncle had been a moderately successful dry goods merchant and built a small family crypt, wherein Ms Brinton placed the urn containing her husband's ashes. (Cremated in a new system that emitted no GHG's.)

*

For several days mail had been coming to Luna, much of it from children, addressed to 'Luna Express, Edmonton.' It was opened, searched, and then brought 'special delivery' by a postal union steward after work to Inspector Tibbetts, who gave it to Luna. After the funeral another bundle came. Amid the letters was a parcel from London, England. After the children finished supper Tibbetts watched intently as Luna (re)opened the package. It contained a handmade necklace—a knotted white string holding small plastic Cracker Jack trinkets, and some colored glass beads, with a silver school pin clipped on—sent by a little boy, John Windsor, 7. A note read "My nanny helped me write this. She will put it in a mailbox so you shall have a necklace if you have to give back your jewels. You are so pretty and brave, I know you must be a princess. When we grow up, will you marry me because I love you?"

"Is that ever sweet," said Zhe, offhandedly.

"The poor fellow has a crush on Luna, for sure," said Milly, who was getting ready to take the Moonflower and her mother back to B1.

"Yeah, that's cute," echoed Luna, in her adult mode.

"Yes, but are you ready for this?" continued the Inspector. "I took the liberty of getting the Post Office to investigate the source. Then we heard that the nanny in question was fired and has gone on Facebook and to the tabloids. Because the boy John is the son of William, Prince of Wales, next in line to the throne of England if Charles is passed over, as seems likely," said Maxine Tibbetts. "So perhaps Luna will be a princess after all, although morganatic."

"What does morganatic mean?" asked Luna, becoming aware of the import of the gift and note. "Is John a nice boy and not too rough? I shall ask Queen Elizabeth."

"Forget morganatic. Remember that New Harmony wants to get rid of royalty," said Zhe, "so that if he marries you he must give up his titles and never be king." Zhe was reeling at this latest setback in the task of keeping Luna psychologically normal. Luna put on the necklace, re-evaluating it sharply upwards after her initial indifference, and wore it to bed that night. On her wrist-top she found pictures and downloadable videos of John Mountbatten-Windsor on the royal website. "Let's keep this necklace in the safe," she told Roxanne in the morning. Unable to reach John at Clarence House, she e-mailed the old queen on her private line, using SpellCheck. "Dear Queen Elizabeth, Could you tell John Thank You? I shall always treasure the necklace and pin. Please say Ask me again when we are big, from Princess Luna of Dragon Nest, pretend daughter of Isis."

The old woman didn't know whether to laugh at the precocity or cry from premonition of an abdication crisis that could spell the end of the House of Windsor. But she sent assurance to Luna that John would be informed, as her romantic side relished being a go-between at her age and in her position. It didn't hurt that her approval numbers subsequently shot up fifteen per cent because of her perceived support of Luna against the wishes of William and Kate.

*

Two armored Humvees, the two MGS's, the Bison, three RCMP cruisers, and the drones formed the escort for the bus and car. (One Stardust Cruiser was being used by Oolayou to drive Boris back to Toronto.) From Edmonton the convoy went northwest for a day and a half, stopping for small audiences in several towns before reaching Grande Prairie, where the bus slowed because the main roads were badly potholed from winter cold and incessant heavy trucks. Here leftist supporters were outnumbered four or five to one by noisy roughnecks, Catholic school supporters, and other demonstrators. At the curvilinear brown brick community college (designed by the renowned Douglas Cardinal), the only interesting building in the boomtown, the prime minister was hit by rotten eggs and tomatoes thrown from behind portable classrooms by pro-Conservative agitators from Peace River who were quickly arrested.

However on native reserves (five were visited), every adult at the rallies promised to vote for the Left. Then the bus turned east and took Highway 2, stopping at four small towns and reaching the town of Athabaska, on the river of the same name, at 4 p.m. on Saturday the 17th. Here most of the three thousand inhabitants welcomed them, some with German shepherds while others held ankh symbols. Many residents worked for Athabaska University, which had some regular students but specialized in providing distance education to 40,000 people a year via the Internet and mail. Bushels of rose petals were strewn in Luna's path by the children of tutors and administrators as she walked from the bus to the university auditorium.

As the bus was leaving town at 8 p.m. it was overtaken by a Black Top taxi from Calgary driven by a bearded and turbaned middle-aged Sikh. The cab was stopped by police at gunpoint, as the convoy halted. Its passenger, a comely young woman in an expensive but rumpled raincoat and a well-tailored but creased suit who said she knew about a threat to Luna, was searched and interrogated for twenty minutes in a police cruiser before Inspector Tibbetts notified Zhe. (The woman gave the cab driver$2000 in cash and he was allowed to leave.) It took time to use the Internet to get a price (C$90,000!) for the watch (a Louis Vuitton Lady Tambour Tourbillon with many jewels and pink, white, and yellow gold pieces in the movement and case) on her wrist and to check the documents in her purse. Zhe walked to the end of the convoy and got into the back seat of a cruiser with the young woman. She was ingenuously beautiful, with no makeup, clear polish on short fingernails, natural ash-blond hair and hyacinth blue irises, good teeth, sensual full lips and a flawless milky complexion. No visible tattoos. Her big bosom and the pearl necklace that dipped into her cleavage looked real.

"My name is Mandy Elaschuk," she told Zhe. "I, uh, work . . . that is I worked fer Frank Connors, yuh know, the owner of Northern Hydrocarbon." Then she flushed and began to cry.

"I'm really just a whore, yuh might as well know," Mandy sobbed. "Just one of Connors' whores."

"How old are you?" asked Zhe.

"I turned nineteen two weeks ago," Mandy replied.

"Go ahead," Zhe directed.

"Well, like I said, last week by accident I overheard Connors' chauffeur, Brad Lyons, arrangin` fer guns fer the Donut Shop gang in Fort McMurray."

"The Donut Shop gang?" said Zhe with surprise, looking at Inspector Tibbetts.

"There were four men," said Tibbetts. "They graduated from shoplifting to armed robberies, mainly of coffee shops, five or six years ago. Led by two brothers, Bill and Bob Bremmer. They always grabbed some donuts too . . . . I guess they are all out of jail by now."

"How did you know it was them?" asked Zhe.

"Lyons called him B.B., and said he could start a chain of donut shops with his money if everything went right," Mandy replied.

"Was Connors with Lyons when the call was made?" asked Zhe.

"No, ma`am," replied Mandy.

"Did you ever hear them talk about it?" asked Zhe, looking for evidence of Connors' involvement.

"No," replied Mandy.

"So you had a dental appointment in Calgary, and got away from the chauffeur afterwards?" confirmed Tibbetts.

"Yeah, I got cash from a bank machine before my appointment," said Mandy. "The first two cabs I hailed thought I was crazy, but Mr Singh trusted me an` started for the highway north. Brad [Lyons] tried tuh follow but some fuzz, . . . sorry, a policeman, saw him pull a Uy [U-turn] over a flower bed in the median in the [black] Lamborghini [Reveton], and stopped him. Mr Singh and me stayed in a motel near Edmonton last night. I paid fer separate rooms. I hardly slept. Then we goes the wrong way this morning."

Zhe made a decision. "I think she's telling the truth," she told Inspector Tibbetts. "Let's bring her along on the bus for now, and get rolling. We're holding up traffic."

"You might need to use the toilet," Zhe told Mandy when they were in the bus. "Here's a robe. I'll borrow pyjamas for you. Take a shower if you want, . . . push the button three times and you'll get a second minute of hot water. Then we'll have a nice cup of tea. I'll put your watch and necklace in the safe." A few minutes later Zhe called Oolayou in Calgary, who called Beloved Morton in Toronto, and Hugo Mann at the CIA. Mann soon came across a NSA decrypt of a short call on Bob Bremmer's cell phone a week before with a reference to paint-ball guns from Pickering, Ontario. NSA analysts had missed the significance. "They may just be paint-ball guns, probably all loaded with red. But check it out," Mann told Oolayou.

The children were napping. Inspector Tibbetts asked Mandy a few more questions while they drank tea and the young woman ate sandwiches. Then Zhe assigned Mandy a berth and suggested she get some sleep.

At 2 a.m. only the driver and his assistant were up, as the bus moved at 70 kph, the top speed of the MGS's and Bison, along the northbound lanes of Highway 63 in shadowy moon-streaked darkness past muskeg and clumps of evergreen in the boreal forest. Luna was coming back from the toilet when she heard a faint sob. She opened the curtain enough to stick her head into the berth from which the sound came. A nightlight was on. The young woman, a stranger, turned to look at her through red and teary eyes.

"My name is Luna. What's yours?" asked the girl in a whisper, getting into the berth and closing the curtain.

"Mandy," the woman replied quietly. "Of course I know who yuh are. Yuh are `bout the most famous child ever, I guess. It's in the newspapers `bout little Prince John wantin' tuh marry yuh."

"Why are you crying?" asked Luna.

"Just lonely I guess. Sad that I've been bad an` wasted my life . . . . An` I don't hev no place tuh stay. No prince, or even a nice ordinary man is gunna want me," Mandy responded through sniffles.

Luna leaned against her and used the corner of a sheet to wipe tears from Mandy's cheeks. The little girl's pyjamas showed scenes on the moon.

"My grandfather Jamie says we can all be redeemed by doing good things. You know what redeemed means, like you get a second chance?"

"Yeah, but where will I stay?" asked Mandy.

"With me. I will tell Zhe you can come with us to Bitumount, and then come back to Home Base. It is very safe there. You will be one of my extra mommies," replied Luna. "Zhe will do what I say or I will ask Turquoise."

"Fer shurr they'll think I'm too young an` ain't a good person," said Mandy.

"If you are my friend, my grandfather will let you stay if I say. He is boss over them all, except Zecutive Council and General Council." Luna said, mispronouncing 'Executive.'

They talked for half an hour. Mandy's tears dried and she felt better. Luna had settled across her chest as Mandy stroked the girl's hair and relaxed. Before falling asleep the child opened the top buttons of the young woman's flannel pyjamas and snuggled her face against Mandy's bare breasts. Anxiety was replaced by hope and then joy at the prospect of redemption, as Mandy cradled the child gently and in turn slipped into the arms of Morpheus.

Zhe found them like that in the morning. Waking, Mandy expected criticism, possibly anger, but Zhe's tone was kindly.

"I see you've made a friend. She sleeps around a lot," said Zhe, smiling at her joke. "Very good. Better button up now. Soon Luna will be too old for this, so we will be discreet about it. Here are some clothes that should fit you." Despite feelings of compassion, Zhe caught herself imagining what uses New Harmony's Magus Players division could make of this young *femme fatale*.

"Thank yuh," said Mandy humbly. "Oh, an` I want yuh tuh know I don't have no diseases. Connors has us checked regularly an` he is very careful himself. A bastard, but clean."

"Still, if you come to B1 you'll have to have tests," said Zhe. "That's a rule for all New Harmony recruits."

"Thet's okay," said Mandy.

"We will be in Fort McMurray soon and you can do some shopping," Zhe said. "We'll be in the parking lot of a hotel, but Inspector Tibbetts will take you out in a car. Luna's grandmother, that's Roxanne, wants to thank you by helping you shop and taking you to lunch with the Inspector. It's Sunday but many places are open."

"I want Mandy to stay with us as long as she wants," insisted Luna, as she awoke, stretching. But there was no objection from Zhe.

"Your will is my command, Most Majestic Imperial Royal Highness," Zhe replied facetiously, smiling as she leaned in to kiss the child on her cheek, and say "Good morning, precious daughter," in Hunanese. She had decided to oppose Luna only on matters of security and diet. And Zhe certainly wasn't going to permit the girl to make her jealous of Mandy and her billowing breasts.

CHAPTER 14
Under Siege in Fort McMurray—Seventh Attempt

The forest having been bulldozed aside, the booming 'urban service area' of Fort McMurray sat like a flattened saddle astride the confluence of the Clearwater and Athabaska Rivers in the Regional Municipality of Wood Buffalo. Coming in, the convoy passed the sprawling Suncor Energy upgrader operation, where bitumen was turned into synthetic crude. Even in daylight its pipes and immense tanks glowed with lights and flames, its stacks pluming smoke. North of town, where once were grassy hills, Syncrude's nearest mine was a giant's black bowl reeking of sulphur, a gaping hole where around the clock in summer heat and long bitterly cold winter darkness five giant-sized tracked shovels loaded a hundred Caterpillar 400-ton trucks with clay and sand to be dumped into the crusher. (From whence large pipes took the liquified sludge to be centrifuged.) The 48'-long trucks, GPS monitored, with tires 22' high, dwarfed their operators. The process required large quantities of water, some of which was collected in large tailing ponds, spotted with oil, that was death to water fowl. "That is what William Blake would call a satanic mill, I think," Roxanne said, when next day she saw it from a promontory called Chretien Point.

A hundred and twenty thousand people, with a median age of twenty-nine, two-thirds of them male, lived in Fort McMurray at that time, ten thousand in trailers and makeshift cabins over muskeg in the woods. Most established residents dwelled in subdivisions around shopping malls, which could be Anywhere North America except for the many big houses with three or four car garages, the numerous cheque-cashing and loan offices and kiosks, and the lack of public buildings and mature trees. City Hall was two eight-storey red brick Lego boxes, already too small for the purpose, joined by a ground level concourse.

Luna noticed that not one adult waved at the bus. Instead many made a gesture with their middle fingers. "What does that mean?" she asked Roxanne. "It's a sign low class people use when they don't like something," her grandmother said. A few dozen children waved, and

Luna responded. Then Luna saw a mother pull her child's arm down and turn with a hard face to deliver harsh words.

Crossing the Athabaska bridge after it was checked for explosives, the convoy came to a halt in the older part of the northwest side of town, pulling into a big parking lot behind the Aurora Borealis Bed and Breakfast. The repaired Cobra helicopter arrived on the scene, settling at the back of the lawn past the MGS's and Bison, rippling the silver leaves of the aspens by the river. The inn was a three-storey three-winged beige stucco structure, with a cedar shingle roof and two turrets, completed in 1950.

"The same year I was born in the old hospital," said the owner, Tantoo Cardinal, wearing a long tie-dyed ten shades of blue hippie dress, as she gave Zhe a quick tour around. "When I made some money in films I bought this place for my retirement. But it badly needs renovation and greening."

It was one of few places in town willing to put them up. In the office, Zhe held Luna up to better see the framed stills of Cardinal in "Dances With Wolves" and many other movies and TV shows. There were also old pictures taken when Fort McMurray was a Hudson's Bay Company fur trading post. Cardinal was a member of the local Historical Society, which often met at the Aurora Borealis.

Because the bus had to be serviced, everyone was checked into the hotel. Off-duty military and police escort were given rooms at the expense of the New Harmony Party, and many took long showers or swam in the pool. Since Cardinal was short of staff, (labor had been expensive and scarce for decades), several political aides and tutors assisted the cook and waitresses. Even the prime minister and Olivia Chow helped soldiers with setting tables in the dining room, and later with washing dishes.

At breakfast, as Piaf's "La vie en rose" came softly from a record player in a side room, Roxanne read to her table from an editorial in the *Fort McMurray Today*. "Just a few days before the provincial election, the Patch is visited by 'important' people, many from Toronto. We ask residents to show their famous Northern hospitality. We are not the money-driven, vulgar hicks the world imagines. Luna is a charming little girl who might one day reject the alarmist socialist dogma of her manipulators, so let's be ladies and gentlemen towards her. Only peaceful demonstrations, please. Remember that the Left are just harmless idiotic dreamers, particularly Prime Minister Jack Layton. Nobody can shut down the tar sands, not even God Hisself, because nobody can wean the world from oil."

At the last minute Luna decide she was not going to the curling rink with the politicians, Athabaska tribal council, Pembina people, and other children. (Where, it transpired, protestors outnumbered leftists ten to one and drowned out the speeches with boos, many mistaking Bliss Akizenzie for Luna.)

"I'm going shopping with Mandy," the girl insisted. Zhe gave in when the crew of the Bison said they wouldn't mind impromptu escort duty.

"You stay low and wear your helmet in the car, mind, so nobody outside can see who it is, and wear your flack jacket," Zhe instructed. She was busy setting up the real-time 3-D model of Fort McMurray, which included cars and humans, that was being sent from the National Reconnaissance Office's radar-imaging satellites. To it was being added CIA and NSA satellite data, input from drones, police and army intelligence, before it was projected on the bus's largest screen. Telephone and directional microphone intercepts were being added. From Toronto Beloved Morton inputted UNECOP and Interpol data and advice. Donut Shop Gang members, some Alberta Freedom Party extremists, and twenty other suspicious individuals, several with America First connections, had been tagged for continual surveillance.

Inspector Tibbetts drove the Stardust Cruiser. Tantoo Cardinal took them not to the Holt-Renfrew in the Peter Pond plaza downtown, but to an eclectic store nearby run by three Jamaican-Canadian seamstress sisters who made jokes about how cold and dark it was in winter, one even reciting bits of Robert Service's "The Cremation of Sam McGee." In fact they had a quilt hanging on a wall portraying the abandoned steamer on the marge of Lake Lebarge, and the embroidered motto: "A promise made is a debt unpaid, and the trail has its own stern code." The Huggins sisters showed Mandy a cotton-hemp robin's-egg blue long-sleeved Guinevere sun dress with UV visor and veil, their own creation, with a black velvet bodice embroidered with European bee-eaters of yellow, orange, red and green, and many colors in between, and the skirt with lines of their swallowtail and maroon African cousins. It fit perfectly, as did a Suzy

Wong side-slit printed silk dress. A caftan from a women's collective in Morocco was next. Then Roxanne insisted Mandy also have an alpaca skirt and 'Gypsy girl' blouse which showed her shoulders and required a strapless bra and lace shawl, for informal occasions. Also a pair of low-heeled black pumps. Roxanne was in a mood to believe in Jungian archetypes, although that was against the Freudian-Marxist line of New Harmony. She wanted to imagine she was in the presence of the nymph Galatea, clay to be molded, or at least Eliza Doolittle, in need of grammar and pronunciation lessons. Roxanne had a Romantic, almost neurotic, side to her personality, which she now indulged. (She was not rich, but had invested the thirty per cent of her father's estate not given to New Harmony in Potash Corporation shares when they were cheap.) And if anyone ever wanted to be remolded, it was Ms Elaschuk.

As Mandy went to the fitting room Inspector Tibbetts handed her a small parcel.

"I don't know why I'm doing this. It could cost me my career," said Tibbetts. The package contained a loaded two-shot over/under nickel-plated .32 derringer in a 'Diamond Lil' garter-belt holster of soft black leather. "This is the safety. Off. On. Like so. At Bitumount I'll give you lessons." She showed Mandy how to wear it, on her inner right thigh. "You'll be a bodyguard for Luna until we leave Alberta. I've filled out the forms necessary to get you a license for the gun. We'll keep it in the safe with the other weapons when you are on the bus . . . . No one will expect such a pretty flower to have a sting."

To hide her identity Mandy wore the bee-eater dress and veil as they left the shop.

A rising breeze from the west blew dust across the parking lot of the Army and Navy Surplus Store as they went in. (Actually, there was little in the way of military surplus.) Mandy bought sensible underwear and socks, work shirts, hiking boots, jeans, and a hat with a mosquito veil, and paid with her bank card. She wanted to show the other women that she was not extravagant, not a stupid tart, . . . that she knew the backwoods . . . For lunch they drove past the Oil Sands Hotel, which they turned down because of its name, to the Athabaska Grill in the Quality Hotel. At first the other customers and staff did not notice the soldiers at the door.

"You are Luna, aren't you?" ventured a waitress with Metis features.

"Princess Luna of *Dragon Nest*," said the child in a matter-of-fact tone. The kitchen door opened and some of the workers watched until the manager shouted "Back to work." Luna was hungry and ate her sole and broccoli with five cheese melt with relish. She was pleased to notice that a piece of Baked Alaska for her dessert arrived without needing to be ordered. Food was put in containers for her escort to eat later, compliments of the management.

Local TV stations filmed Luna leaving, wearing a flak jacket and helmet, but didn't ask for an interview. For their indifference Luna gave them a weak little wave, with a reserved Unscrewing a Lightbulb motion of her hand. The TV cameras then focused on Mandy in her bee-eater dress and visor, perhaps hoping the wind would snatch her veil away. Luna took her hand and hurried her to the car protectively.

On Sakitawaw Trail (Hwy 63) there was a delay while a long cylindrical coker on an immense flatbed truck was given priority. Inspector Tibbetts used the time to get updates from Zhe on her wrist-top about the Donut Shop Gang and others under surveillance. She learned that dozens of skinheads were on a train coming from Edmonton.

The *Luna Express*, containing the other children and the prime minister and local leftist politicians, and the rest of the convoy, met them at the next stop—the Oil Sands Discovery Centre, in the southeast part of town on fifteen acres next to MacKenzie Blvd.

As the Cobra circled 300 metres overhead, Centre officials led the VIP's into the glass and steel main building. Massive as a big dinosaur, an old yellow 150 tonne heavy hauler with tire three metres high, dominated the main gallery. There was a 15 minute film on the history of the oil sands and a ten minute simplified demonstration of the extraction of oil from sand by the hot water separation method. The children, invited to touch, got oily hands.

An employee in a costume and make-up, Dr Noseitall, was there to answer questions.

"When are the oil sands going to shut down?" asked Luna, without receiving a reply. "I guess he doesn't know it all," Luna told her Math and Science tutor.

Outside in the Industrial Artefact Garden, Luna noticed that ravens and swifts were nesting in the obsolete machinery, whiting some areas with their droppings. She saw dozens of nests of straw in the rusting 850-tonne bucket-wheel excavator. A huge drag-line bucket with behemoth chains, from the days when surface coal mining methods were used, shimmered in the sun's heat despite the breeze. Luna took wrist-top pictures of her retinue around the prime minister with the old hulks in the background.

Meanwhile Inspector Tibbetts had been notified by Zhe that Brad Lyons, driving Connor's Lamborghini Reveton, had been spotted coming into town. Two of the Donut Gang were on the move.

The wind from the west was stronger, coming in gusts, sporadically bearing the rotten-egg smell of hydrogen sulphide.

*

For ten dollars Bob Bremmer has a neighborhood boy take a note to Pierre and Johnny Boy by bicycle. As he pedals through back alleys and around a golf course the breeze puffs the lad's nylon jacket out like sails. He crosses the bridge over the Horse River and makes for a new apartment building near the old Abasand subdivision. He holds the glass door of the building against the pull of the wind as he enters the lobby. He closes his eyes during the elevator ride, to better feel the motion. The two men seem nervous, and insist on giving him a twenty dollar tip. He boldly takes a swig from Johnny Boy's beer bottle as he leaves the apartment.

"Go to the cottege [sic] near Lake Antoine," the note in the envelope reads. "Under the back porch find dufel [sic] bag holding eight sachel [sic] bombs with timers and two rifles with extra clips. Green spray paint. Flashlites [sic] and your camoflage [sic] clothes and wigs and scarves. When you get to the pumping station, Brad said to get in the lites [sic] about a hundred feet from the nearest camara [sic], and write Green Daughters slogens [sic] on the gate, Death to Tar Sands Pigs, Death to All Warming Criminals, and sign GDofRD." Bob writes. "P. S. You don't need to put on dresses, because the Green Daughters wear camoflage pants and jackets. Burn this paper now."

Pierre smiles, showing his decaying teeth from his OxyContin habit. He uses his lighter to burn the note in an ashtray, and puts out his cigarette. Johnny Boy, the youngest at 25, also needs dental work. His broken front teeth (from fights and playing hockey and lacrosse), the pimples on his cheeks, and the rattlesnake tattoo on his neck, mar what is otherwise a handsome face on a muscular six-foot frame. He has brown skin and long black hair to his shoulders. They go off in a rusted gray '88 Chevrolet station wagon, leaving a little trail of blue smoke as the vehicle accelerates. Wind snatches the smoke, whisking it away.

*

That evening, after calling her parents, Luna goes to Mandy's room and finds her lying on the big brass bed in a velour nightgown, a dictionary beside her, determined to read the copy of *A Vindication of the Rights of Women* given to her by Roxanne. After brushing each other's hair a hundred strokes, the child again unbuttons Mandy's pyjama top to use her breasts as pillows. "I can hear your heart beat," Luna says, Nietzschean in her bold innocence. Passively Mandy allows it, only saying feebly, "Soon yuh will be too old fer this." But she hugs the girl tenderly, running her fingers through Luna's hair as they fall asleep. Wind creaks the wooden roof and rafters.

Zhe enters the room and wakes them at 3 a.m., touching Mandy's shoulder and putting on a light. Zhe is wearing her flak jacket and helmet and carrying a machine gun. Her face is grim.

"I have a job for you," she tells the young woman. "One of the Donut Shop guys has been arrested. He and another attempted to blow up the big Suncor pumping station south of town several hours ago. They were going to blame it on the Green Daughters of the Red Dawn . . . . They were foiled because we were following them. Thanks to you . . . . The other one is dead."

Mandy listens, wide-eyed, as Zhe continues. "The one we arrested is John Gabriel, . . . Johnny Boy is his nickname. His mother was Dene, an alcoholic who died when he was ten. Father unknown. Grew up in foster care in Edmonton, . . . not fetal alcohol syndrome but psychologically troubled, passed through ten different foster homes, and youth detention for stealing cars. Then prison for armed robbery and wounding . . . . Gabriel refuses to talk. He says he is no stool pigeon. So we must use extreme measures to make him say what he knows. Many lives could be at stake."

Zhe pauses to pull aside the curtain, looking out the window to ensure that sentinels are in place in front of the hotel.

"Inspector Tibbetts is having him brought from the [local RCMP] detachment cells. To an upstairs room in the back wing," Zhe goes on. "We can work on him better here than in jail."

"Are you gunna torture him?" Mandy asks fearfully, frowning.

"Worse than that," replies Zhe, with a quick small smile. "Because there is an old Chinese proverb that one can catch more flies with honey than with vinegar."

"What?" said Mandy. "I think they said that in the Ukraine too."

"You are the honey, honey," replies Zhe. (Beloved Morton had made this suggestion from Toronto half an hour earlier, knowing it broke a 1979 General Council directive against using recruits in Magus Players types of operations before their psychological assessments were complete.)

"You have time for a bath," says Zhe. "Put on the low cut blouse and skirt. Don't bother with a bra. Use a little flower-oil perfume."

Luna is awake, listening. She goes to the toilet and then bathes with Mandy, soaping the young woman's back, pouring too much bubble-bath powder into the tub by mistake, giggling as it bubbles over a bit. Zhe combs Luna's hair and puts in the Egyptian clips, dressing her in a cobalt blue silk dragon robe over a vermillion brocade high-collared jacket embroidered with gold threads, and matching formal pants and slippers. Luna loans the ankh pendent necklace to Mandy, and wears the young woman's pearls in a double loop around her neck.

John Gabriel, unshaven and looking tired, is in an orange jumpsuit. His feet are shackled. One wrist is handcuffed to the bed, on which he sits. In his other hand he holds a mug of hot chocolate. The women pass a guard and enter the room with Luna.

"Mr Gabriel, you are in the presence of Luna Cheng-Ramsey, aka Little Dragon, the first and so far the only child born in space," Inspector Tibbetts tells the prisoner.

He looks at Luna, who is standing two metres away, and then averts his eyes in shame.

"Is he a bad man?" Luna asks, going to sit in a wicker armchair.

"He tried to start a big fire to waste gasoline and pollute the atmosphere. Oolayou could charge him with conspiracy to commit an environmental crime. Plus he shot at police before he surrendered. That's attempted murder," Zhe tells Luna, forgetting to use simple words.

"You must say you are sorry and maybe you can be redeemed," says Luna earnestly to Gabriel.

"I . . ." the man is overcome with emotion.

"You can change from bad to good if you want," says Luna, emphasizing the last 'you.'

She tells him about the inmates who sent her a model of the *Titanic*. She stays another ten minutes, taking the opportunity to gobble down one of the Tim Horton donuts—chocolate glazed with chocolate icing—bought by Inspector Tibbetts for the occasion. (Luna was rarely allowed such quantities of refined sugar.)

Then they leave Gabriel alone with Mandy for an hour. She puts an album of Steppenwolf's Greatest Hits on the old juke box in the corner. She turns off the overhead fixture and sits beside him on the bed. She lights a joint contributed by Jamie Ramsey, and holds it to his mouth. They smoke in silence for five minutes.

"Dude, yer in big trouble," she starts, in a kindly tone.

"I should possibly maybe have a lawyer then," he says warily.

She ignores that and shifts her shawl so that more of her bosom shows. Her figure is dappled with colors projected by the lampshade—pictures of the Rockies.

"If yuh don't talk, it will go hard on yuh. `Specially if yer gang hurts the kid. Don't yuh see this special little kid, an` the people around her, kin stop war an` stop global warmin` an` save the world?" asks Mandy.

"Nobody can fuckin' save the world," he says, defiantly nihilistic.

"Anyhoo, now is yer chance tuh help yerself," she says. He could see most of her breasts. "If yuh talk, no UN `vironmental charges. New Harmony leaders an` the Prime Minister will ask the Crown Attorney fer reduced Canadian criminal charges an` the judge fer a light sentence in a safe slammer down East near where I'll be. Yuh will have witness protection after that. But yuh gotta tell the Inspector everythin`. This mornin`."

Her subtle perfume engulfs him. Never has he been so near such a beautiful woman, classier than in *Playboy* magazines. Even her feet and pink toenails are beautiful. At the same time he knows by her grammar that there are no class barriers between them. Her voluptuous breasts brush against his arm. She kisses his neck lightly. "Lay down," she urges.

"I'll visit yuh in jail. Fer Luna I would marry yuh, an` there would be conjugal visits," says Mandy impulsively. "Fate give me a chance tuh change, an` now yuh kin too. Tuhgether with me, who is also a poor sinner."

She disrobes slowly, gracefully. Then she embraces him and lets him cup her breasts with his free hand. By their swaying softness he, a connoisseur, knows they are natural. She sees his erection forming, as she unzips his jump suit. Zhe has left condoms in the drawer of the night table that holds the lamp. Mandy goes on top, and later lies beside him without speaking, holding his free hand with both of hers, until Zhe and Inspector Tibbetts return.

Zhe helps Mandy into a robe, and she leaves. There is a pre-dawn glow in the east.

*

For a long minute Gabriel stared at Zhe and Maxine Tibbetts. They stared back at him. Then he talked.

Gabriel revealed a plot to break into the hotel that (Monday) evening and let off poisonous gas. He knew where twenty more C7 assault rifles, four hydrogen cyanide canisters in aluminum cases, fake military uniforms and credentials, hazmat suits and gas masks, and thirty hand grenades were secreted—in an old school bus once used to transport tar sands workers, parked behind a trailer owned by Bob Bremmer's former wife, off a side road about three kilometres from the cottage near Lake Antoine.

Despite the wind the Cobra swooped down to seize the lot. Ten skinheads from Edmonton and six Alberta Freedom Party members in two cars and a van were arrested when they approached the property two hours later.

Gabriel said that Svetlana Mayakova had provided the weapons, disguises, and $40,000, with the promise of $3 million each if the plan to kill Luna succeeded.

The Bremmer brothers were arrested without resistance, leaving their apartment at 11 a.m. But the forty paint-ball rifles paid for by Connors were not found, having been moved and distributed to various agitators. Brad Lyons had evaded surveillance, leaving the Lamborghini in an underground parking lot.

(Gabriel had seen Lyons with Mayakova several weeks before. But there was no evidence that Connors was involved with the assassination attempt.)

"You are worth a thousand radar-imaging satellites," said Zhe to Mandy, as the latter stood beside the window of her room to wave at the cruiser taking John Gabriel to segregated RCMP cells in Edmonton. As they went to lunch Zhe guessed that Mandy was worried about making good her promises to Gabriel.

"Don't worry, you don't even have to think about him again. Put him out of your head," said Zhe. "Things you say in bed to an assassin dog don't count."

"Yuh will need him for the trials. So I'll string him along till then," said the young woman, shocked, and knowing, as Zhe apparently did not, that the new Mandy would have to do more than that. *A promise made is a debt unpaid* . . . echoed in her head.

The rally scheduled at Keyano Community College in the afternoon was cancelled. At 2 p.m. Luna and the prime minister met two widows of firemen killed in the Green Daughters attack on Exxon's Firebag operation in the spring. Then there were hugs, kisses, and nose rubs from Luna and the other children as Layton and Olivia Chow, their aides and RCMP escort were driven to the airport where a small Ministry of Defense Challenger stood ready to take them to Toronto. Gusting wind did not prevent takeoff.

Late in the afternoon by creating a diversion Lyons was able to drive the Lamborghini out of the garage and onto Highway 63 southbound, where he was spotted. Soon he was being chased by police cruisers and the Cobra. Forty kilometres south of town the Lamborghini went over spiked belts at 230 kph. The outer rubber shredded but the car continued at 180 kph on the hard cores of its tires. Ten minutes later a hastily constructed barricade with commandeered trucks of the southbound lanes failed when Lyons slowed, drove across the median into oncoming northerly traffic, and then back into the southbound lanes. But by then the Cobra was close and shot a Hellfire laser-guided missile into the pavement in front of the speeding Lamborghini. Lyons lost control of the vehicle as he hit the hole and careened off the road, down a slope of small fir trees and muskeg. By chance the car hit a shoal of limestone covered with rotting leaves and turned upside down, coming to rest in three metres of oily water. Lyons drowned, pinned in the wreck, before the Lamborghini could be pulled from the pond.

The car was put on a trailer and taken to the RCMP crime lab in Edmonton, where in the following days several fingerprints and a hair follicle with the DNA of Svetlana Mayakova were found. Computer-updated five-year-old pictures of Mayakova were sent to Interpol, other police forces, and the media, as arrest warrants for conspiracy to murder, attempted murder, and UNECOP environmental charges, were prepared. RCMP in Churchill, Manitoba, were watching Russian ships in the harbor.

Inspector Tibbetts was focusing on Frank Connors' role when she was diverted by the angry crowd building up around the Aurora Borealis.

*

They began as individuals, many fueled by liquor and false rumors that a Left election victory on Thursday would be followed by a total shut-down of the tar sands with no compensation. Many people in town had lost money as tar sands stocks dropped another 20% during the day, even as oil hit $230 a barrel. With the prospect of a Left victory in Alberta, the Canadian dollar was in free-fall.

They began as divers individuals. For instance, at the Newfoundland Lobster and Steak House Lounge, Danny Dolin cut into a tender strip of sirloin. He could see much of the parking lot, which contained dozens of new SUV's, Hummers, and pickup trucks—including his own Cadillac Mountaineer. There were no older vehicles and of course no hybrid or hydrogen vehicles—their owners would have been teased unmercifully. He was a stock broker, age 52, with all his money in tar sand companies. He'd been drinking more than usual.

"It's a helluva sad day," he said to a client, Shawn Perry, 37, who was eating a caribou steak with French fries. "Friggin` Stalinists, shuttin` us down." Perry had just come off shift from his job driving a heavy hauler for Syncrude. His tar sands stocks had lost $180,000 in value since the spring. His house, in a ten-year-old subdivision, had fallen in value by half in three months.

"I shudda sold in March," Perry said for the tenth time that day, ordering another rum and coke. "Maybe I'll sell now and go back tuh the Rock. But the wife an' kids sez no way."

"I come by chance to Come By Chance, but I left on purpose, bye," said Dolan, using one of his favorite jokes. "I'se [I was]so poor if the moose hunt dinn't go good, we dinn't have no meat. I ain't gonne [going] back tuh thet, bye."

"Lardy tunderin` Jeezus, I hopes the Americuns invades and takes over Alberta," said Perry, dipping a piece of lobster in butter. "Thet'd suit me fine."

"They say a crowd is gittin` big, `round the hotel these Toronna creeps is using," said Dolan.

"Less [Let us] check her out on the way tuh the Boomer [Boomtown Casino]."

Meanwhile, two students in the Mechanics course for future tars sands workers at Keyano Community College were arguing in the cafeteria with two students in the musical instrument repair course. The summer semester had begun, so the cafeteria was crowded.

"Now you'll see, this town's gonna die. To please Mueslix-eating yuppie Eastern bastids. No jobs. No town. You pansies must be pleased," said one of the would-be mechanics, a shortish chunky young man, to the instrument repair students.

"Even if it ruins the Canadian economy, the tar sands must be stopped," said one of the instrument repair students, a thin tall young man with a wispy beard and John Lennon glasses.

"I'd like to jump over the table and kick your Commie arses," said the other Mechanics student, a tackle on the football team.

"Why don't you brave boys go down and join the mob around the Northern Lights Hotel?" replied the tall instrument student. "If you want to be morons, about it . . . although the girls at Melons

Aplenty [a local strip joint with booths for private 'dancing'] will miss you."

"That's a good idea, shit face," said the footballer.

At the same time, a GM salesman was drinking with a friend, a garbage truck driver for the municipality, in the clubhouse of a new course on the northern edge of town.

"Jeez, the wind was carrying the balls. That's my worst score in two years," said the car salesman.

"At least there wasn't any black bears on the back nine this time," said the garbage truck driver, a man in his mid-thirties with a brush cut.

"I couldn't concentrate worth a shit," said the auto salesman. "Business has been down so much, it depresses me. Everyone is putting off buying a new vehicle, in case the Commies win. I never shudda taken the speeded up mortgage payments on the house, . . . every two weeks, . . . it's killing me."

"Someone should really do sumthin' about these Eastern bastards," replied the truck driver.

"Afterwards let's go over to their hotel and see what's going on. There is a big crowd, I hear," said the auto salesman.

Elsewhere, as dusk fell, Sam and Joe Rizzo, 16 and 17, students at Immaculate Heart of Mary High School, with their parents' and their (visiting) Italian grandparents' blessing were carrying anti-Left signs as they took part in a torchlight parade of Catholic students from the school to the Aurora Borealis. Soon they were joined in common cause by hundreds of (Protestant evangelical)students from Christ the King charter school, angry that their alma mater must become secular or close. The Wilson brothers called out to two young female cashiers coming off work at Wal-Mart, who came with them. As the parade passed Paddy McSwiggin's pub a dozen youths inside gulped down their drinks and then ran laughing to catch up with the marchers. Some were sloshed by open bottles of beer in their jackets.

"The weasel Communist prime minister has left but the leader of New Harmony is still here," their Religious Studies teacher called to Sam Wilson and his friends.

"Yes, the old hippie socialist full of his One-World mystical crap," the Gym teacher shouted.

Two roofers with a big pot of warm tar on wheels behind their pickup, coming home late after a few drinks at the Islander Hotel, decided to follow the parade. There were some long 2-by-4's in the back of their truck.

"They can't take the bread out of our mouths and get away with it," one of the roofers said to the other. In their thirties, they had come from a small northern Ontario town a decade before when the sawmill shut down.

Also in the unruly crowd around the hotel were real tar sands workers, paid agitators, aggrieved shareholders, angry Conservatives and Alberta Freedom Party members, assorted skin-heads and several Neo-Nazis from Edmonton.

Violence started when a balding old man with glasses came out of the hotel and slipped through the crowd until someone shouted "That's him. That's Jamie Ramsey." The unfortunate man, actually a dishwasher, was seized and his hands tied. His protestations went unheard. By chance it was near the roofers' truck. "Tar and feathers!" several members of the mob shouted. So the elderly man was stripped to his underwear, his arms and legs were tied with rope and he was hung from a 2X4 and carried about. Tar was brushed on and feathers from an eider down pillow, from the truck of a woman with a bad back, were dumped over the victim. Finally he was rescued by a determined phalanx of police and soldiers with batons and shields to protect them from flying rocks and bottles.

At this point Zhe and Inspector Tibbetts decided to send out a loudspeaker cruiser escorted by a MGS's, with recordings of the Riot Act read by the reeve of Wood Buffalo region. "You are being videoed and will not escape prosecution for criminal offences. Please go home. The Eastern politicians have gone, and only Luna and her party remain. Deadly force will be used if necessary to defend them," it added. The RCMP made numerous arrests, but couldn't break up the crowd. For despite the tough message, it was too windy to employ tear-gas and Zhe had prohibited the use of live ammunition or even rubber bullets against the demonstrators.

In the shadows several masked youths were handing out scarves and thirty paint-ball rifles donated by Frank Connors via Brad Lyons and Bob Bremmer. Others in balaclavas shot out the street lights with air rifles and a .22 pistol. The moon, in its last quarter, gave little light. The beige stucco walls of the Aurora Borealis, even the roof, were soon blotched with red, which in the dark looked almost black. Then came fireworks, arcing Victoria Day air burst rockets and illegal cherry bombs thrown high in the air. Stones and bricks penetrated shutters and shattered windows, as the mob with one mind vented its fury on the Aurora Borealis.

Zhe gave the order to evacuate the hotel and board the bus, which was heavily guarded at the rear of the hotel. Staff were taken out in the Bison, which pushed cars and pickups out of its way, followed by a Humvee taking the few other guests to another hotel. Ten minutes later, as wind fanned sparks on the shingles, flames appeared in two places on the roof. The wet paint ignited with a woosh, running blue and yellow fingers down the sides of the building. For a critical fifteen minutes the crowd prevented fire trucks from getting near the building by barricading streets with their vehicles and sitting on the ground. By then it was eleven p.m. The owners of the old slate-roofed mansion on the big lot to the west were preparing to leave if necessary, although the wind was blowing towards the garden center to the east, where staff were using garden hoses to wet the barn and sheds on their property.

After supervising the evacuation Tantoo Cardinal gathered some clothing and a few precious things in a suitcase, refusing to cry. She was the last to board the bus.

"We must break out now," Zhe told the driver. "The MGS's will push open a path."

As the bus drove over the lawn next to the adjacent mansion, crashing through a picket fence, convection currents lifted a large (three metres by four metres) piece from the roof. By bad luck it landed on the top of the bus near the middle, and stuck. The faster the bus went, the more the wood glowed and flamed in the dark, amid a barrage of rocks and bricks from both sides. After five minutes, as the bus and its escort got temporarily clear of the angry crowd, a fire truck extinguished the blaze and soldiers use hooks to pull it down. Then, as some of the mob in their vehicles approached, (having detoured on side streets around police barricades,) the bus and its escort continued along Thickwood Boulevard, approaching Sakitawaw Trail (63).

“Will I be going north or south?” asked the driver. Zhe and Inspector Tibbetts were sitting near him, next to Tantoo Cardinal. Luna was on Cardinal’s lap, consoling her.

South, over the Athabaska, down Highway 63 past the airport until smaller roads led to the safety of the Canadian forces base at Cold Lake? Obviously the rational choice. Or north, to the uncertainties of a rag-tag collection of victims and New Age flakes in an isolated derelict ghost village?

Just then Zhe received a ‘priority red’ encrypted e-mail from New Harmony’s Executive Council; which had just seen images of the fire on TV and Internet. “Enough. Cancel Bitumount trip. Return to Home Base immediately via Cold Lake and northern Manitoba,” it said, terse as a telegram. Seconds later a similar message came from Han-Spar.

“The Executive Council and Han-Spar say we must go home now,” said Zhe to Luna. “Would that be okay?”

“No way!” said Luna emphatically, pouting, frowning and preparing to cry. Zhe paused, watching the child. It was obvious she would react with fury if disappointed.

“Say the satellite dishes were damaged and their messages were garbled,” Zhe told the assistant. “When they call back, don’t acknowledge.”

“Turn left and go north on Sagitawaw,” Zhe informed the driver. “After we go over the Clearwater bridge, the MGS’s will block it.”

Highway 63, reduced to two lanes, ended in Fort MacKay, 64 kilometres to the north. Zhe would rather face the distant wrath of Executive Council and her superiors at Lop Nur and Beijing than the tears and recriminations of the child beside her. So the bus sped toward Fort MacKay.

In Fort McMurray authorities were stopping and Identocam-ing the occupants of vehicles around the Clearwater bridge. Amid the local goons were two former DEA agents with outstanding warrants. Several other men were connected to Bud Munk, the Big Oil lobbyist. More members of the Alberta Freedom Party were jailed, for throwing rocks at police. At the federal cabinet’s direction, the town was put under martial law until after the election.

Because the other soldiers and police officers were needed in Fort McMurray, only the Cobra and four RCMP officers (including

Inspector Tibbetts) in two cars accompanied the bus and Stardust Cruiser. Finally the wind stopped.

*

The hamlet of Fort MacKay was officially home to 736 people, mostly natives from the reserve. (The inhabitants had to get used to the constant hum of machinery from the heavy oil operations which surrounded the settlement, and the pop of chemical gas cannons set to keep birds from landing on the ubiquitous oily tailing ponds.) Although it was after midnight hundreds of people of all ages had gathered around the Snow Goose Motel. Mandy held Luna up by a street lamp so that the crowd could see her and take pictures. Inside, Tantoo Cardinal introduced them to the owners, a Cree family. Five elders came in to meet Luna and her grandparents.

The elders had a lot of complaints. "The [tar sands] operations give good jobs, but we cannot eat fish from the Athabaska River. Some are mutated and got two mouths or extra fins. Downstream from Fort McMurray the river has a real stench. The hunting isn't worth a shit for hundreds of miles now . . ." trailed off an old man wistfully.

"Some of the holding 'ponds' are really vast lakes held by some of the largest dams in the world. Some of the mercury, arsenic, and lead gets in the river with the oily water, and so the Mikisew First Nation in Fort Chipewyan have high rates of cancer," said Celina Harpe, a woman in her eighties. "They can fill in the holes but the streams are gone, with the berries and the birds we knew . . . ."

"Then there are the GHG emissions producing global warming," added Jamie Ramsey. "And the sulfuric acid rain that falls in Manitoba."

"Well, that's what this election is about," said Roxanne.

"No more fossil fuel," said Luna, yawning in Mandy's arms.

Next day Zhe and Inspector Tibbetts left Luna and other children with Mandy and the Science tutor. The latter reminded the children that there are no gods and goddesses. "They are concepts invented by humans, whatever the people tomorrow will say. A concept is like an idea, something in human heads," she said. "The concept of god in the Old Testament is a fierce tribal god who punishes the tribe's enemies. Then Jesus changed the concept to a loving inclusive non-violent god." To escape the lecture the excited children ran outside to watch every time the Cobra landed or took off for the five kilometre trip to the little turf airstrip near Bitumount.

They knew tomorrow would be Summer Solstice, the longest day of the year.

"We are going in just before dawn tomorrow. So have a big nap this afternoon. And early to bed tonight," Roxanne told the children when she and Ramsey returned from Bitumount and Lunaville.

After supper there was a rally in the hockey rink. The visitors were shocked to see a small counter-demonstration outside by a small group which wanted to exploit the extensive tar sands on the reserve.

The youngsters were in bed by sundown, but so noisy and excited that Mandy was assigned to calm them down. They were on two queen-sized beds put side to side in a motel room, so Mandy lay down near the middle in her white and pink flannel pyjamas as the children pressed around her. She read to them from a copy of *The Old Man and the Sea* purchased that afternoon for her by Roxanne in a used book store in town. One by one they dropped off to sleep, Mandy last.

CHAPTER 15
Summer Solstice at Bitumount-Lunaville: Eighth Attempt

It was dark except for street lamps and a few headlights as the Cobra rose above Fort MacKay. In her crashball but with its door open, Luna wiggled with anticipation and happiness as she talked to Roxanne and Mandy. Behind them Luna could see Sanjay helping Mitsy with the mosquito veil which hung from her straw hat. The children were wearing runners, jeans, shirts and nylon jackets. Ira Swartz was filming for UNTV. A few minutes later the Cobra approached the 300-metre-long grass landing strip in the bush east of Bitumount.

"Groovy," said Meritaten, when she noticed that the airport lights below formed the outline of a large ankh symbol. She photographed it with her wrist-top and reached to show Luna, who could not see from her crashball. The lights had been positioned by a Welcoming Committee appointed by Nitawik, a 25-year-old Metis woman five years past a vicious gang rape and beating. Responsibility had turned Nitawik from a frightened rabbit, to use her own words, to a competent manager of the money and materials sent by Milly Moosomin. Although she would always bear the scar from a broken beer bottle across her left cheek, Nitawik was accepted as leader by all the main factions, and was good at resolving disputes and keeping order with ten elected Monitors. She was a petit woman, soft-voiced, doe-eyed, too busy now to dream of revenge.

Against the early morning chill Nitawik was wearing a cream and teal dress and sweater-coat (knitted by the Textile Collective of which she was a member from alpaca and angora wool sent from Home Base and the base near Regina by Milly Moosomin) patterned with Blackfoot dancing figures.

To cement Nitawik's authority Zhe insisted she be the first of the Welcoming Committee to greet Luna, and ride to the sunrise ceremony with the child and her grandparents in the first of the electric carts. Because she was chilly Luna got on Nitawik's lap, pulling the woman's sweater-coat around her as she was hugged and held, the sort of instant bonding at which the child excelled. They were driven along a narrow gravel road, newly surfaced and packed, past the large conifers which loomed darkly on either side. It was more than a kilometre to Fitzsimmons' Peak, a hill named after the promoter who with a crew of seven men developed a small-scale hot-water separation technique at Bitumount in the `thirties before selling his International Bitumen Company and fleeing the country ahead of creditors.

In the second cart rode a green-robed self-styled Green Digger Christian minister, Monica Weldon, 42, representing a congregation of forty. The Green Christian position was that while Luna was not herself divine, her coming was a sign from God. Sophie Bloom, 35, leader of the New Age/Wiccan group of Luna worshipers, feeling slighted, was in the third cart with Bliss, Mandy, and the Science tutor. Ms. Bloom had promised her group than Luna would bless them in the church (old equipment shed).

In the fourth cart Lily Doucet, 46, with henna-red hair, in a pale lemon velvet dress, a self-styled prophet/therapist who had led fifteen former psychiatric patients and seventeen former outpatients of Alberta Hospital Edmonton to Bitumount in bitter weather in an old school bus in January. Lily used what she called redemption therapy, and had been promising her group that Luna would forgive and bless them.

Next to Lily sat Peace, 24, a neo-hippie in a T-shirt picturing The Doors under his Joseph coat of many colors, wearing sandals but no socks, in clean but tattered jeans, his face shaven except for a shaggy moustache, his tangled and dangling thick dreadlocks smelling of the marijuana recently smoked in the dark forest by flashlight. Peace was a chess enthusiast, having been in the chess club and a dozen tournaments during his three years at university in Edmonton. He had dabbled in Philosophy until he had a breakdown while studying the ideas of Soren Kierkegaard. Kierkegaard argued that one discovered God by an irrational 'leap of faith' by virtue of the Absurd, by virtue of the Absolute Paradox that the Infinite and Eternal were once historically incarnate. But Peace's attempts to imagine himself in Abraham's position, his knife poised over Isaac bound on the altar, . . . a Knight of Faith at the highest ethical level willing to murder his son if the deity demanded, had caused Peace to stop functioning for a while. For if there is no God, he reasoned, then the Abraham figure, who is important to three religions, was criminally insane. But now, two years later, Peace was somewhat recovered, and was primed to argue with Jamie Ramsey over his atheism, and challenge him to a game of chess.

Nitawik included Peace because he was respected by the Vegans for being a vegetarian, by the artists because he helped them with the murals and frescoes and by mixing paints, and by the Ceramics Collective (whose work was an important source of income for the settlement) because he could find the right sort of volcanic ash they needed to glaze pottery. Peace was also Nitawik's bridge to the old hippies from the Qu'Appelle Valley in Saskatchewan. And he was her only connection to the Outlanders on both sides of the river who seldom came into the village—the Luddites, who theoretically wanted to destroy all machines that use fossil fuels or require the use of fossil fuels for their manufacture; the Moles making a crude underground complex in response to the Warming; the nudists; apolitical homeless men and women who resented all authority; Roma with forged Canadian documents; and several undocumented Americans and Mexicans, . . . and their children not sent to the Lunaville school, not in the spring nor now, in the summer term.

The fifth cart carried Ernie Aitkins, in his nineties, the garrulous unofficial watchman who'd left a retirement home in Calgary in the mid `nineties and wandered for three years before arriving at Bitumount. He had survived in the manager's house, now newly reshingled, rewired, and resupplied with electricity to augment the wood stove. The old man was talking with Annabelle Martin, a woman about his own age who after high school had been the Postmistress of Bitumount for a year and a half (1949-50), while her father worked as an engineer. She too had come out of a retirement home (in Victoria, B.C.), two months before, accompanied by her granddaughter, Leah Lucas, 31, who had just finished a Ph.D. in Anthropology at Northwestern University in Chicago. They were staying in Aitkins' house, at meal times cooking chicken and fish for the old man and the guest workers who craved meat enough to listen to Aikens' rambling yarns. (Vegetarian diet was the norm in Lunaville, with the exception of some First Nations people.) Annabelle had recently donated a stamp collection worth at least $100,000 to Lunaville. Her collection of envelopes with the Bitumount postmark (1940-51) was on display in the new Lunaville-Bitumount Post Office and Communications Centre, next to blowups of the proposed new Luna (Canadian) stamp.

In the pre-dawn, as more of the path became visible, the RCMP officers turned off the headlights of their mountain bicycles. They were clad in jeans, lumberjack plaid shirts, and denim jackets. They and four armed soldiers in helmets and body armor on electric ATV's stayed close to Luna. (No one expected trouble in a village of victims that venerated Luna. But Zhe worried that the census taken two weeks before was incomplete. Some people had avoided Nitawik's census team, while dozens of others had since come down the Athabaska on homemade rafts. The latter were seen by the crews of fuel-cell electric barges and boats bringing building materials and supplies from the Waterways docks in Fort McMurray. However, out of respect for the nature of Bitumount, Zhe decided not to Identocam the residents.)

As the carts passed some inhabitants sank to their knees and bowed their heads. "She has truly come, Savior Child!" some cried rapturously. "Luna, Light of our Lives! Hosanna!" others shouted, waving willow branches. Then they rose joyfully to follow the procession. Others, just as enthusiastic in their way, waved and called her "Moon Child" or "Space Girl" to show respect but not worship. "A Thousand Years to Little Dragon," some shouted, as though saluting an empress.

Approaching the heights, there was a brief stop while the children changed their clothes for the ceremony. They donned the gold-embroidered white cotton robes of ancient Egyptian royalty, and were painted with eye shadow. Luna put on her ankh pendant and a child-sized headdress of Isis, with a sun disk between Hathor's horns, made of painted balsa by three women in the Woodworking Collective. Her hair was page-boy in front, loose over her shoulders at the sides and back.

Then the convoy started again, more sharply uphill, past rows of wind turbines and solar collectors in open spaces. More trees were visible now, mostly conifers—balsam fir, black and white spruce, tamarack and jack pine, alive with the chatter of squirrels. There were hardy deciduous with small leaves such as white birch, larch, and poplar. Some birds sang. On the ground last year's old grass could be seen amid the new growth. Blood-red branches of alder shrubs grew in thickets amid the evergreens. As day came, white clusters of flowers of mountain ash beside the path became visible in detail.

The south side of the top of Fitzsimmons' Peak looked east and west. (It was here the promoter came on Sunday afternoons to write his mawkish poetry extolling Nature and/or meet native women.) A natural amphitheater of stone ridges and tiers of wooden seats, augmented with folding chairs and ground sheets, provided seating for the four hundred people present.

Many were visitors, such as the sixty students and teachers from Lakehead University in Thunder Bay, on their way downstream on a 3,500 km voyage to the Arctic Ocean. Their four 36' birchbark freight canoes, replicas of those used by fur traders, authentically decorated from Kreighoff and Kane paintings, had arrived by coincidence the previous evening. The 'voyageurs' were sitting on tarpaulins at one side, so as not to deprive the inhabitants of seats. Several wore buckskin jackets, coonskin hats, and carried (unloaded) black powder rifles and bags of pemmican.

In addition there were many Lunaville-based workers and many residents in attendance. The District Returning Officer from Fort McMurray, a woman come by a First Air flight several days before to prepare for tomorrow's provincial election, wore a pith helmet, khaki pants and jacket. Nitawik noticed some 'Outlanders,' most of whom lived on the west side of the river, who rarely came to the village. They included mystic Hindus, several Buddhists, and the nudists, eleven people now dressed in brown hooded friar robes and moccasins because of the morning chill and wet grass, who sat together.

At 5.19 a.m. the solar rim appeared on the eastern horizon. Those seeing for the first time the scarred landscape left by the nearby Fort Hills projects recoiled in shock. To the east and south, as far as could be seen, 50,000 hectares of carbon-absorbing boreal forest had been reduced to a bleak terrain which resembled a First World War battlefield in France after a long bombardment, a brown and gray barren wasteland of shattered earth and large holes filled with tailings and oily water. Erosion from heavy rains had erased roads and overflowed the murky ponds, which were laden with mercury and other toxins. The blasted ground was devoid of vegetation except for a few places where trees had been replanted and streams recreated by reclamation workers from Lunaville. In the distance to the south two large JESS Heavy Lift blimps, powered by helicopter blades, were carrying equipment out.

With cruel irony, the treacherous Trojan-horse gift of hydrocarbons from the Lower Cretaceous was bringing Armageddon.

"Carthage was not so badly treated when its fields were salted by the Romans," said the Science tutor indignantly.

With a jolt Ramsey thought he saw men waving and walking on water, hatted or hooded Christ-figures of some abject army desperate to surrender, . . . but they were thousands of scarecrows set on anchored barrels bobbing on the oily scum of hundreds of tailings ponds. The distant popping sound of propane cannons set to keep water fowl from landing completed the hallucination. Peace, looking for a chance to speak to Ramsey, came close.

"Didn't Hegel say that everything contains the seeds of its own destruction? The rats are prospering however, eating dead waterfowl, even swimming down to drag them up," said Peace. "They dig deep burrows and 'hibernate' in winter when food is scarce. Of course they have many birth-defect deaths and mutations."

"The horror, the horror!" replied Ramsey. "Don't let the children know."

For relief Ramsey turned his head and looked south-west. The Athabaska River—placid water veiled in morning mist, sand bars, and tree-covered islands in the stream—was a kilometre away. Peace pointed out the larger buildings of Bitumount amid trees on an embankment on the near side of the river, better preserved because of their tin coverings. The powerhouse was on a slope near the river. The separator unit, its two stacks still standing, was visible past the refinery and reservoir tanks. The adjacent Fuller domes of Lunaville looked like golf balls.

As Luna stood and walked to the microphone, sunlight sparkled on beads of dew on the grass beneath her feet. Saying the Morning Prayer to Aten, she noticed drops rolling down several spider webs beneath the benches. As she finished, her eyes fell on one of the wild Outlander children about twenty metres away, a dirty buck-toothed boy of eight, with a quiff of brown hair, restraining a muzzled black pup on a leash. Luna wondered why the creature was muzzled.

(It was in fact a three month old male wolf cub, given to the boy by a stranger who brought whiskey and spent a week in May with his slatternly mother after repairing their tar-paper hut north of the airport. Its parents had been poisoned with strychnine in a wolf reduction campaign that was supposed to slow the decline of large ungulates such as caribou.)

Then there was music over the loudspeakers. "Here Comes the Sun" and "Imagine" were followed by the "Finlandia Hymn" with the religious words, "Democracy (is Coming to the USA)" by Leonard Cohen, and Buffy Ste. Marie's "Universal Soldier." After a pause, the Science tutor read the "Credo for a New World" by the heroic Jim Prentice. Then she read a long statement explaining that New Harmony and its allies were science-loving atheists who respected and supported paganism in order to undermine patriarchal religions such as Christianity, which were built upon pagan foundations. It was boring to the children. Luna took off her Isis headdress because it was heavy, and ran her fingers through her hair.

Just at that moment the wolf cub chewed through the binder twine cord that was his leash. With his paws he quickly pushed off the muzzle. With a yelp he ran around joyfully, chased by his master and other boys. By chance the pup ran past the green-robed Digger Christians and through a half dozen Environment Canada scientists, to the children around Luna. With Sanjay's help Luna grabbed his collar, getting her face licked for her trouble as she held him. She felt his soft black fur, noticed the white spot in the middle of his forehead, and admired his handsome pointed ears, his precise pearly little dagger teeth.

"No, dear. It could possibly have rabies," said Zhe, reaching in a bag for a disinfectant cloth to wipe Luna's face. The child soon pushed Zhe away, for embarrassing her in front of her friends.

The boy owner approached to take back his pet.

"Bad Spot. Bad boy," he said, ignoring Luna as she returned the squirming pup.

"Please tell that fellow I would speak to him," said Luna to Nitawik, and the departing boy was summoned, with Spot straining at the end of the re-tied twine. "His name is Alf," said Nitawik by way of introduction.

"What do you want to trade for him?" Luna asked the boy.

"Spot ain't fer sale," the ragged boy replied, wiping his nose on his shirt sleeve. His face around his mouth was smeared with bits of jam and peanut butter, his hands muddy and his fingernails broken and dirty. "He's a friggin` wolf, not no lady's lap dog," he snorted.

"I would tame him," said Luna confidently.

"Yer crazy as a coot owl," replied the boy.

"Some nice jewels, Alfred?" asked Luna, thinking of one or two of the hair clips or a broach.

"Jewels is ferr gurls," he said dismissively.

"What then?" she asked, "Baseball `quipment, comic books, computer games, . . . a nicer house? I will order it for you. Or do you want money?"

"Nuttin`," he said quickly. "Not for sale."

"But I am a goddess and you must trade or sell him if I ask," said Luna imperiously.

"Poo, yer jist a famous kid," scoffed Alf. "Yah shit an`piss an' fart like everybody. If they [there] wuz [were] goddissis, they wunna shit 'n' piss."

Luna and her friends were shocked by his rudeness, but noticed that Zhe and Nitawik did not intervene. Alf ran away with the pup, and that seemed to be the end of it. The crowd began to disperse.

"That boy is a blunt rascal, but he is right. A wolf would be too wild for Home Base," said Zhe. "He could never run free."

"But we need to replace Anubis," said Luna.

"When Spot gets big he might try to eat you up like Little Red Riding Hood," said Inspector Tibbetts, looking different in a dress, but Luna wouldn't smile at the patronizing joke. Wolf or not, she coveted the animal. Thinking of ways to get the pup, she payed little attention to the scores of kneeling adorers and worshipers who craved her blessing as she left the amphitheater and started back.

The procession went past the airstrip and approached Lunaville and Bitumount. Temporarily the fastest growing place in Wood Buffalo Region, Lunaville was then a dozen geodesic domes of various sizes, six portables (one used as a medical dental clinic, one as a schoolroom, two by Greenpeace, the WWF, and the Sierra Club), five prefab cabins, a small Environment Canada weather station, and two Quonset huts used by Pembina observers and scientist with the UN Intergovernmental Panel on Climate Change. The planned underground complex was staked out. There were dormitories for the tree-planting brigades, the experts trying to save boreal fauna, and the soil ecologists.

The four short gravel roads of Lunaville were to be named by the children that morning.

Jamie Ramsey felt that protocol demanded that the first stop on Luna's tour, even before breakfast, must be to the dome which housed the 'First Ten' to come to Bitumount. The building was home to Mary Vincent, 52, whose forearms had been chopped off by the man who raped her as a teenager. Ivy Redbird's tongue was cut out and one side of her face burned by a jealous former boyfriend. Tina DeAngelis, 27, from Toronto, was in a wheelchair after a rapist threw her from a tenth floor balcony. (A cedar hedge saved her from death.) Mina Hussein, 23, of Calgary, had been badly whipped by her father for dating a non-Muslim. Three other women were incest survivors. The elderly sisters of Helen Betty Osborne, the Cree teenager raped and killed with a screwdriver by her four assailants in Le Pas in 1971, acted as mother figures to the others.

But Luna saw the sign in the window—House of Women Only. She stopped. "Does that mean Jamie and Sanjay can't come inside?" she asked Nitawik.

"I guess so, if they wouldn't mind," said Nitawik uncomfortably. "These women were all badly hurt by men."

"But *I* mind," said Luna. "I won't go in if my grandad isn't welcome," she declared. "Jamie never hurt them. He loves women, `cause I will be a woman, and he loves me," she added with impeccable if self-centered logic.

So there were hurried discussions inside. Nitawik was embarrassed, almost angry, at the women.

"Really, these guys are too young and old to hurt you," she said. "Stop nursing the tempting memory of your pain. Let it go and you can live again," continued Nitawik, her rhyme (in words unconsciously taken from Buffy Sainte Marie's recording of Ed Freeman's "The Angel") buttressing the meaning.

After a few minutes the sign came down. Mary Vincent, tears streaking her cheeks, extended her prosthetic hands to lead Sanjay and Ramsey into the dome. Luna met all the women, curtsying in respect and shaking their hands. Mary Vincent poured tea for everyone from a Spode teapot into cups with traditional Chinese scenes, and pieces of fruit were offered to the guests. Inspector Tibbetts pointed out a picture of Helen Osborne in a shrine area, and lifted Luna up to see. "It is permanent stain on the RCMP that her murder was not investigated properly, and the guilty men punished quickly," said Tibbetts, wiping away tears. Then the children went into a bedroom and changed into their casual clothes. The adults talked for twenty minutes about how the lot of women would be improved during the Transition, as racism and patriarchal religions faded and all girls were well educated, while the children played with two cats and a ball of yarn from Mary Vincent's knitting box. Tantoo Cardinal invited the women to visit her hotel when it was rebuilt.

As they were leaving, Luna pulled on Zhe's arm.

"Zhe, I want to have a tea party in the afternoon, with sweets. I want to invite all the children. And that boy Alf with Spot," Luna said.

"I'm sure a tea party can be arranged, but no one can force the boy to come," replied Zhe.

"We'll make a special invitation to say he can have cakes and cookies to take home with him," said Luna. "And a boat ride, or something like that."

"Okay," said Zhe, smiling inwardly at the little schemer.

The next stop was at the House of the Blind and Deaf. The Science tutor reminded Luna of the American Sign Language she knew, and the child did her best to communicate with the deaf. Luna insisted that the blind touch her, and run their fingers over her face, her hair and shoulders.

There was a picture of Helen Keller with her tutor. Luna asked Sue Li, a small Chinese-Canadian woman in her twenties blinded by acid thrown by a spurned boyfriend, to explain who Keller was.

In one corner there was a seemingly senile old man in a rocking chair in pajamas and nightgown. He wore dark glasses which gave him a mole-like appearance. "His name is Bert, but he likes to be called Tiresias," said Nitawik with a small lift of her of her eyebrows.

"Because I tire easily," he said to Ramsey, smiling engagingly. "You know I was at Thebes [Greece] long ago, below the wall, among the lowest of the dead. I have foreseen, foresuffered all," he said in an earnest tone, reaching out to clutch Ramsey's right hand with both of his.

"He's recalling bits of T. S. Eliot, that's what," said Roxanne, who remembered the lines from college. "*The Waste Land.*"

"I knew Achilles, Alexander, Caesar, Napoleon, all the great ones. Now I'm pleased to meet you and these other world historical figures," said the man to Ramsey, with no hint of irony or air of flattery. He touched her head and took Luna's hands in his, and seemed to go into a trance. Then he looked anxious.

"You are in danger here, golden child. There are gypsies, tramps, and thieves. Fly away, pretty daughter of Isis, fly away now." He paused and continued. "After that, during the War to End All Wars, beware the Shan Plateau. Ask for extra bodyguards and tanks, when you hear the name, if they insist you go. You will be in peril on the Shan Plateau, in Burma," he said, letting free her hands. "I see it clearly though I see not. Fly now," he ended.

"Stop, you are frightening the child," said Zhe. "Tell me or Inspector Tibbetts if you know anything specific, more than stereotypes."

"Sorry," he said meekly, turning to put a one-sided 78 rpm disk on the Victrola beside him. It was a 1921 RCA recording of Borodin's "Dance of the Polovtsian Maidens" by the Berlin Orchestra. Despite the static, the children were fascinated and listened to the end because they were familiar with "A Stranger in Paradise." The old man did not speak again, except to say goodbye.

For breakfast, in the portable that served as a cookhouse, there were slices of pineapple on pancakes ground from wheat sent by Milly Moosomin from the New Harmony base near Regina, and maple syrup from the base near Nominingue, Quebec. The strawberries were homegrown, and the milk (fully tested) from the two cows in the new prefab barn.

The staff clapped and cheered as the children walked in. As grace, Luna thanked them for making the food, and wished that everybody in the world had enough to eat. (There were riots over increased grain prices in four countries as she spoke.) Before leaving, she signed photographs of herself and gave them to the cooks and servers, and then to many of the workers and Lunavillers present.

Continuing the tour, the visitors quietly looked at six wounded wolverines recovering in a wire-fenced shaded area behind one of the Quonset huts. The reclusive animals had trees and stumps to hide in. There were other rescued animals and birds in the barns. Members of the Wildlife Rehabilitation Society of Edmonton were busy de-oiling fifty mallards picked up that morning on dawn patrol on the eastern edge of the Fort Hill wasteland.

At the Lunaville-Bitumount Post Office and Communications Center, there were thousands of e-mails and hundreds of letters and parcels for Luna. One letter was from John Windsor, assisted by and mailed by the assistant chauffeur, expressing envy at her adventures and alarm at her perils. "If I used the second chauffeur's e-mail for messages to you, would spies know?" John asked.

"Ask the Queen to tell him to try it," said Zhe, smiling. Sorting through the gifts, Luna kept a few of the clothes for herself and her friends.

"I'll give the rest to the kids here," she decided, and the clothes were boxed and taken to the commissary by Leah Lucas, the former postmistress' granddaughter.

It was a school holiday because of Luna's visit, but many of the thirty-three students were assembled to greet her. After they toured the classroom, Nitawik asked Luna and her friends to name the streets. They soon came up with Aten Avenue, Think Of The Poor Road, Wolverine Lane, and Stop Warming Way, getting older children to help with the spelling as Bliss wrote them on the blackboard.

The largest Fuller dome contained the dental/medical office where a nurse/dentist was on duty, and Nitawik's office and apartment. Luna used a computer to print notices of her tea party for children nine and under at 4 p.m. She made an invitation for Alfred promising a boat ride and sweets if he came with Spot. Sanjay and a soldier were dispatched to deliver it. After changing into a favorite blue vicuna-hair dress decorated with Egyptian gods and goddesses, and putting on the ankh necklace again, Luna sat by an easterly window in Nitawik's suite for forty minutes (with short breaks) while Andre Blais, an Impressionist artist inspired by van Gogh and the Canadian Group of Seven, sat for her portrait. He took photographs to assist him in finishing it later.

"Could you put the wolf cub beside me, from photos or remembering?" asked Luna at the end of the sitting.

"Yes, why not?" laughed the artist, as Peace helped him close up his paints.

Several hundred people followed as Peace and Nitiwak led Luna (hatted and freshly sun-screened) and her procession to the adjacent ghost town of Bitumount, despite it being a contaminated site according to a provincial government website. The visitors saw the metal sign put up after the place was abandoned in 1958, its paint cracked and peeled like birch bark, rendering it illegible except for 'Alberta Historical Site' at the top.

The first cluster of buildings was comprised of the bunkhouses and bungalows, of wood and mostly in bad shape, overgrown with weeds and brush. About half were burned or decayed beyond recovery. The cookhouse and laundry building survived however, having been protected by green tar paper. They had been cleaned and repaired, for temporary dormitories. The tin-clad separator building, its twin smokestacks still held with guy wires, contained most of the original equipment. The saw mill where Bitumount's lumber had been cut in the `forties was largely intact. The refinery, an elegant silver cathedral of pipes and tanks, stood atop the embankment above the Athabaska. There were two rusted street signs for Sulphur Alley and Diesel Road. The old powerhouse, part way down the embankment, was humming with activity, having been refitted with hydrogen fuel-cell electric generators and new lines. Electricians and roofers were hard at work.

In a long shed, originally a machine shop, Andre Blais and his helpers had been painting a mural on sheets of plywood along the inside of the walls. The "End of Empire" began with a portrayal of American atrocities, starting with Wounded Knee. The next panel portrayed the destruction of villages and the killing of hundreds of thousands of non-combatants by US forces in the campaign (circa 1900) to pacify the southern Muslim areas of the Philippines. The starvation and carnage caused by American military support of the right in Greece 1947-49 came next, followed by the use of nerve gas bombs in Korea in the early fifties. Guatemala-1954 showed the CIA deposing a democratically-elected government to usher in decades of murderous right-wing tyranny in the region. A panel depicted the torture chambers of the CIA-installed Shah of Iran. Then the My Lai massacre in Viet Nam, and the carpet bombing of

Cambodia (and Laos), begun under Johnson, which produced the Kymer Rouge killing-fields. Then Chile in 1993, showing the CIA assisting the military dictator's henchmen in rounding up thousands of labor leaders and pro-Allende politicians in soccer stadiums to be gang raped (if female), tortured, and killed. Another panel showed Palestinian refugees in crowded camps, victims of (US-backed) Israeli apartheid.

Next was "9-11," a large painting of the twin towers pierced and burning. Scenes of American forces bombing Afghanistan and torturing in Abu Ghraib prison in Iraq appeared on the next two panels. Then there was a blank sheet, followed by a panorama of Easter Island at the height of its folly—showing stone heads being rolled on logs and rats eating birds' eggs. Then another blank.

It was followed by a panel (the 17th) where Blais' painting of Luna, the UN headquarters and moon behind her, wearing the Isis headdress with Spot in a silver and turquoise Anubis collar beside her, was to be copied, doubled in size, with Prentice's Credo in one corner. On subsequent panels there were sketches and plans for pictures of the Transition in progress, depicting UN forces defeating American and Russian imperialism and all the dictatorships, to make a powerful UN world government.

Chandlers, potters, weavers, woodcarvers, furniture and soap makers worked in the same shed. At one end a museum of Bitumount artifacts had been started by the graduate student in Archeology sent from the University of Alberta Edmonton campus for the summer by the provincial government. The children were weighed, individually and then together, on a balance-beam scale two metres high. The other stuff impressed them less: kerosene lanterns, truck engine blocks and crankshafts, parts of wood stoves and primitive (clothes) washing machines from the `thirties and `forties, rusted steel milk cans and wheel barrows, earthenware pots and mason jars, and an upright marine steam engine. On the Internet the student, Sai Woo Foxworth by name, had found hundreds of pictures taken in Bitumount in the archives of the University of Alberta. She had received permission to reproduce many of them for the museum. One jumped out at Ramsey. It showed a gaggle of float planes on the Athabaska which brought executives of the Anglo-Iranian Oil Company, Royal Dutch

Shell, Jersey Standard (later Exxon), and Secony Mobil) executives to visit in June of 1950, when the process was proven to work.

Zhe wouldn't let Luna enter the old equipment shed where her worshipers awaited, scooping her up and carrying her lest she run in. "We mustn't encourage them," said Zhe, and Ramsey concurred.

"Sorry, honey, Executive Council is against it. They threatened to charge me with reactionary behavior at next General Council if I let it happen," said her grandfather. "They'll say I'm not a real socialist."

"Won't the people waiting for me be sad?" Luna asked.

"The Science tutor has explained to them how our enemies could misuse such a thing against us. America First politicians and right-wing media will say we are creating a cult of Luna worship. The Left will say we are pandering to religion. Everyone will say it is hypocritical to promote a *Kumari devi* [living goddess] here while deploring it in Kathmandu," said Zhe, forgetting to use simple words.

"What if I just went in and said 'Hello'?" Luna asked.

But Nitawik objected.

"Lily Doucet and Sophie Bloom were bad," said Nitawik. "An hour ago they tried to bribe Alf's mother with alcohol to take the wolf cub from Alf and give him to you. If you would bless their followers, . . . A monitor caught them delivering the bottles . . . . We can't reward their bad behavior."

Luna digested this thickening of the plot. "Those ladies could get Spot for me?" she asked.

"Not any more. It wasn't right so we stopped it," said Nitawik.

Luna had to accept this for the moment. Anyway, she had glimpsed the river and was eager to see it up close. So Nitawik led the way out of Bitumount, turning down the embankment road past the old excavations, now terraced with gardens, to a staging area above the new docks. To the south were the remains of the original wooden docks, too rotted to be used. Past that on the sandy shore, strung out part way up the bank, amid cat-tails and willows, were three derelict barges and a small side-wheel river boat. The dilapidated boat reminded Mandy of the old steamer on the marge of Lake Lebarge in the poem, and her promises to John Gabriel.

It was hot now, the sun overhead in a mostly cloudless blue sky. The river seemed to sigh in the heat, sweating oil and tar. "The water smells a bit like a gas station," said Desiderata. Luna saw the empty electric barge that was being prepared to take the children on a short trip down river later in the afternoon. Her cartouche had been painted on the sides in gold and black paint. A portable toilet was carried on. Under a canopy of green canvas rows of child-size benches were being bolted to the deck, next to a stack of small life preservers and pint-size silver survival suits. "Please have a life preserver for Spot too," Luna said There were several canoes tied to the barge.

But first came lunch, sandwiches in a tent set up in the staging area, organized by the parents of the fifteen young children in the village. Their offspring met Luna and her friends, who had many questions about life in Lunaville, and a few questions about Alf and Spot. Afterwards the village youngsters napped with the visitors on air mattresses put down in the tent. The side flaps were opened to receive a cooling breeze from the east. Luna slept for three hours, lying against Mandy, who was wearing her bee-eater dress, reading a book when not dozing. Several soldiers were having naps too, while one stood on guard by the door. Everything was peaceful, in a dragon-fly droning summer sort of way.

As the children slept, Lily Doucet and Sophie Bloom and their robed followers walked down from Bitumount to see their goddess. Nitawik decided it was only fair to let them come into the tent quietly five at a time to see Luna sleeping.

After treating them with such consideration, Nitawik was annoyed when they knelt in rows outside the tent after seeing Luna and wouldn't go away, cluttering up the staging area. Her anger flared and Nitawik was at the point of having the monitors or police and soldiers move them. But then she was ashamed of herself, and wondered if she were becoming authoritarian.

At that point Luna awoke, saw her worshipers, and declared that she would speak to them. Zhe started to tell her what to say but Luna put her hand over her guardian's mouth and then stood on a chair outside the tent. She was still wearing her blue dress embroidered with Egyptian gods and goddesses, and the ankh pendant.

"Please stand up, dear people. You mustn't pray to me, or worship me . . . . I'm just a kid," Luna declared. "Not a goddess, I guess. That's just a game. I'm not even a real princess, you know, that's just pretend. My Mommy Turquoise told me again last night, and she is very smart. So it must be true. She is helping make Apollo City on the moon with my father and other smart people."

As the child repeated and expanded on the theme, they slowly stood, one after another.

"Turquoise said I could bless you, as long as I said I was just a kid. So I bless you and hope you will be happy," said Luna, raising her hands above her shoulders for a moment. "She said Thank You for working to save the land and don't worry so much about your own problems."

Slowly, as if coming out of a trance, they left singly and in small groups. Lily Doucet and Sophie Bloom both knew, with a measure of relief, that they had lost their flocks.

Because there had been no reply from the boy, even though she had written RSVP at the bottom of the page, Luna sent Sanjay and a policeman to find Alf. Ashamed to admit that neither he nor his drunken mother could read the invitation, the boy almost threw a stone at Sanjay. Then he retreated into the smelly hovel that was his home. But Sanjay was so deferential, addressing him as 'Mister Alfred' and 'Sir' through the greasy blanket that served as a door as Luna had instructed, that soon Alf was coaxed out to talk and before long was soaping in a bathtub in Nitawik's apartment, and helping Sanjay give Spot a bath he did not want. The boys took turns toweling Spot as he tried to nip them. After that Alf was fitted with a used shirt and denim pants, and new socks and running shoes made in a Fair Trade factory in Edmonton, from the commissary nearby.

After everyone put on UV cream, policemen and policewomen in swim suits escorted all the children aboard the barge. Two armed soldiers manned the lines and jumped aboard as the barge's engine pulled it into the middle of the languid current. With the motor shut off, the craft drifted past the wooded sand bars and holms. Water testers waved from a rowboat.

A kilometre downstream on the western bank a thick fold of limestone was exposed, rising ten metres from the water, topped by a metre of soil—enough for a mat of jack pines and fir twenty metres high. Ravens were the only birds they saw in the trees. A kilometre further along, as the limestone gave way to banks of sand and shale, two moose, a male and a female, were spotted browsing in a distant swale. The children watched with binoculars. A bit later the Science tutor thought she saw a whooping crane.

"Possibly it was a heron," Nitawik said to her, smiling inwardly. "I think the whoopers are all up in the delta in Wood Buffalo Park busy raising families now."

Luna put on white gloves and poured tea (made from purified water heated in a Petrolia solar samovar) for the other children, assisted by Mitsy and Bliss. At Luna's request Mandy was especially attentive to Alf, feeding him slices of mango and mangosteen. The lad had never seen such a beautiful woman up close, smiling and leaning against him, and was instantly smitten. Alf let Mandy stroke Spot's head and feed him morsels from a chicken sandwich. Feeling sorry for him, Mandy impulsively gave Alf a hug and a kiss on his cheek, her lilac perfume and hyacinth eyes bewitching him. He glanced at Luna, to see if she were jealous. But Luna smiled at him as serenely as a queen as she poured tea. Later she showed Alf how her wrist-top worked. A news item came on as she was flicking through TV stations.

"She's a four billion dollar baby," a CBC announcer said. Zhe heard it and paused to listen. "The total of money raised for UNICEF, UNHCR, and UNESCO by Luna dolls, her lines of children's clothing and educational toys, and her charity appearances has just topped four billion Canadian dollars," the announcer continued. "In a New York speech the Secretary-General called Luna 'the precious little beating heart of the United Nations.'" Pictures of Luna and the *Dragon Nest* appeared on the screen.

"How much is four billion?" she asked the Science tutor.

"Four thousand million," said the tutor, writing it on a napkin. For a moment Alf felt the gulf between him and Luna, wide as the river. How he envied the urbane Sanjay, as he took him aside to ask what the United Nations was. "If I gives Spot to her, I guiss I could git another pup," Alf confided to Sanjay. "Don't she deserve `im fer bein' so brave?"

"You are very generous," replied Sanjay, a little disappointed at his capitulation, "but not even Luna will be allowed to keep a wolf in Home Base."

Alf went to Luna and whispered in her ear. "Okay, ya give me a hunnert dollers fer tuh git another pup, an` Spot is yers."

Then a Mountie in swimming trunks and a shirt took Alf and Sanjay in a canoe for half an hour, letting them do most of the work with half-sized paddles. Luna took the opportunity to hold Spot's new chain leash, hugging and playing with him, laughing when he chased his tail.

"Don't get attached to him," Roxanne warned, "because there is absolutely no way he's coming back with us. It would look bad, you taking the poor boy's prized possession. Plus the creature is too wild for Home Base. Animal rights people, our allies, would howl. You live in a goldfish bowl, my dear, and must be careful what you do. It's a price of being famous."

As a joke Ira Swartz, taking a break from filming, put the Rolling Stones' "Blinded by Love" on a portable player. There was a verse about Marc Anthony and Cleopatra that applied to Alf.

"I need a hundred dollars. He will sell Spot for a hundred dollars," Luna whispered to Mandy, knowing Roxanne would not approve.

"Ah, jeez, Sugar Plum, I can't go against Zhe and Roxanne, an` maybe get kicked out of New Harmony before I get in," replied Mandy. "Please don't ask me tuh stoop tuh folly."

So Luna tried Ira Swartz, taking him aside for a moment. He too found an excuse, leaving her frustrated. All the police and soldiers claimed to have left their money in the barracks. "All my money goes to building Lunaville," claimed Nitawik when asked, thinking quickly. "I need my money to rebuild the Aurora Borealis," added Tantoo Cardinal.

*

Meanwhile Jamie Ramsey had gone off with Peace into the dense bush behind Bitumount, past the old tailings pits—slated to become a water purification system of lagoons and marshes. On a slope of muskeg, glacial till, and reclaimed tailings Peace had planted dozens of marijuana plants amid ferns and saplings. "They are from cuttings taken from a dynamite BC mother," he said, "which I started indoors. They were two feet high when I put them in a month ago." The plants had grown another thirty centimetres since then, being well watered, well fertilized, reveling in long hours of sunshine and on track to be big as bears. "The price has dropped a lot out here since it was legalized, and the quality gone up. I'll get about sixty bucks an ounce for this, if it doesn't get seeded from the hemp we use in land reclamation to fix nitrogen."

Peace's prefab hut was in a glen on a winding trail off the road to the airport. It was small, about four metres square, but had two big windows fitted with screens to let in light and air. The scent of sandalwood pervaded. Several shelves were filled with works of Philosophy and Psychology. One wall was covered with psychedelic posters and album covers from the `sixties. There was a pile of original *Zap Comix*.

"Well, this takes me back," said Ramsey. "Roxanne and I were lucky enough to get to Woodstock, you know. Along with some others at York University who later became directors of New Harmony."

"How I envy you. I've read about it and seen all the pictures and film, of course," Peace replied. "Too bad it's been turned into a theme park, sanitized of sex and drugs."

"Yes, there is always an element of fascism in theme parks," replied Ramsey.

They smoked from a small hookah, sampling several British Columbia strains including that from which the daughters outside had been taken. Then because their mouths were dry, Peace brought out a two litre bottle of Diet Coke (which he knew Ramsey liked despite its political incorrectness) kept cool in a pail of ice from the big refrigerator in one of the portables in Lunaville, and two mugs.

"In the mid `sixties we'd drive down in the evenings from York U to Yorkville. We'd meet friends at Webster's Restaurant and go to the Riverboat or the Mynah Bird. Joso let us play speed chess at the back when he and Malka weren't singing, if it wasn't busy, because the tourists liked to see it," Ramsey said, nostalgically.

"Yes, I have heard these names," said Peace.

"Of course it was soon commercialized. Soon the Mynah Bird had a Paint the Nude for Ten Dollars operation going on upstairs, and businessmen were coming for that," said Ramsey. "Then the city engineered a fake hepatitis epidemic threat to evict the hippies and usher in developers."

Peace put on music from an old CD boom box, pieces that pleaded for primitive beliefs and irrational leaps of faith—against the atheism of the New Harmony planning group. His selections were designed to soften up Ramsey emotionally before they discussed it. "God is Alive, Magic is Afoot" with words by Leonard Cohen and music by Buffy Sainte Marie, was followed by the haunting voice and echoing bells of "The Angel," which Peace had shared with Nitawik. The third was a Mormon Tabernacle choir version of the original words to the "Finlandia Hymn," already heard that morning. The line "God walks abroad in garments of might," was the most explicit deistic Christ reference in it, but ". . . a throne, eternal and high," also offended.

"Okay, so better words need to be found for a UN anthem. But we must maintain a Marxist view of organized religion, and hope that religious institutions and beliefs fade away. Organized religion may do some good, but is one of the superficial differences among humans which must be overcome, . . . transcended, . . . if universal Species-Being is to be achieved," stated Ramsey. Peace wanted to talk about Kierkegaard but Ramsey didn't.

"Kierkegaard is interesting for having the last philosophically interesting argument for the existence of God, after all the others had been refuted. But he was self-obsessed to the point of insanity, and needed some regular sex and a family, and to stop worrying about his alleged sins, which were maybe just masturbation, if you ask me," replied Ramsey brusquely. "Religious existentialism is still religion, unprovable metaphysics that will not fit with science."

They sat on folding chairs at a card table. Peace set the chess clock (actually two clocks in one case) for an hour each. After he won White in a coin toss, they set up the two armies of four inch wooden Staunton pieces facing each other on the oil board. Ramsey started the game by pushing the button on his side, starting Peace's clock. Peace moved his King's Pawn to the fourth rank (e4), and pushed the button on his side of the case to start Ramsey's time. The first twelve moves went quickly as both sides hurried to contest the center with pawns while developing bishops and knights and castling king-side.

The mid-game was slower. Ramsey discerned that his opponent could see further ahead than he, and had studied *Modern Chess Openings* more recently and more assiduously, and played more tournament games. Peace would not likely play defensively. So Ramsey prepared his king-side for the Oedipal assault which soon began, matching every new attacker with pieces kept in strategic reserve. But inevitably the pawn bodyguard around the black monarch was weakened.

Exhibiting great mobility, Peace next launched an invasion on Ramsey's Queen-side flank, hoping to draw defenders away from his king. Ramsey was not fooled, however, and committed just enough resources—two rooks and a knight—to hold the side. When Peace shifted back to hunting Ramsey's king, he again met stiff resistance and there were exchanges of material as Black tried desperately to reduce White's forces. By now each played had used more than half his time.

After a feint in the center, Peace again pushed toward the Black King, sacrificing his remaining knight to dispatch two bodyguard pawns. With a hastily assembled retinue, Ramsey's king fled a series of checks along the first rank into a bunker of rooks, shielded by his powerful consort, the Black Queen. Peace's assault on the bunker faltered after twelve moves, and he had to retreat quickly in the face of a counterattack. His last bishop was waylaid and pulled down by two pawns who died in the action.

Now Ramsey gathered his remaining forces to advance a queen-side rook pawn to the eighth rank, attempting to promote it to another queen. This pawn was blocked by a rook, but Ramsey's white-square bishop moved along the diagonal (to g1) to support the pawn and trap the blockading white rook in the corner. It was something he had learned from Beloved Morton, who favored defense and pawn promotion over attack, even against weaker players. Ramsey started to push another pawn, forcing exchanges where he could to increase his edge in material. When Ramsey had three minutes left, and Peace only a few seconds, the latter resigned.

"Quite a battle," said Ramsey. "After that the War to End All War will be a piece of cake." He hoped he did not sound condescending, because he liked this young man who reminded him of some aspects of his youthful self. After another smoke from the hookah and more talk, they walked back to the staging area near the dock. Dozens of picnic tables had been brought in, for a self-serve supper from an iron cauldron full of chile, various beans and other vegetables, and bits of salt fish.

*

The children returned from their cruise. Luna was leading Spot on his leash despite being unable to borrow the money. Beside her, Alf was carrying two cloth bags of sandwiches and sweets. "I'm almost too full fer supper," he said, before eating a bowl of chile.

"Jamie, lend me a hundred dollars," Luna pleaded, as Mandy held an umbrella to shield her from the declining sun.

"Oh, honey, if it's to buy the wolf, I can't do that. I do hope you will understand. You are getting mature enough to understand these hard facts," Ramsey replied, flattering her. "But I tell you what. We can leave money with Nitawik to get a pre-paid cell phone with camera for Alf, and he can send you pictures of Spot as he grows up."

"I don't think he can read or do numbers," said Luna. "Maybe he can't use a phone."

"He wants to learn to read and do arithmetic. He wants to attend school," said Sanjay.

"Well, it would be better than nothing, but . . ." Luna was still hoping she could keep the pup.

Soon the children lay down for a rest before the sunset ceremony at Fitzsimmons' Peak. (The plan was to spend the night and leave next morning.) Mandy lay down next to Luna and the other children, pulling sheets over them as cooler evening breezes came off the river. Spot and Alf fell asleep on an air mattress nearby, after the later boasted that he wasn't tired, as "Greensleeves" and other soothing music emanated softly from a player. Zhe was in the Communications Centre on an errand when Luna awoke at 8.30 because Spot growled.

A Roma man and woman had entered the tent, pretending to be cleaning up. They were Outlanders who had been seen a number of times during the day by security staff. Choosing a minute when few adults were present, the male got near the soldier by the door. When she wasn't looking he pulled out a large wrench from under his jacket, knocked off her helmet and struck the back of her head. Her thick hair, bundled to conceal the fact that it was longer than regulations permitted, saved her life, but the blow knocked her unconscious. By then Spot was biting at the male assailant's boots, only to be kicked hard against the side of the tent. Brandishing a knife, the woman advanced on Mandy, who sat shielding Luna in her arms.

"Let the girl go and you won't get hurt, pretty missy," the woman hissed at Mandy.

"Your gun," Luna whispered into Mandy's ear, guiding her right hand beneath the sheet, beneath her bee-eater dress, to the holster on her right thigh. Mandy cooly slipped out the derringer, remembering to push off the safety with her thumb. With two hands she leveled the gun as she'd seen in movies and hit the woman, who was nearer, in the shoulder, shattering her right clavicle and shoulder-joint and knocking her to the ground. Turning her wrists, Mandy hit the man under his left armpit as he lunged at her. He was still alive, a look of disbelief on his face, as he dropped the wrench and fell to the carpet near Alf. (The bullet had gone through the man's heart.) He was olive-skinned, big-nosed, tanned on his neck and face, with long black hair and a red bandana around his neck. Luna watched his eyes go blank.

Hearing the shots, soldiers and police ran in half a minute later and subdued the writhing woman. They administered First Aid to her and to their comrade, who was regaining consciousness, wondering where she was and why her scalp was bleeding so badly. Mandy, after being so brave and effective, dissolved into tears. Maxine Tibbetts sat to hold and comfort her, giving orders over her shoulder. The area was secured as a crime scene and Ira Swartz was called in to video for forensic purposes. Between sobs, Mandy blurted out what had happened. Luna and Alf noticed that Spot could not walk, and was whimpering in pain, so they carried him to the mattress beside Mandy. Unfazed by the violence, Luna held Mandy's hand for a while until she quieted.

The male, a 43 year old Romanian national named Florin Ralulescu, as was later established, was dead. His body was put on a stretcher on an electric cart and carried aboard the Cobra at Bitumount airport. The injured soldier and the female prisoner went on the same flight, with Tantoo Cardinal and Alf. They were taking Spot, suffering from a broken left front leg, to the best veterinarian clinic in Fort McMurray. Once in town they would use the Stardust Cruiser, which had been given to Cardinal for all her trouble.

"Tantoo will get a cell phone or a wrist-top for you," Luna told Alf, outside the tent as he left for the airstrip, shading her eyes against the western sun. By then she was in her flak suit and blue UN helmet, surrounded by soldiers and police in body armor and helmets. Any adult approaching her was being Identocam-ed and searched.

"I hope you will call me every day, and show me how Spot is doing. You arc my friend, Alfred."

"I wull call," he said. "Nitawik sez I wull live wit' her an` go tuh school, and Mom wull git help not tuh booze." (He did not know that Mandy, recovering her composure with a small glass of brandy, had taken her Louis Vuitton Lady Tourbillon watch off her wrist and given it to Nitawik to sell and invest for the futures of the 'under-parented' children of Lunaville such as Alf.)

Luna held out the back of her right hand to have it kissed, and then touched Alf's shoulder with a cattail as he knelt.

"I dub thee Sir Alfred of Lunaville who looks after Spot," she said. "Arise Sir Knight." She stroked the pup's tail as he was carried by, his leg in splints, and waved as he and Alf set off for the airstrip in a cart with Tantoo Cardinal.

*

Tricked into thinking she was dying from loss of blood, the woman, Florica Cuza, 39, confessed to Inspector Tibbetts that she and Ralulescu had met a Russian woman who called herself Ivana (who fit the description of Svetlana Mayakova) in Edmonton, where they'd been sleeping in a park, early in June. (They had accepted a C$40,000 down payment, with the promise of five million after Luna was killed, to be paid in Churchill.) There was a stolen motor boat fitted with a spotlight hidden upriver, their intended means of escape after dark.

Zhe almost decided to cancel the sunset ceremony. But the Chinook helicopter coming from Cold Lake would be at least an hour, and since Fitzsimmons' Peak was near the airstrip, and the children needed to be occupied, . . .

Most of the village came with them to see the blazing sunset. "Evening" by the Moody Blues was appropriate, but "Canadian Sunset" by Andy Williams, meant as a joke, fell on a solemn audience. Ten shades of red and five of purple, mingled with ochre and orange, radiated over the dark forest on the western horizon, painting pink and mauve the underbellies of cloud banks above. As the sun dipped, Luna recited the Evening Prayer to a dying Aten, raising the shield of her helmet for a few minutes as she stood at the microphone. The ruined land behind her had sunken into shadow. By 9:56 p.m. the orb was gone.

"Nights in White Satin" by the Moody Blues was playing as Luna's cart left the Peak in the gloaming. Orders to return to Home Base immediately were pouring in to Zhe and Ramsey as news of the latest attempt leaked out. Frantic Han-Spar executives who wanted her to visit China before elections in 2019, earnest UN officials who wanted their golden goose back in her nest, worried New Harmony Executive Council members not afraid to question Ramsey's judgement, well-meaning suggestions from President Winfrey and other political allies, and finally Turquoise from Apollo City with a mildly sarcastic tone which he knew masked anxiety, saying "After the delay, Chou and I are coming down in two weeks and we're rather hoping Luna will still be in one piece."

"The Chinook is ready," Zhe was informed, as they approached the turn to the airstrip. "The Cobra will go ahead to scan for missiles or anything else. There are two drones helping."

"Okay, let's go home," Ramsey said, sitting next to her. Much of the crowd followed them to the airstrip.

There was the barest sliver of balsamic moon as they boarded the big helicopter. The lights forming the large ankh were spontaneously augmented by hundreds of people holding flashlights and by several small spotlights, as the Chinook rose from the ground. Luna insisted upon watching from a window until the ankh faded, finally letting herself be placed in her crashball by Zhe.

Two F-35 Harrier Stealth Lightnings on a training mission escorted the helicopters for the last one hundred kilometres. An hour and a quarter after leaving Bitumount-Lunaville the Chinook put down on the tarmac at the Canadian Forces Air Weapons Range north of Cold Lake, near the main dormitory and administrative center. General (as she now was) Molly Moosomin welcomed them with an honor guard and a hastily assembled reception for half an hour in the mess hall. Hundreds of people from the town and from local reserves had been allowed in, after being searched. (Military regulations required that even visiting children, of which there were several dozen, be searched before coming on base. This was not ordered by Luna's handlers, as the right-wing media claimed.)

The cheering was thunderous as Luna and her sleepy friends were carried into the main mess hall. The service men and women sang "For She's a Jolly Good Fellow," and then a band with an hour's practice did "Rockin` Little Angel." Finally everyone sang the UN Hymn with the original politically incorrect words. As Luna saluted the assembly, applause swelled. It was obvious that all ranks anticipated playing significant roles in the UN War to End All Wars, looking forward to being the last generation of armed forces.

The *Luna Express* was ready. In the bus Luna got into her pajamas and said goodbye to Maxine Tibbetts, with much hugging, kissing, and nose rubbing. "Thank you for keeping me safe, Timbits," Luna said. Ominously, the Inspector had been ordered to report to her superiors in Edmonton asap.

*

The big blue bus, familiar to the public from television and Internet, left Cold Lake along Highway 55 with an escort of two RCMP cruisers, each containing two officers. It soon crossed into Saskatchewan and continued south-east through the night, through small towns and Prince Albert. Even in the smallest settlements many people came out beneath streetlights to wave and hold up ankh signs as the bus went by. At 10.30 a.m. as they approached Neepawa, Manitoba, pop. 4,298, Ramsey remembered that Margaret Laurence, a writer he admired, grew up in this little prairie town, the inspiration for the fictional Manawaka. He wanted to pay homage. Zhe agreed, so the bus turned off the Yellowhead Highway (as that part of the Trans Canada was called) onto a tree-lined side street (First Avenue) and parked near Laurence House, which was just opening for the day. Everyone on board the bus and the policemen in the escort were glad of a chance to stretch their legs.

Soon the mayor and various officials showed up. As other locals began to gather, Luna (in straw hat, embroidered turquoise hemp overalls, and Blue Jays T-shirt) posed for a photographer from the

Neepawa *Banner* on the front steps of the verandah of the house, a two storey beige brick building, fancier than most in town because of the decorative stone pediments above the windows. Inside, the staff would not accept money from Ramsey and his company. The curator and two college students hired for the summer showed them around and got Luna to sign the special visitors' book and pose for pictures with them. "My grandchildren will be so sorry not to see you," the curator said to Luna. Roxanne bought Mandy a copy of *The Stone Angel* in the gift store.

The mayor implored them to come to the Lily Festival, if only for twenty minutes, and Luna agreed. By chance one locally-developed yellow and orange variety was named Starburst Luna, after her. She was rewarded with a bushel of such exotic new varieties of bulbs which genetic engineering hath wrought, which two policemen carried to the bus. Seeing Mandy with a book, some wit in the crowd loudly made a sly variant on the old joke about leading a whore to culture (horticulture), causing the young woman to cringe and veil her face. (Details of Mandy's past had surfaced when a former foster parent, angling for money, telephoned an Edmonton radio station the day before.) It seemed so unfair and cruel that Zhe resisted an urge to wade into the throng and collar the man at gunpoint. Instead she and Roxanne led Mandy back to the bus, ending the tour.

"Chin up, my dear," said Roxanne. "You are a twice a hero, plain and simple. In Home Base you will be treated as such. No nasty labels. If anything you will be regarded as a victim, which may be another trap."

"Off with the head of the silly bastard," Luna mock ordered, raising eyebrows in her entourage. They wondered what other slang she had picked up from Alf.

Most of the population of Portage la Prairie, which was much bigger than Neepawa, turned out to glimpse the small face in the window of the bus, before it picked up speed again on the highway.

In Winnipeg in the afternoon hundreds of thousands cheered Luna's progress, as the mayor and local officials joined the impromptu parade. The Science tutor ran off the bus at a brief stop and purchased a clutch of local newspapers from a boy on the street. The headline on the front page of the *Winnipeg Free Press* read: ATTACK

IN LUNAVILLE: DRAGON GIRL SAFE, RETURNING HOME. Below that a smaller banner—ALBERTA VOTING TODAY ON FUTURE OF PLANET. LOONIE DIVES AGAIN AMID STOCK MARKET CHAOS. There were pictures courtesy of UNTV of Luna in her Isis headdress, Luna wearing white gloves pouring tea on the barge, and Luna with Spot and Alf. There was one of Alf straining to carry Spot into the Cobra. Pictures of Mandy with Luna, taken from TV footage shot outside the Quality Hotel in Fort McMurray, appeared next to a potted history of Bitumount.

In the evening the bus passed Virden, Manitoba, a small town off the Trans Canada Highway. Half the town's population lined the highway, so the bus slowed and Luna waved from the front window, held by Zhe. At the border two Ontario Provincial Police cruisers replaced the RCMP. In Rainy River before midnight people of all ages lined the route five deep on both sides of the road. Toronto media called it 'Lunamania.' Meanwhile the object of all this attention, after waving from the front through Rainy River, viewed the many pictures sent by Alf of Spot with a cast on his leg, surprisingly agile on three legs, a final time before going back to sleep between her grandparents.

During the night Ramsey received an encrypted message from Harry Katz. A New Harmony spy within the RCMP had learned that Maxine Tibbetts had been demoted two ranks with loss of pay by a trio of white male Tory superiors in Edmonton. They had a long list of alleged misdeeds; destruction of RCMP vehicles, providing a firearm to an unlicenced civilian, removing a prisoner (Gabriel) from cells for unapproved interrogation techniques, consorting with a prostitute, . . . Ramsey promised Katz that he would call the prime minister that day to complain.

Very early risers in Thunder Bay ran out of donut shops and service stations to wave at the bus. Some people came out of their homes and apartment buildings in pajamas and nightgowns, while others watched from windows and balconies. The election results had come from Alberta: after recounts in five close ridings, it was announced that the parties of the Left had defeated the Conservatives, taking 51 of 84 seats in the legislature, sweeping the cities and larger towns and taking 43% of the popular vote. The strong showing (7%) of the Alberta Independence Party, which had an option of

American statehood, and the Wildrose Alliance, took votes from the Conservatives.

Premier-designate Joan Nakashima, a Calgary Liberal, a professor of urban planning, was already receiving death threats.

During the day TV news helicopters occasionally flew above as the bus traversed the north shore of Lake Superior before coming into an exuberant Sault Ste. Marie at 1.30 p.m, where people danced to "Rockin`Little Angel" and partied on the sidewalks as she went by.

Late in the afternoon they reached the village of Espanola (Spanish). Because of reports of many Toronto-based *paparazzi* ahead, at Ramsey's suggestion Zhe ordered a turn south, through Whitefish Falls and the picturesque hamlet of Little Current, where the road crossed the Northern Channel to Georgian Bay. There was a short wait for the swing bridge to let boats pass, and then on to Manitoulin Island.

They went south, often slowing because of the many cyclists, to the port village of South Baymouth. On the way the children twice got out to buy blueberries from Anishnabe children, as the Science tutor pointed out exposed dolomite, eskers, and kettle lakes in unforested areas. The native children were surprised each time Bliss asked in Anishnawbe if any hawberries were ripe. Security arrangements having been made, at South Baymouth they drove aboard the 300-vehicle ferry *Chi-Cheemaun* ('big canoe') at the last minute for the last (sunset) trip of the day to Tobermory. Surprised tourists, including many Americans, clamored to see Luna. (Except for a retired dentist from Ohio, who had tar sands stocks in his portfolio, who was removed to a makeshift brig after he shouted "I hope someone gets to the little bitch.") Surrounded by police, she sat in a deck chair on the main deck with her friends, wearing flak jacket and helmet. Passengers with small children were allowed to come close and speak to Luna without being searched and Identocam-ed. The captain invited her to the bridge for twenty minutes, where she told him about Boris Larinov and the *Kapitan Lebnikov* while she autographed pictures for the First Mate's children. Nearing Tobermory, from Flowerpot Island to Big Tub Harbor the ferry was followed by the boats of native fishermen, lake-going yachts, expensive motor launches, and the glass-bottom boats that took tourists over the many wrecks in the area. In Tobermory harbor the children asked for ice cream from a candy shop on the hillside, so armored police escorted them up and down the steep steps. People clapped and cheered as Luna, her chin smeared with jamoca almond fudge ice cream, boarded the bus.

Now came the last lap, down Bruce Peninsula on Highway 6. Traffic in both directions nearly all stopped to watch and wave at the bus, slowing its pace. It was dusk when they reached the Owen Sound by-pass, lined with parked cars from the Drive-in theater to the Inglis Mill waterfall and Highway 10. Despite the damage that would be done to Canada's economy by stopping the tar sands, horns blared and people waved. Amid the ankhs, several signs advertized German shepherds for sale or free. Many children held Schoolgirl Luna dolls. A group of teenagers sang "Rockin' Little Dragon, come on down from the sky, . . .", making up their own words.

Just then Zhe got a call from Maxine Tibbetts. "Yesterday I was busted down two ranks in Edmonton, and contemplated quitting," Tibbetts said. "Then today I was summoned to HQ in Calgary. Top brass in Ottawa had intervened and I was restored in rank, and then raised to Superintendent. My former superiors in Edmonton are taking early retirement. I was assured the Force will be loyal to the federal government, whatever happens in Alberta. I'm to head the task force looking for Mayakova and investigating Frank Connors. The best part is that secretaries and junior ranks stopped work and gave me a standing ovation as I left the building."

"Will wonders never cease?" said Zhe disingenuously, knowing about Ramsey's call to the PM. "Anyway, congratulations! Luna wants to talk to you, . . . here she is."

Twenty minutes later the tower in B1 came into view. Soon the bus was being saluted by guards at the front gate. Sitting up front, Luna returned the salutes. "I must visit Moonflower and her mother in their barn, and then see Boris and Oolayou before I go to bed," she informed Roxanne as the gate closed behind them. Zhe took off her body armor and heaved a sigh of relief. "You'll bunk with me until you get settled," she said to Mandy. "I have a small apartment in the tower, and larger quarters in the egg. Welcome to Home Base, my dear."

* * *

Now, Dear Reader, a pause. Historical Committee 203 will take a vacation and then come back to finish its work. If you do not already know how Luna got a sister, campaigned in America, Mexico, and Peru, spearheaded the UN invasion of Burma in the first large battle in the War to End All Wars, and survived more attempts on her life, you must read further volumes when they become available.